INSIDE BRITAIN'S ULTRA SECRET M.I. 6

"Miss Autland, I know this is a shock, and I'm truly sorry."

"But why? Why did my father come back into it?"

"Lark was afraid to trust anyone else. David felt compelled to make the contact. Lark had firm intelligence on Russian penetration into the Secret Service. You must not think, Miss Autland, that your father was called into service and sacrificed for nothing."

"Thank you for trying to put it in perspective for me, Mr. Barnsworth . . ."

"Well, actually . . ." Barnsworth cleared his throat. "Lark made another request. He asked for the only other person he feels is above suspicion. Perhaps he sees this mission as a legacy." There was silence. "Lark asked for you, Miss Autland."

Avon Books are available at special quantity discounts for bulk purchases for sales promotions, premiums, fund raising or educational use. Special books, or book excerpts, can also be created to fit specific needs.

For details write or telephone the office of the Director of Special Markets, Avon Books, Dept. FP, 1790 Broadway, New York, New York 10019, 212-399-1357. *IN CANADA*: Director of Special Sales, Avon Books of Canada, Suite 210, 2061 McCowan Rd., Scarborough, Ontario M1S 3Y6, 416-293-9404.

LEGACY OF FEAR

K.T. ANDERS

*To Willa
Here's to good reading
on Fire Island.
K.T. Anders*

AVON
PUBLISHERS OF BARD, CAMELOT, DISCUS AND FLARE BOOKS

LEGACY OF FEAR is an original publication of Avon Books. This work has never before appeared in book form. This work is a novel. Any similarity to actual persons or events is purely coincidental.

AVON BOOKS
A division of
The Hearst Corporation
1790 Broadway
New York, New York 10019

Copyright © 1985 by Katie Anders
Published by arrangement with the author
Library of Congress Catalog Card Number: 84-91204
ISBN: 0-380-89515-3

All rights reserved, which includes the right to reproduce this book or portions thereof in any form whatsoever except as provided by the U. S. Copyright Law. For information address Avon Books.

First Avon Printing, January, 1985

AVON TRADEMARK REG. U. S. PAT. OFF. AND IN
OTHER COUNTRIES, MARCA REGISTRADA, HECHO EN
U. S. A.

Printed in the U. S. A.

WFH 10 9 8 7 6 5 4 3 2 1

FOR

FRANK
who sometimes believed

and

VINCENT
who always believed

That sweet and sounding name of patria becomes an illusion and a curse.

—George Gissing
By the Ionian Sea

CHAPTER ONE

"Human beings are always going to muck up the neatness of machines," said Peter Barnsworth. He rocked in the high-backed chair of burgundy leather, his palms making small circles, almost caressingly, on the overstuffed arms. The elegant chair dominated the otherwise dismal government-office furnishings, an upholstered monument to its owner's elevated position in the bureaucratic pecking order, although the acknowledgment had not come from the government. It had been a gift from his wife. Nevertheless, Peter relished it as his private status symbol in the gray, anonymous world of British Intelligence. Of course, he'd have all the trappings if he ever became Chief. But his public school had been unimpressive. He'd been Head of Section for twenty years; it was probably as far as he would go. His chair, therefore, was all the dearer.

The man sitting across the desk from him watched his hands working the leather in the old, familiar gesture. Peter Barnsworth had not changed much in seven years, he reflected: he was still blessed with a shockingly lush head of salt-and-pepper hair and mercurial blue eyes. Knowing that Peter needed little encouragement to get to the point, the man let his silence and raised eyebrows pass as his reply.

"You, for instance," continued Barnsworth, taking the cue and turning to the computer terminal at his desk. "At the touch of a finger, here you are." He punched the keys and the screen sprang to life, green worms squiggling across a dark, muddy pond.

"Age: 53," he read aloud. "Height: 6' 2". Weight: 200. . . ."

"195 actually," interrupted the man. "I dropped five—summer's coming."

"Exactly," said Barnsworth, hands in the air. "That's

exactly the sort of thing I mean. You've mucked up my machine." He frowned slightly as he played on the keys, making the correction. The other man nodded. He remembered that Peter Barnsworth had always liked his information up to the minute. The computer terminal was new since he'd last been in this office, but its appearance was no surprise. State of the art technology was indigenous to the intelligence business. It was the consummate toy for a man of Peter's proclivities.

Satisfied, Barnsworth began reading again. "Divorced: one daughter." Here he paused, shot an oblique glance at the man opposite him, received no reaction, and returned to the screen. "Background: MI6 field agent, code 10, nineteen years. Compulsory retirement: identity exposed. Current status: seven years MI6 liaison with CIA, based in Washington D.C." He turned to face the man with a gesture.

"You see, all very neat."

"A triumph of technology."

"Of course. . . ." said Barnsworth as he snatched a yellow paper from the confusion spread across his huge, government-issue desk. "Of course, I can't give the computer *this.*"

The man eyed the paper in silence, pondering before he stepped into the snare. "Do you ever play it straight, Peter?" he asked at length, running a hand through his thinning hair.

Peter assumed his wounded puppy look. "I say, you don't think I'd try to put one over on you? I'm simply a conduit, old boy . . . a conduit to Thespian."

The two men locked eyes for a long moment. Barnsworth kept his pitifully sincere. The other man's eyes narrowed as a telltale flush of color singed his cheeks, betraying his interest.

"I rang you as soon as it came in yesterday," said Peter, magnanimous now that the fish had seen the worm. He relinquished the paper, reached for his pipe, lying in the ceramic ashtray on his right, puffed experimentally, then re-lit it as he watched the man's eyes move across the page.

The cablegram read: URGENT STOP HAVE NEW SCRIPT CAN ONLY USE OLD ACTOR STOP WILL NOT REPEAT NOT ACCEPT SUBSTITUTE STOP AUDI-

TION AT 1100 HOURS TUESDAY THE 15TH AT THEATRE IN THE PARK STOP NO OTHER ACTORS TO BE INVOLVED PLEASE MAKE ALL ARRANGEMENTS SIGNED LARK.

"He can't be serious!" said the man called Thespian. "I was cashiered from field work, remember? My picture is in every secret service file around the world. Christ, Peter," he continued as the other man said nothing, "I was the star of a best seller, an intelligence service exposé. That CIA bastard got MI6 involved, then blew us to the universe! I'm not only a celebrity spy, I'm a household word—with as much chance on a live mission as a fox on the opening day of hunting season."

"Quite so, of course. Totally impossible."

"How do you know it's authentic?"

"Cyphers said it came through with all the proper idents."

Thespian studied the serious face before him, its sharp angles softened by a liveliness in the blue eyes that was barely under control.

"It's absurd," he said, vaulting from the chair and walking to the window. His memory bridged seventeen years to the day he recruited Lark, a discontented colonel in the Russian KGB. For ten years he had run the penetration: a decade between two men who addressed each other only as Thespian and Lark, but who had formed a relationship that moved from professional wariness to deep, mutual respect, which in an ordinary business would have been a close personal friendship.

"Why the bloody hell would he ask for me?" said Thespian as he watched the flow of London traffic splashing through the dousing rain in the circus below. His view was partially blocked by the back of a huge letter "O" covering a fourth of the window, part of a BOAC sign that hung on the facade of the building. He swung around to face Peter. "It's been seven years. He adjusted to the new people, didn't he? Why me, now?"

Peter rocked in his chair, one hand holding his pipe, the other working the leather. "Yes, yes, he adjusted. Quite upset at first, as you know. But we've had no problems. His cover held. He's been giving us high-grade stuff, piece by piece."

"You don't suppose he wants to come out, do you?"

"He would hardly need you for that, old boy. Not the sentimental sort, do you think?"

"But he must know it's dicey, even after seven years."

"Yes, he must." The ensuing pause filled the room with Lark's presence.

"Actually, all I need from you . . ." said Peter, giving the computer terminal a brief nod, "what I can't seem to locate in the files is . . . ah . . . the location of the 'theatre in the park.' Then I can send his regular case officer."

"Sorry, old man, we never turned it in. It was our emergency location. Sort of double indemnity insurance."

Peter was silent. The moment balanced between them as delicately as a counterweight scale. Thespian gazed out the window again, wrapped in his memories, this time oblivious to the hubbub below.

"Lark," he said softly. "Lark . . . damn it, why?"

"He must have something extraordinary." Peter's shrewd eyes watched Thespian closely. "He's not the sort to get a wind up unless it's top of the line, do you think? Of course, you know him better than I."

"No, he's not the sort."

"Curious request."

"Bloody shame I'm blown."

"I was certain you'd want to give it a miss," said Barnsworth, nodding as he puffed his pipe. "But I felt honor-bound to inform you. The most sensible path, of course, is to insist upon regular channels."

Thespian regarded him silently. He could feel the pulse beating in his neck; adrenal rush, a body response forgotten for seven years, boiled again in his stomach. "I've never been your most sensible agent," he said softly.

Peter Barnsworth leaned forward as if he hadn't heard correctly. He placed his pipe in the ashtray.

"My dear chap, don't tell me you're actually. . . . ? Oh, no, no." He gestured to the computer. "You're quite right. It does say retired from field service. I couldn't possibly ask you to take this kind of assignment."

"Precisely," said Thespian. "You could only haul me over here, wave the bait, and hope."

"That's a bit unfair. . . ."

"What's your current date code?"

12

"Ahead two hours, back five days." Peter was trying hard to mask his pleasure.

"That makes it 1 p.m. on Thursday the 10th. Day after tomorrow." Thespian hoisted himself from the chair. "Good show. You bagged the weasel. Now it's time for the good little ferret to do his own hunting."

"And the theatre in the park?" ventured Peter.

"In the Italian Alps, near Aosta. That's all you get. I'm still smarter than your bloody machine."

"Betty can take care of any arrangements you need."

"I'll have to collect some hiking equipment. Can you trick me up a passport? I'll need another name."

"It will be ready in the morning."

Peter walked with him to the door. "I forgot to ask how your flight was."

"I don't know how Lindbergh had the patience. Now we do it in seven hours with two meals and a film and it's still too damn long."

"You didn't take the Concorde?"

"I'm an environmentalist."

Peter shook his head. "You see—attitude. It can't be programmed into the computer." He meant the clump on the other man's shoulder to be affectionate, but it came off rather awkwardly. "I'm not certain what we've got here. Do your best to stay in touch. You know the routine. Under the circumstances, it's impossible to give you any support out there."

"I know. I'm a . . . volunteer." Thespian waved toward the desk. "Not even in your box."

Peter winced. "Do be careful."

Thespian flashed a token smile, his mind already absorbed by the details of his plans. In the outer office, he stopped at the desk where Betty sat hunched over her typewriter.

"Well, old girl, just like the old days. Give me some petty cash vouchers. And I'll need reservations—plane, hotel, car. I'll ring you this afternoon with specifics."

"I'll be here." She handed him the chits. Her eyes went to Peter, standing in the doorway, then returned to Thespian with a wry smile.

"Welcome back to the business," she said.

Thespian saluted her with the umbrella he'd taken off

the coat rack, tossed his raincoat over his arm, and let the door bang behind him.

Peter turned to his secretary. "Betty, tell Documents it's a go on that passport I ordered. Oh, and make a computer entry: Theatre in the park is in the Italian Alps, near Aosta."

With a thoughtful glance at the door, he retreated into his office.

CHAPTER TWO

David Payne, whose code name was Thespian, steered his rented Fiat through the sleepy village of Courmayeur. The tourist crush was still a month away; he had the mountains practically to himself. It was good to be back in Europe, he thought, as his gloved hand swerved the wheel to avoid hitting a young shepherd and his flock who were just emerging onto the roadway. Especially good to be back in the Italian Alps. The scenery was spectacular, if somewhat gentler than Switzerland: tiny, red-roofed villages snuggled between mountains arrayed in spring greenery, white-capped peaks presiding in the distance. His mood matched the surrounding grandeur.

Directly upon leaving Peter's office in London, he had experienced the high that came with a new mission. He was alive again, senses tingling, mind concentrated into a pinpoint of light. He sighed. How unfair of Fate to rob a man of his chosen career! How unfair to spend years becoming the best in one's field, only to see success destroyed by the malice of an ego-wounded ex-agent who wanted revenge on the system, ignorant of the lives he smashed in the process. He had never even met the man who had set his name down as a spy for the world to see. A depersonalized assasination.

As the road curved, the sun suddenly splashed the opposite mountain with early morning brilliance.

David Payne felt confident as he reviewed the precautions he'd taken to cover this meeting with Lark. Traveling as Richard Westley, English businessman on holiday, he had flown into Geneva from London. A convoluted route by car into the French Alps had ended at Chamonix, where he checked into a hotel, prepaying his bill for the night. Then he had spent the afternoon hiking in the mountains, turning and twisting through forest and ridge to liberate himself from any watchful eyes. At precisely 6 p.m., he returned to the cable car station in Chamonix, barely in time for the last ride up the flank of Mont Blanc.

There were few passengers. He slipped into a seat at the last moment, nodding pleasantly to the two sturdy Germans wearing backpacks. The other passengers looked harmless enough: a giggly young couple and a docile, middle-aged couple with two listless teenagers.

The ascent was breathtaking, as the cable rose as much as 2,000 feet between support towers. All but the German hikers were hushed and more than a little shaken when the suspended car stopped on firm ground at the second station, Aiguille du Midi, at an altitude of 12,602 feet. The other passengers huddled together at the belvedere, ready to return to Chamonix, purposely ignoring the 125 miles of Alps sprawling at their feet across the boundaries of three countries. As David Payne followed the Germans across the narrow, chasm-spanning bridge leading to the third cable car, he felt humbled by the mountain. National self-interest was absurd, he reflected; man's very existence was ultimately insignificant.

Across the glacial fields, at the Pointe Helbronner station, he showed his passport as Richard Westley, then descended along with the German hikers, aboard two less precarious cable cars, to the village of Courmayeur, Italy. It was dark when he arrived. After the Germans waved goodbye, Thespian picked up the hotel reservation and rented car for Richard Westley, had a delightful meal in an elegant restaurant, and fell into bed, satisfied that he had not been followed. Although his body was ready for rest, his mind wouldn't let go; it took him a long time to fall asleep.

Now he glanced into the rear view mirror as he had been doing all morning since leaving Courmayeur. There was no sign of another car keeping a discreet distance behind him. He felt safe.

As he wound down into the valley, he thought again about Lark. What could have prompted him to insist upon this contact? If he didn't know the man better, he would suspect a trap: he still had some residual value to the Russians and they probably would enjoy an in-depth chat on MI6-CIA liaison. But he trusted Lark. The Russian must be frightened. Of what? What did he have that couldn't be passed to his case officer?

Signs of civilization cropped up along the roadside: carefully tended vineyards, a scattering of houses. He recognized the large, white building on the left as the cheese factory, remembered the smooth taste of the local Fontina.

The theatre in the park, high above the valley floor between Courmayeur and Aosta, was a deserted mountain cabin that had been used as part of an escape route for POWs during World War II. He had chosen to approach it from Aosta, the larger town, where his presence would be least noticed. The cabin had been a fallback meeting place with Lark and he hoped it was still deserted. He judged he would be there by noon.

He entered Aosta and drove straight to the car park in the center square. Amidst the mass of parked cars, he didn't notice the man sitting in the gray Citroën who pulled a hat over his face as the Fiat came to a stop.

Taking his walking stick and rucksack from the trunk, Thespian strolled along the main street and turned past the ruins of the Roman amphitheatre. A stocky man, walking on the opposite side of the street, had made the last two turns with him. Suddenly wary, Thespian stopped, leaned against the side of a building and consulted his map. The man didn't seem to notice him, but kept walking and turned the corner. Thespian lingered for two minutes, then cautiously approached the corner. The man was not in sight. Relieved, he continued out of town on a path that plunged into the forests and meadows of Valle d'Aosta. There were no other hikers.

The morning air was fresh and fragrant. He enjoyed the exercise. He hiked for five miles, rising higher and higher into the mountains, pausing, turning back, circling. There was no one behind him. He felt more invigorated than tired when, at 12:15, he came upon the hut. It was a squat, wooden structure, so dwarfed by the surrounding white pines that it seemed to appear suddenly—invisible from the path until one was almost upon it.

In the shadow of the trees he circled the hut, quietly checking the forest floor for signs of human presence. The sun shone directly above the treetops, dappling the ground. Satisfied that nature was undisturbed, he approached the structure from the rear and peered into the opening that had once held a pane of glass. The windows and doors had long since yielded to the elements, as had portions of the roof. Rotting timbers hung disconsolately; sunlight spilled in from above. The hut had two rooms. From his position he could see the entire back room. It was empty save for a cupboard almost eight feet high built against one wall. Thespian smiled.

He moved to the front of the cabin, keeping low, checked the window opening, then stepped to the threshold. The front room was as he remembered it, only more aged by neglect.

Suddenly he tensed: A distinct scraping noise was audible from the rear room. As he stood, statue-like, it came again. He flattened himself against the wall to the left of the doorway, pulled a knife from the side of his hiking boot, and waited. Thirty seconds ticked by. The scraping grew more pronounced. Thespian acted. With a clatter of boots, he hurled himself into the room, knife poised, eyes sweeping the space. The adversaries faced each other in astonishment. The frightened marmot that had been gnawing in the corner froze, its coarse, brown fur blending into the dark wood behind and beneath him. The animal blinked, then bolted, leaving Thespian to lean against the doorjamb with a sound between a gasp and a short laugh. At least his instincts were undulled.

He looked around the room thoughtfully, waiting for his body to readjust to peace. The cupboard beckoned like an old lover. He gently pushed aside the slanting door and reached down to the bottom. The worn piece of wood, soft from dampness and age, lifted out easily to reveal another wooden bottom, this one with two blocks in the back corners on each side. He reached for them and turned them slowly on their pivotal pegs. Thus freed, the heavy plank lifted out.

An opening large enough for a man to slip into yawned before him. Taking the flashlight from his knapsack, he directed it into the hole. The beam penetrated about four feet, revealing a dirt floor. There were no footprints in the packed earth. Satisfied, he replaced the wood over the opening, turned the blocks, then fitted the false bottom in place. Little had changed in seven years.

He returned to the front room, stationed himself to the

side of the window, and checked his watch. Lark was due in fifteen minutes.

Only an occasional bird call broke the stillness. Thespian kept his eyes on the path, ears straining. The sound of a cautious step close to the hut brought him into position, knife ready. The sun spattered a pattern across the threshold. Soundlessly, a form filled the space: a roundish, balding head perched atop a chunky body in rumpled camping clothes. The two men stood motionless, holding each other's gaze, as the calendar flipped back seven years. The men embraced.

"I wanted to give you enough time to feel comfortable," said the newcomer, his English good, but accented with heavy Russian rhythm.

Thespian pounded the Russian on the shoulder. "Are you hinting that I'm rusty?" he said.

"No, no. You're good. But I'm still in the business." The Russian wagged his finger. "I have to be better." Their eyes evaluated each other, taking in every detail.

"I hope you took precautions," said Lark.

"Yes. No record of my presence in the Italian Alps. I'm Richard Westley, on holiday."

"Good. How are you?" asked Lark with genuine concern.

"Fine. And you?"

"My life goes on."

The rush of warmth between the two men threatened to embarrass them both. Lark continued in a lighter tone. "As well as can be expected, that is: I've had to learn to live without our dialectics. Your successors are part of the new breed—all business. There are no philosophers left in the services."

"And you haven't converted them?"

"No. There wasn't a flicker of interest when I mentioned Utopian Socialism or Robert Owen. They had never heard of either. John Stuart Mill? They should be ashamed that a Russian knows more about him than they do."

"The world is moving on."

"Their loss. I couldn't pursue it. I think my enthusiasm is waning with middle age."

"Word has it your efficiency has not been impaired."

"Hmmmm." Lark looked around the cabin, pursuing

some private thought, then focused back on Thespian. "Thank you for coming," he said. "I had no right to ask."

"Old habits die hard, even when you've been put out to pasture."

Lark smiled, his face becoming even rounder as his cheeks puffed outward. "And how *is* life in the pasture?"

Thespian nodded. "Is that it? You're ready to come out?"

"No," said Lark after a pause. "I'll admit it's crossed my mind lately. The law of averages: my number must be coming up soon." He shook his head. "Months of debriefing, hours sitting behind a desk . . . I'm not ready yet. In any case, I wouldn't drag you here for that. One day I'll appear, like the ghost of Banquo, in Barnsworth's office. He'll have to make a few changes in his computer!"

Thespian noted that his smiling face looked almost boyish, except for a certain sadness in the eyes.

"But if I wanted to come out now, this would guarantee me a soft berth," continued Lark as he rolled back the cuff of his jacket and picked at the stitching of the lining. Carefully, he worked a roll of microfilm through the opening he had made. He handed it to Thespian, who held it mutely in his palm.

"I have little room in my life for sentimental reunions," said Lark. "There was no one else to trust."

"But. . . ."

"No one." Lark paced to the other side of the small room, then returned, keeping clear of the window. "You're holding a copy of pay records from KGB headquarters. It contains the names and photographs of people in six networks operating right now in England: undercover case officers and penetration agents with their informers who are working for us in Parliament, various government offices, even MI6."

Thespian whistled softly.

"I can vouch for its authenticity," continued Lark. "It's from Archives at Moscow Center."

"Treasures from the vault!"

"Exactly. Worth a hiking trip, wouldn't you say? I didn't have time to see precisely what I was photographing. I wouldn't recognize most of the names anyway; they're Denisenko's networks."

"You think your case officer's name is there?"

"I don't know. Probably not. But I can't afford to trust whomever *he* might trust. You Brits like to go through channels. By the time this got to London, who knows how many people might have seen it. If Moscow even hears of its existence, it will kick up a storm that could lead to me. I'm not going to be another Volkov handing myself over to Kim Philby!"

"I see your point."

"I don't know who's on that film, but I know who's *not* there. You. And I know it will go from you straight into Barnsworth's hands. It will even bypass his computer."

"My god," said Thespian, overcome by the enormity of the information lying in his palm. "When you do come out, I'll personally see that you get a medal."

Lark's laugh was a low, inhibited sound. "Yes, a medal. I'll definitely need a medal! Or . . . why not a knighthood? We gave Philby the Order of the Red Banner."

"Done." Thespian was laughing, too.

Lark ran his eyes over his former colleague's face for a long moment, as if imprinting it on his memory. "By the way," he said, "I met your daughter."

"My daughter!"

"Yes. Humorous, isn't it? The two secret parts of your life coming face to face. Of course, she didn't know who I was."

"Where would you. . . ."

"It was at one of those perennial *détente* talks in Geneva about three years ago. She was interviewing the wives of some minor Russian diplomats, getting the human side of politics: how did the Russian women enjoy shopping in the West? What did they think of fashion? What restaurants did they like? All very subversive. I was there to make sure the Party line was being properly translated. She was charming."

"Little did I know I'd be a proud father so late in life. How in bloody hell did you find out about her?"

Lark shrugged. "She looks like you. Same intense green eyes."

"Come on, you. . . ."

"Never underestimate the tentacles of the KGB, even around a blown agent. I've been keeping track of her career."

Thespian looked alarmed. "If I thought she was in danger because of me. . . ."

"No, I removed her name from the records. I doubt that anyone else knows about her. She's not in danger." Lark held out his hand. "I'm sorry to get you involved again; I hope you understand. Good luck."

Thespian grasped his hand firmly. "Yes, I understand." He held up the microfilm in his other hand. "Thank you." There was an awkward moment of silence: too much to say, yet nothing. Lark turned abruptly, stood to the side of the door looking out, then stepped into the sunshine. With a brief look back over his shoulder, he disappeared into the trees.

Thespian remained in the front room as a flock of birds swirled overhead, chattering to each other, then the forest returned to stillness. He had never felt so alone in his life; he mourned for an irretrievable past. Slowly, his fingers closed over the microfilm in his palm as the solitude of the mountains pressed around him.

The top button of his jacket came apart into two pieces under his able fingers. He fit the microfilm neatly into the loose half, then popped it back into place on the garment. It looked no different from the five other buttons in a line below it.

At the cupboard in the back room, he carefully lifted out the two planks in the bottom, then climbed through the opening, dropping onto the dirt floor. He positioned the false bottom on a tilt, so it would slam down as soon as he had twisted the pegs on the underside that controlled the blocks. In a moment, the boards were in place over his head, their secret safely concealed.

The beam of his flashlight was reassuring as the total darkness assaulted him and the rooty, damp smell of earth filled his nostrils. I hope you're clear all the way, he thought belatedly. It was necessary to crawl on his hands and knees for about twenty feet, the protruding roots scraping his sides. Then the tunnel enlarged enough to permit him to stand. The floor was packed down smoothly, but gave no indication as to when the tunnel had last been used. How many Allied soldiers had escaped the pursuing Black Shirts through this tunnel? The decaying supports held no souvenirs. The old Italian mountaineer who had first brought him here was long cold in his grave. Time passed, politics changed, but man was always in need of an escape route.

There was more root growth on the sides and overhead than he remembered. Frequently he was forced to stoop or crawl, using his hunting knife to hack a larger opening. Tiny crawling things scurried from his intruding presence. He stepped over the remains of several small animals, and once he thought he saw a hare scampering ahead out of the range of his light. At several points, small cave-ins or slides partially blocked the passage with dirt and rocks, but he was able to climb through. Sweating, he would pause on the other side to catch his breath in the close, earthy air and tell himself it was foolish to have chanced the tunnel after all these years. Was *he* looking for a sentimental reunion?

Gradually the angle of the tunnel began to level off and progress was easier. There was a sharp turn, a steep drop, then the passage was terminated by a stack of logs wedged floor to ceiling. Thespian ran his hands along the rough wood, testing. It took several minutes before he located the loose log and pushed it through to the other side. The opening was large enough to scramble through. He heaved the log back into position, jammed it hard into place with his shoulder. Now he was in a shallow, natural cave formed by the overhang of rock and the side of the hill. He had been in the tunnel for over an hour.

The clean air refreshed his lungs and the light, even through the filter of foliage, seemed dazzling. He could see flecks of sky and sunlight at the mouth of the cave, fifteen feet in front of him, the way barred by fallen timbers, dead bushes and encroaching growth. He went forward slowly, as twigs snapped underfoot and branches clawed at his arms and legs. He tripped on some scattered bones, remnants of an animal meal taken in a safe shelter.

He had almost reached the entrance when he heard it and he froze instinctively. The sound repeated. Clang! Clang! He tried to see through the mosaic in front of him. Clang! It was a bell, very close now. Could he be seen? Had he been heard? The bell seemed to be directly in front of the cave, but he could see nothing. He tensed. The next sound made him smile; it was a distinct "moo-ooo."

He crept through the remaining bushes. He was still partly screened, but now he could see out. The cave was set into the side of a steep rise; below it lay a small meadow. In front and a little below him, a cow grazed on the wild grasses, the bell around its neck swinging noisily with each nod of its head.

Thespian watched as a little boy came into view, brandishing a stick. He addressed the cow cheerfully as he prodded its flanks. With a baleful look, the cow plodded along the path; the little boy continued his monologue. Thespian waited until the bell was only a tinkle in the distance, then, cautiously thrusting through the bushes, he emerged into the sunlight.

The meadow sloped gently downward, ablaze with a scattering of wild rosebushes. He wiped sweat and dirt from his face with his sleeve. Skirting the meadow, he found the path leading back toward Aosta.

He had been lucky, he told himself: anything might have happened in that tunnel. It was stupid to try to recapture the past. The old days were over. Lark had been right: there was no room for sentimentality. He understood the Russian's reluctance to quit, but hadn't he done enough? Why couldn't he get out now, live a free life? But even as he wished it, Thespian knew that life outside Russia would never truly be free for Lark. He would always be looking over his shoulder for the KGB. As he walked, he couldn't shake his melancholia.

He was puffing by the time he reached Aosta. Going directly to the car park, he stowed his rucksack in the trunk, then crumpled into the driver's seat. He had been in the mountains for over four hours. Yesterday, his decoy hike had lasted five. Seven years behind a desk had robbed him of stamina. He would have to spend more time at the gym when he returned to Washington.

Five minutes later he got out of the car and headed towards a telephone booth on the side of the ornate City Hall building. He searched his pockets, but realized he didn't have a telephone token. The shops along the square were still shuttered for the afternoon siesta. Reluctantly, he headed down a narrow street leading out of the square.

The interior of the post office was deserted except for a woman behind the counter reading a book. She didn't look up, although the bell over the door jangled as he entered.

"I'd like to send a cable," he said in Italian, somewhat too loudly.

She nodded, pushed a pad across the counter to him without raising her eyes. Thespian wrote quickly. The woman tore herself away from the book long enough to accept his money, then immersed herself again.

Thespian cleared his throat. "This will go out right away, Signora?"

She nodded, eyes still buried. Thespian remained immobile before her. With a deliberate sigh, she picked up the paper, walked to the Teletype machine, and began transmitting. Thespian returned to the street.

He automatically recorded the presence of the gray Citroën with French plates across from the post office. Someone was sleeping on the passenger side of the front seat, a hat pulled down over his face. The car had not been there when he entered the post office.

Walking quickly, Thespian returned to the car park, and climbed into the Fiat. The gray Citroën did not enter the square. He pulled into the road leading out of town, checked the rear-view mirror. No gray Citroën. His nerves were working overtime.

He drove aggressively, his mind churning. He should be able to make the 6:30 p.m. flight to London from Geneva with no problems. This was going to blow the lid off London. And Washington. Positive identification of moles in British Intelligence, not to mention other government offices, and he had proof—actual records of payments made by the Russians. Unconsciously he touched the button of his jacket. If only he could read the film right now! What names were there? This could be one of the biggest intelligence coups of the century. No wonder Lark had felt vulnerable.

Courmayeur flashed past, and soon he saw the signs for the Mont Blanc Tunnel. Perhaps he should stop in Chamonix and take one of the ski flights back to Geneva; he might be able to pick up some time that way.

Traffic had been light and there was no one in front of him when he pulled up to the blue toll booth outside the tunnel. The officer leaned out to take his money, then leisurely leafed through his false passport. Thespian tapped the steering wheel impatiently. He was amused to see the large, sturdy peasant frame draped in Italian macho: the uniform was unbuttoned nearly to the waist revealing the usual assortment of chains, a shark's tooth, and the ubiquitous Italian Christian cross. A gadgety Japanese watch circled one wrist, a gaudy ID bracelet the other. Then he noticed the rings: a cheap, square-cut turquoise and an onyx on the left hand, a bulky gold pinkie on the right. Thespian shook his head. At last, with a grin, the officer slapped the little book back into his outstretched hand. Thespian winced.

"Hey, my friend, careful with the jewelry," he said in Italian. The pinkie ring had a sharp corner and had nicked his forefinger. The guard was grinning in apparent incomprehension. Thespian pointed to the ring, then to his own finger. "This is not a contact sport," he said. The guard nodded. Thespian shifted gears and entered the Mont Blanc Tunnel.

He had driven about two miles when he began to feel dizzy. The lights, running in strips on the ceiling, blurred; he shook his head and the spell passed. The tunnel seemed well ventilated, but he rolled up his window and turned on the air conditioning as a precaution. There were still no cars in front of him. He checked the rear-view mirror. Only one car, about one hundred meters behind him. His eyes snapped back to the mirror. A gray Citroën? A vague unease nagged at him. He stepped on the gas, hoping to get through the tunnel as quickly as possible.

Although the interior was lit as brightly as daylight, he began to experience waves of dimmed vision. He was forced to slow down to keep control of the car. A spreading pain gripped his chest and he was having difficulty breathing. A kernel of fear knotted his stomach. At this high altitude, still weary from the exertion of hiking and the reduced oxygen in the tunnel, could he be having a heart attack? The tunnel seemed endless, but he didn't want to stop at one of the rest areas; better to get into the open air. He had gone five and a half miles. Two more miles to go. He felt nauseous. A stomach cramp forced him to hunch over the steering wheel as beads of perspiration dotted his forehead. His vision alternately blurred and cleared; his head felt like the target of a wrecking ball.

One mile to go. Would the tunnel never end? He was having trouble keeping the car in its lane. The gray Citroën was no longer in sight. Ahead, he could see a huge, white disk blocking the road, realized it was the end of the tunnel, and stepped on the gas, fighting for control.

Then he burst into the sunlight. He rolled down the window; but gulping the fresh air didn't seem to make any difference. He swerved the Fiat onto the shoulder and rolled to a stop. Dizziness and nausea robbed him of the energy to crawl out of the car.

Light bounced reflectively off its windshield as the Citroën emerged from the tunnel. It pulled up on the verge about ten yards behind the Fiat. Thespian tried to focus on the rear-view mirror. There were two men in the front seat. With a gesture out his window, he motioned to them. They remained in the car, looking forward impassively. The man on the passenger side looked like the guard from the toll booth. The Citroën had French plates.

Realization hit him like a jackhammer. He stared at his forefinger where the guard had nicked him. A small, black circle was forming around the minute puncture. Whatever they used was working fast. He looked into the rear-view mirror again; the men remained motionless. Waiting, he thought. The bastards are just sitting there waiting for me to die.

It was impossible, they couldn't know! He was certain he hadn't been followed from Courmayeur this morning. How had they picked him up in Aosta? Why? A chance identification with liquidation for past grievances? Unlikely—he had more value alive. They must have known about the meeting with Lark. Vertigo sucked him into its spiral. He was panting like a parched dog. At least he wouldn't make it easy for them.

He tore the top button off his jacket and put it into his mouth. Gathering all of his saliva around it, he swallowed hard. The button felt enormous. He gagged. Bile and button slid back into his mouth, tasting foul. Forcing himself, he swallowed again. The button stayed down. He was breathing in short gasps now, his peripheral vision completely black.

The two men sat impassively in the car behind him. There was no other traffic on the road. How could they have known? Lark . . . Lark wouldn't have . . . couldn't have set him up? The world became a tiny dot of light at the center of his vision. He died confused, loath to distrust his friend.

CHAPTER THREE

Room 309 at the Hôtel du Lac in Geneva overlooked the lake and the Jet d'eau, but the two men standing face to face in the middle of the room were oblivious to the view. The decor was in deep red accents on tones of gray, and the two men were the embodiment of the designer's vision: the taller, handsome man was livid, his anger splashing across his ashen-faced companion.

"He's what??" he shouted in disbelief.

The shorter man shifted uncomfortably, taking the weight off his throbbing ankle. Armchairs drawn up at the window tempted him, but he had not been invited to sit. He ducked his head to avoid the glare of the taller man, whose features were twisted around blazing dark eyes.

"I'm sorry, Major Nikolayev," he whimpered. "It was a normal dose; it should only have knocked him out." He knew his career in the KGB was probably over and was terrified by how his boss would decide to end it. As a Georgian, he abhorred cold weather.

"Tell me slowly," said Nikolayev.

"I picked him up in Aosta, exactly as you said. . . ." The man paused, deciding not to mention the three-hour gap when he had lost him in the mountains. He was a good tail in a car, even on foot in city streets, but he wasn't a goddam mountain goat. It wasn't his fault he had twisted his ankle badly only ten minutes after Payne left the trail and entered the deep woods. But the Major didn't have to know everything.

"He sent a cable from Aosta," he continued. "I couldn't stop it, but I got a copy."

"Read it to me."

He fished in his pockets, pulled out the rumpled piece of paper and read. "TRUMBULL REAL ESTATE 21 PARK LANE LONDON ON 6:30 FLIGHT MEET ME AT AIR-

PORT STOP HAVE HARD EVIDENCE OF MAJOR DAMAGE TO RESIDENCE FROM MOLES AND TERMITES STOP PLUMBING STILL LEAKS PRIORITY TIGHTEN ALL TAPS TO PREVENT FLOOD SIGNED RICHARD."

"Idiot! You should have stopped that cable!"

"I didn't get there in time. I thought he was looking for a token for the telephone. The woman had finished transmission when I went in."

Nikolayev turned his back in disgust. "Go on."

"He started back toward the border, just as we thought," continued the Georgian, truly frightened now as he addressed his boss's broad back. "So I radioed ahead. Yuri took the place of the guard at the Mont Blanc Tunnel, the drug in his ring." Despite his fear, he couldn't contain a snicker. "That crazy Yuri and his costumes! He wore so much jewelry no one would even have noticed the ring."

Nikolayev did not turn around. The man continued sulkily.

"Payne came through the toll booth using the Westley passport and Yuri hit him with the ring. It should have taken about fifteen minutes for him to get drowsy, then pass out. When he stopped on the French side of the tunnel, Yuri and I pulled behind and waited. He slumped over and we went in. He was . . . dead." He said the last word softly, as if to lessen its impact. "Yuri said he must have had a bad heart or something. Or maybe it was the altitude." Suddenly he saw a way out. Maybe he wouldn't end up in Siberia after all.

"You know," his tone became aggressive, "drugs work differently at high altitudes; someone should have . . ."

"We're discussing *your* performance, Kosov," said Nikolayev sharply. He studied the man before him. Physically, Kosov looked as if he had been assembled from a spare parts factory. Although he had a stocky build, his face had a pinched look, as if the head belonged to another body and were annoyed at sitting on top of this one. His narrow, pointed nose, and the absence of the normally prominent Slavic cheekbones, gave the unfortunate illusion that someone had pulled his chin too hard, causing all the features to slide downward. The frightened eyes avoided direct contact.

Nikolayev frowned. He had worked with Kosov many

times. While the man was not overly intelligent, he was competent, a good watchdog, and he knew how to obey orders. This was his first major mistake; it was out of character for a man with his training.

Kosov was due to be rotated back to Moscow after this assignment. It was no secret he was eager to return home; there was something about a stillborn baby while he had been away and, as a result, his wife was having a nervous breakdown. Kosov's concentration clearly was not on his work.

"What did you do with the body?" asked Nikolayev, already feeling defeated.

"Yuri drove Payne's car, taking the Chamonix exit. I followed in our car. We pulled into the trees and searched him thoroughly. The car, too. Nothing. If he *had* something, we would have found it!"

Nikolayev's skeptical expression gave him no encouragement.

"So," continued Kosov, "we drove to a ledge, put him in the driver's seat of his car, started the engine, and pushed it over the side." He shrugged. "We couldn't cross the border with a body."

"And you didn't think to contact me?"

"Well, he was already dead. Whatever he knew, he won't be passing it on."

"He certainly won't," said Nikolayev icily. "But *we* won't know what he knew, or where he got his information, will we? You are positive he made no contact in Aosta?"

Kosov shifted uncomfortably. His ankle was killing him.

"Well?" said Nikolayev.

"We did lose him for a short time in the mountains," he mumbled.

Nikolayev suppressed an overwhelming urge to smash the pointed little face.

"Get out!"

Kosov scurried out the door, crab-like, afraid to turn his back on his boss. Nikolayev reeled, sank onto the bed. Incompetent fools! He cracked the knuckles of his left hand noisily.

When he had heard, in London, that David Payne was being reactivated to meet with a Russian informer, he'd followed up with surveillance as a matter of course, not knowing where it would lead. Now he knew that Payne had been given information concerning KGB penetrations into London intelligence. The hounds were barking at Nikolayev's own back door. Was his own identity revealed in the information?

Years of careful maneuvering had established his cover in England as the owner of a small, slightly vague but profitable trading company which had rewarded him with excellent contacts in the British government. These he had gradually expanded to include MI5 and MI6. His friends in London had no inkling that he was a career officer in the KGB. To save his skin he had to find out what the information was, who had passed it, and where the informer got his knowledge. Damn them for losing Payne!

Nikolayev lay still on the bed, the sweat rolling off his body despite the breeze coming across the lake through the open window. He felt like a naked man at a masked ball, exposed, yet unable to identify his enemies. Whom could he trust? Who was leaking information from Moscow? Every time Nikolayev made a report, was he giving information to a traitor? He would have to contact Barakov in Internal Security. He dreaded the idea. Barakov's reputation was a legend in KGB circles: he was a man to avoid. But Nikolayev had no choice.

He shuffled to the desk, took out several sheets of stationery and began writing. He'd have to convince Barakov to let him take charge of the situation from London. Of course, he'd have to tell Barakov that Payne was dead. A delicate situation. Barakov was not a man to tolerate failure. Still, logic dictated that Nikolayev be given the authority to investigate: He was in the best position to monitor MI6; he was an agent in place, cover established. Even Barakov would have to admit that. A security man suddenly nosing around London would draw ire like a fly on a birthday cake.

A slow smile spread across Nikolayev's face as his angular scrawl filled the page. If he handled this properly, if he could deliver the traitor to Barakov, he'd rate a promotion. And by God, he deserved to be a colonel! He was 35; his father had been a colonel at 32. Nikolayev had a legacy to live up to.

He wrote rapidly.

CHAPTER FOUR

Yegeni Vassilovitch Alexiekov closed his eyes in a futile attempt to erase the vision before him. The late afternoon sun, streaming through the wooden slats at the window, focused like a spotlight on his mistress's more than ample behind as she bent over from the bed to put on her slippers. He heaved a mighty sigh. It seemed to him that all the Russian women he knew were fat. In more philosophical moments, he told himself they were Rubenesque, but in truth lumpy thighs and pendulous breasts were all that he could remember of a long chain of women. He opened his eyes in disgust, preferring even the reality of Helenka to the nameless parade of bodies in his memory. She was at least good-hearted, if somewhat stupid.

But why couldn't he have a woman with slim ankles and a narrow waist? He dreamed of high, pointy little breasts. He saw plenty of them all over Europe. But when he traveled he was not a free man. Prudence limited his western contacts; his social life revolved around the gangrenous Soviet colony in whichever country he was visiting. The women were either the bored wives of other Soviet officials who were looking for a behind-the-door thrill, or calculating partners provided by the KGB who filed their reports after each assignation. He avoided them as the tiger avoids the scent of the hunter. Only among the lusty peasants near his dacha, three hours outside of Moscow, was he free to choose, free of the cloak of KGB suspicion. He grunted in frustration.

Helenka waddled to his side of the wooden-framed bed, her mind and body flaccid in the pleasant afterglow of lovemaking.

"Cookie," she gurgled, caressing his face.

Yegeni flinched at the nickname. He would have preferred a more dashing sobriquet, but supposed at fifty, balding, with overeating and the force of gravity working on his body, there were precious few to choose from. Helenka leaned down to give him a wet kiss, her breasts landing on his chest like heavy dumplings.

"Do you want some sausage, Cookie?"

"No, Helushka, I must go to sleep for a bit." He rolled away from her patting hands and closed his eyes again. He loathed himself for coming back to her, but after all, what were the alternatives? True, his wife Natasha had a lithe, trim figure, although her attractiveness was marred by the set of her mouth and a hardness in her eyes. Nevertheless, his marriage was a sham. He had not made love to Natasha once in the past twelve years, not since she had been promoted in the KVD, the Soviet Counterespionage Organization. Now she actually outranked him.

The subject of divorce had never surfaced. It would be political suicide, both were realpolitik enough to know that. In the eyes of the state, theirs was the perfect marriage: a KGB husband and a KVD wife. The security of that combined power disgusted Yegeni.

But the whole New Class stratum of Soviet society, of which Yegeni was outwardly a paradigm, disgusted him. His father, an officer at the Ministry of Foreign Affairs, had groomed him carefully for power, sending him to the best schools, choosing his friends from among the well connected, teaching him how to win favor with foreign goods. Early on, Yegeni learned that privileged Party members represented a system by which they did not live—for the rewards of praising Communism were the trappings of capitalism. He had learned the lesson well: now he watched holiday parades in Red Square on his 21-inch Sony; his dishwasher came from Sweden; his brand of American cigarettes, chosen with a certain ironical satisfaction, was "True."

He didn't know how the seeds of disenchantment had sprouted and bloomed. Perhaps he was sated with the perks of power. Perhaps he traveled too often to the West, or was seeking some inner satisfaction. Once, on a trip to Paris, he read Solzhenitsyn. His appetite, whetted, grew insatiable; he developed a passion for underground literature. In Europe, he found forbidden works by Pasternak, Dostoyevsky and Amalrik that awakened a fierce patriotism for his homeland. He wanted a better future for the Russian people than that promised by the Party.

And so he had found a way to fight—not for Soviet Russia, but for Mother Russia, the homeland. In the interest of his fight, his life and status had to be preserved. That included his marriage to Natasha.

Yegeni was careful to choose lovers who posed no threat to Natasha's position, so the facade of their marriage remained intact. His loyal peasant women wanted nothing more than the fresh oranges and extra rations of milk he could provide. They satisfied his physical need. But why did they all have to be fat?

Yegeni sighed into his pillow. He usually felt more relaxed after lovemaking, the knots of tension momentarily eased. He breathed deeply, willing his mind to go blank. But sleep would not come. Instead, his mind played a film clip of the events of the past two weeks like a loop, endlessly repeating while he automatically checked for the tiny flaw that could destroy him.

Fate had presented Yegeni with one of those odd moments in life when happenstance shapes men's destinies more than they know.

He had been at his office at the KGB Center, outside Moscow. Here, in the bureau of the First Chief Directorate, was the control point for all Soviet clandestine activities abroad.

In Department A, the Disinformation Department, Colonel Yegeni Alexiekov was currently in charge of fomenting discontent among the NATO countries. His activities included supporting European opposition to America's missile base program, fanning anti-American sentiment regarding arms control, and aiding antinuclear demonstrations. He had been ordered to trim the budget on all his operations. This meant reviewing the personnel on every project in each country. He had only one more week to complete his recommendations.

A cloudy Monday morning had made it somewhat cozy under the harsh ceiling lights as Yegeni walked into the sub-basement vault that was Department 15, Central Archives. For security reasons, records in the field were sketchy, making Department 15 the only repository for complete information on all foreign operations. It was storage for pay records, photographs of all operatives and their contacts, identities of suborned foreign nationals and KGB personnel assigned abroad, and the whereabouts of expatriates.

Security was tight and elaborate. The highest clearance was required to enter the sub-basement level: photo identity at the checkpost, fingerprint clearance to enter the actual room, and signature for files. Data could be requisitioned as a computer display or printout, but strict compartmentalization limited the information solely to the reviewer's immediate area of authority. A record was kept of every requisition and the period of time the file was in use. The entire area was under constant surveillance by television cameras.

The bars on his uniform gleamed in the light and Yegeni nodded as the guard at the checkpost compared his face to the photograph on his badge. He walked through the gate toward the heavy lead door marked with a large number 15 and placed his right hand on the lighted glass panel. The computer automatically matched his fingerprints with those allowed access. A light buzzing sound indicated he had passed and the door locking system had been released. He entered the inner sanctum.

As he signed for his file under the watchful ceiling cameras, Yegeni felt a hand on his back. He turned to see the jowly smile of Dmitri Denisenko, a boyhood chum with whom he still had a firm, if infrequent, friendship. They had been Pioneers together, joined the Communist Youth Organization, Komsomol, had gone to school together, and had qualified for the elite Institute of International Relations. Although the demands of their different areas of responsibility often kept them apart, they socialized when they could, and occasionally ran into each other at the Center. With age, Denisenko's youthful idealism had converted him into a hard-line Party hawk; yet, despite the polarization of their views, Yegeni still had affection for his burly friend. He gave Denisenko a hearty grin.

"Dmitri! I haven't seen you for months!"

"The Center keeps me busy. But you, my friend, are never here, it seems."

"A field officer is always traveling. It keeps me thin." Yegeni patted his ample frame. Denisenko guffawed. Gourmet meals were de rigueur for traveling KGB personnel.

"What do you think of these cuts?" continued Yegeni, as the whir of electronic machinery halted and the clerk handed him a folder of computer printouts.

"I don't like it. We may need more activity in the Middle East, but the pulse is still in Europe." Denisenko was from Department 3, First Chief Directorate, controlling KGB operations against the United Kingdom. "I have six excellent penetration networks in London giving me top-grade information. I can't afford to lose any of it. But I'm supposed to trim the fat. What fat? I run a lean organization." He shook his head. "Information costs money." He handed the file clerk his requisition.

Still chatting casually, both men retreated toward study carrels with their papers. Yegeni passed on the latest dirty joke he had heard in Paris about a woman in a bar drinking beer. Denisenko threw back his head with a roar of laughter, slapping his side. The clerk at the counter looked up in sharp disapproval before turning his back.

"And I have one. . . ." A deep cough cut off Denisenko's words. Yegeni pounded him on the back, but the spasm continued. Each inhalation caused the coughing to become more violent, until his face was florid, his eyes bulging.

"There's a water fountain in the hall," said Yegeni, alarmed, as he led him toward the door. As he thumped on Denisenko's back, Yegeni's file folder slipped to the floor.

Jerking violently and gasping for air, Denisenko pulled away and stumbled into the hall, his own file tumbling, scattering papers behind him on the shiny, black floor.

It seemed to Yegeni that he was in the center of a very bright light, that the world had ceased to exist. With dead calm he looked at the two folders at his feet, their contents spilling out in a confused jumble. A quick glance confirmed that both Dmitri and the clerk were out of view.

Yegeni stooped, at the same time sliding his left hand into the pocket of his pants. Leaning forward so that the curve of his back was to the ceiling camera, he brought his hand out of the pocket and rested it on his left knee, as if to support himself as he bent over to collect the scattered papers. But it was not his own file that he sorted. A thin, gold cigarette lighter was deftly hidden in his left palm. With a nearly imperceptible movement of his thumb, he clicked the shutter of the miniature camera as he shuffled one paper after another into position, all the while keeping an ear tuned to Denisenko's diminishing coughs in the hall.

It was an opportunity unparalleled in Yegeni Alexiekov's seventeen years of service. Denisenko's six networks of Russian agents and their informants in London passed across the field of his camera lens. It was information to which Yegeni normally would never have access. He caught a glimpse of names, photographs and numbers as he clicked furiously, not even taking the time to digest what he was seeing, only anxious to photograph as much as possible. In the center of a whirlpool, his movements were controlled and precise. Suddenly he was aware of silence from the hall. He fumbled to find his own papers, scooped them up with his right hand, then slid his left hand back into his pocket just as Denisenko reached his side, puffing heavily from his ordeal. Yegeni made a point of stuffing his disordered papers back into their folder.

"You frightened me. Have you seen a doctor?"

"Yes, yes," groaned Denisenko, holding his aching chest as he bent to retrieve the confusion of his own printouts. "I'm supposed to stop smoking. I think I'd rather cough." He apparently didn't sense anything amiss in the disarray on the floor.

"I've found American cigarettes to be milder."

Denisenko gave him a thumbs up sign with a wide grin. "What are you smoking now?"

Yegeni's smile was beatific. *"True,"* he said.

Denisenko nodded. Both officers knew that American cigarettes, as well as numerous other items not available to the general public, could be purchased by members at the KGB Club in Building 12 across the street. The bond of privilege united the two men as each settled into his own cubicle to study his file of operations and reshape his budget.

Yegeni shifted restlessly in bed, exhausted by the continuous replay of his thoughts. He couldn't find the flaw and he needed to sleep! After the delivery of the film to Thespian in the Alps yesterday afternoon, he had driven straight to Milan, where he caught a plane to Trieste, using a false passport. From Trieste, he slipped over the border into Yugoslavia on a tourist bus. He then drove to Ljubljana, where he put in a token appearance for the

Party business that had provided his cover, switched to his own passport, flew to Budapest, and on to Moscow. It was a three-hour drive from Moscow to his dacha. His nerves were strained and he was bone tired. Helenka had helped to take the edge off his tension. Now, why couldn't he sleep?

He must have drifted; he had no idea how long Helenka had been shaking him and whispering urgently in his ear. He rolled away from her, but she was insistent.

"Yegeni! Wake up, wake up! There's someone to see you. A man in a uniform. He came in a black car with a chauffeur. Wake up!"

Yegeni jumped out of bed, grabbing for his clothes.

"Did he say what he wanted?"

"No, only told me to wake you . . ."

"Stay in here, don't come out." He looked at her face, eyes wide over puffy cheeks. "It's all right, Helushka, I've done nothing wrong."

Not exactly true. Had the ceiling cameras recorded his sleight of hand? He had covered his motions with his body. Had he slipped up? His clothing fought him as he dressed. Adjusting his collar, he walked down the corridor to the low-ceilinged front room.

The man in the uniform stood facing the windows, his back to Yegeni. He was tall, with a thick bush of black hair that was combed straight back, and powerfully built, although muscle tone was running to fat now in his later years. At the sound of footsteps, he turned. His high forehead and round, wire-framed glasses gave him an intellectual look, but his eyes lacked a scholar's wisdom. They were small and hard, black flecks of magnetite.

"Comrade Barakov!" said Yegeni with surprise and more than a little dread. "I was not expecting you. I'm sorry, I was sleeping."

"An urgent matter, Comrade Alexiekov. The telephone was not secure."

Yegeni motioned him to a chair. "Please," he said.

Barakov lowered his husky form into the overstuffed chair by the stone fireplace. Yegeni sat in a straight, wooden chair opposite him.

Yegeni always felt uncomfortable in Barakov's presence, although they were of equal rank and close in age. Barakov was a colonel in the Internal Security Department, charged with investigating treason and espionage within the ranks of the KGB, as well as penetrations by foreign intelligence. Even the most loyal Party hard-liners were nervous when Barakov appeared. Yegeni burst into a cold sweat. Barakov always got his man—or rather he always got *a* man. Yegeni suspected that if Barakov had an inkling of wrongdoing, or wrong thinking, he would not hesitate to create a victim, guilty or not.

Barakov's reputation for ruthlessness was well deserved: He had informed on his own father for protesting the Soviet invasion of Czechoslovakia in 1968. His father had been sent to the Serbsky Institute of Forensic Psychiatry for "treatment." He had never come out.

"How was your trip?" asked Barakov.

"Tiring," said Yegeni, wondering why Barakov was keeping tabs on him.

"The castle in Ljubljana is quite magnificent."

"Unfortunately, I rarely have time to be a tourist."

"A pity, when one has so much opportunity for travel." Barakov's face was a mask, his eyes hooded. When he spoke, only the muscles around his mouth moved.

"I seem to spend most of my time in airplanes and offices." Yegeni forced a laugh. No documentation could trace him from Ljubljana to Italy or back again, and his presence in Yugoslavia had been carefully calculated to give maximum cover to his real activity under the guise of Party business. He decided to put an end to the fishing expedition.

"You mentioned an urgent matter, Comrade Barakov. I assume I can be of assistance?"

Barakov ran his hand through his thick, dark hair. "We have an ugly situation on our hands," he said.

Yegeni waited.

"I have reason to believe there is a penetration."

"In what area?"

"Someone with access to London operations."

"London," said Yegeni, in what he hoped was a thoughtful tone. "There are several people under me, in Department A, who would be involved with London projects. How do you know this?"

"An English agent died near the Mont Blanc Tunnel on his way to London with information."

Yegeni ordered his mind to move to pastoral images—

gentle fields of wildflowers, blue cloudless skies. Anything to fool his nervous system and prevent physical reaction, to keep the blood from rushing to his face, to keep his breathing even.

"And you think he got that information from one of ours?"

"I'm working on that assumption."

"What was his information?" Yegeni's lips felt dry, but he refrained from licking them.

Barakov looked mildly surprised at the question. "Information on London operations," he repeated.

"That leaves the field rather open," said Yegeni in exasperation. "Nearly every department in our Directorate, and in most others, has *some* interests in London!" What game was Barakov playing? "Do we have any background on the English agent?" Please don't let it be Thespian, not Thespian because of me. Who else was operating in the Italian Alps? There could be hordes of agents.

"I've put that through proper channels," replied Barakov. "However, I believe I've come up with a reasonable candidate from our side."

Water was a good image. He could feel the coolness of a pond, deep, still water. If he concentrated hard enough, he could see the grassy banks; Barakov dissolved into velvet grass and pebbles seen through shimmering ripples. From this oasis of calm, Yegeni's voice floated out, disembodied.

"Who?"

"Dmitri Denisenko."

"Denisenko!" A jolt back to earth. He had expected to hear his own name.

"You are acquainted with him, I believe?" said Barakov.

"Yes. We've known each other since our Pioneer days."

"You have maintained the friendship?"

"We see each other occasionally."

"You have seen him recently?"

Delicate ground. This was beginning to feel more and more like an interrogation. It was possible that Barakov didn't know about the meeting at Archives. It was equally possible that he did.

"At the Center, last week. I ran into him." If Barakov had seen the tapes from Archives, he was covered. "We spoke briefly about the budget cuts. He had a dreadful cough." All true and duly recorded on camera. Quicksand from here on in. How much did Barakov know? Yegeni could feel the dampness in his armpits. He moved his elbows out on the sides of the chair, hoping Barakov wouldn't notice he was sweating.

Barakov seemed bored now. He sauntered to the spindly, handpainted sideboard, surveyed the bottles, and selected Stolichnaya. He poured out a double shot.

"Do you mind?"

Yegeni was on his feet at once. "No, please, help yourself." He, too, poured himself a vodka.

"Why Denisenko?" asked Yegeni.

"Denisenko controls six important networks in London."

"Many people have interest in London." Yegeni instantly regretted this remark. He had several projects in London; he had fallen neatly into Barakov's trap—if it was a trap.

"I'm sorry to burden you with this. I know your trip was tiring." Barakov's voice oozed smooth concern.

Yegeni decided to brazen it out. "If this is true—and I must say I hope it is not—why are you telling me? I have no authority over Denisenko."

Barakov smiled for the first time, a maneuver which only pulled back his lips to reveal his even, yellowing teeth and left his eyes unwarmed.

"Nooooo," he said, holding the word just long enough for it to sound slightly patronizing. "I thought, because you are not in his department, but are friendly with him, that perhaps you could investigate a little for me. Socially, I mean. Draw him out. Discover any psychological sponginess that might indicate where his sympathies lie."

Yegeni nodded. It was not unusual for the KGB to ask its members to spy upon one another.

"Yes, I suppose I could do that. I am traveling a lot, but I could arrange to see him more often socially when I'm in Moscow."

"Good."

"Can you give me any more specific information? It might help me to lead the conversation, know what I'm probing for. . . ."

"I don't have more information at this time."

"Was Denisenko, or whoever, in direct contact with this English agent you mentioned?" He had to know more!

"Your involvement, Comrade-Colonel, is character surveillance. Get closer to him."

Time for retreat. "Like a fox romancing a chicken," said Yegeni, using one of Barakov's favorite phrases. He raised his glass and downed the last swallow of vodka. Barakov revealed his teeth again; it shivered the hairs down Yegeni's back.

"Needless to say, this conversation is to remain between us." Barakov strode to the front door.

Yegeni nodded slightly. Famous KGB phrase, he thought, as he watched Barakov slide his bulk into the back seat of the long, black Chaika. The chauffeur saluted smartly and climbed into the driver's seat; his passenger looked neither right nor left as the car roared out of the gravel drive, the miniature green KGB ensigns with the hammer and sickle flapping on each front fender. Yes, leave it to Barakov to try for the psychological advantage. Yegeni turned back to the house.

He couldn't see the satisfied smile on Barakov's face, or know that he was on his way to an apartment on the Nevsky Prospekt, there to play the same scene before Dmitri Denisenko, this time casting Yegeni Vassilovitch Alexiekov in the role of traitor.

The next morning, the buzz of his Seiko alarm clock chased the long night of disturbing dreams from the edge of Yegeni's consciousness. He rolled over with a groan. Helenka stirred beside him. He patted her gently, told her to go back to sleep. Lying in the dark, watching the first finger-thin glimmer of dawn light the sky out his window, he wondered why he felt compelled to make this trip. Logically, it was an unnecessary risk: he would have to do some fancy paper shuffling to justify an urgent trip the day after he had returned. He didn't have a plan, hadn't the faintest idea what he could accomplish; he only knew he had to be in the right place, and his intuition rarely led him astray.

He kept a low profile at Sheremetyevo Airport, although he had to pull rank to get a seat on the crowded plane. He recognized no one, thankful for small favors.

The Aeroflot steward distributed the morning Geneva newspapers left on the plane from the flight in. News censorship for those arriving or departing the U.S.S.R. was redundant: great pains, however, were taken to insure that not one scrap of newsprint left the aircraft on Russian soil.

He might have missed the article had he been able to sleep on the flight, but every time he closed his eyes, his brain began hammering at him, driving worry and fear like a spike deep into a post until it split. He immersed himself in the papers for distraction. The article was buried on page 14. The lead read: "Man Killed in Automobile Accident Outside Mont Blanc Tunnel." It was a short article: a car had missed one of the turns on the descent from Mont Blanc to Chamonix and fallen 400 feet. Apparently the accident had occurred on Thursday, although the wreckage was not found until Friday afternoon. The driver had been killed instantly. He was identified as Richard Westley, British businessman.

Yegeni felt sick. He made his way to the lavatory, splashed cold water on his face, then stared at himself in the mirror. He knew now what he had to do; he hoped merely to get there in time.

The police chief in Chamonix was sympathetic, but helpless. Yes, he understood that Monsieur represented the family of the deceased, but this was Saturday, the proper paperwork must be performed and the morgue office was not open until Monday. And besides, he had received a call from London that the widow would be here to claim the body, so he couldn't do anything until he heard further. Perhaps Monsieur would like to take advantage of the weekend to enjoy the mountains, try his luck at the casino, or do a bit of skiing on the high slopes? Early June was the best time to be in Chamonix. . . .

Yegeni fumed; the chief was apologetic. Chamonix was a small town; there was not adequate staff at the morgue for weekend operation. Certainly Monsieur could see the body for identification, but removal was out of the question until Monday. Yegeni went along to the morgue.

The smell of formaldehyde grew stronger as he followed the clerk down the stairs into the body-storage room. The echo of their footsteps bounced off the green tile walls and floor. One side of the room was a wall-size filing cabinet, each drawer neatly labeled. The clerk was accommodating: the remains of Mr. Westley were in drawer 7, but *mon dieu*, the body was very badly torn in the crash. He shook his head sympathetically. Yes, he understood deep personal loss. Monsieur could definitely have a few moments alone with the body. He would wait upstairs in the office. He pulled drawer number 7 open, shook his head again, and withdrew.

A draft of cold air wafted around Yegeni as the drawer opened. He stared at the sheet covering the body—the cliché of death. Slowly, he lifted the white fabric.

Lark squeezed his hands into fists, his knuckles white from the pressure. The body was ragged, a gouge in the torso spilling internal organs like so much spaghetti from a bowl. The rib cage was broken; the third and fourth ribs protruded at right angles from the form. Bits of glass from the windshield were imbedded in the badly smashed face.

When Barakov had begun playing cat and mouse, Yegeni realized that the microfilm had not been recovered. Indeed, Barakov may not even have been aware of its existence or there would have been no need to kill Thespian. As he stood above the mangled body, Yegeni suddenly knew where the film was, knew what he would have done in Thespian's place. He hated the thought of what he had to do.

The equipment lay on a cabinet near the autopsy table in the adjoining room. He quickly selected the scalpel and tongs, slipped his hands into a pair of rubber gloves. As he approached the body, his resolve wavered. But he had to get the microfilm. The scalpel touched flesh, bore down. It required more pressure than Yegeni had anticipated. The sternum was in the way, and he had to use his hand to probe underneath it. He was forced to play elaborate mind games to get himself through the procedure.

The button was lodged in the esophagus, halfway between the throat and the stomach. Yegeni withdrew his hand, fought the nausea that bubbled acrid liquid into the back of his throat. He popped the button apart; the microfilm lay undisturbed in its shell.

He washed his hands in the sink in the corner for a long, long time, wiping tears from his cheeks. I'm sorry Thespian, for that—and for this. I'm sorry . . . I'm sorry . . . I'm sorry.

The plane ride back to Moscow was interminable; he was the passive victim of his turbulent thoughts. How had they traced Thespian? He had no way to develop the microfilm to find the traitor. He would repay them for this, he vowed. Somehow, he would get the microfilm to Barnsworth in London. Thespian's sacrifice would not be wasted.

He thought his rage was spent by the time he completed the long drive to his dacha. He had kept the accelerator floored for most of the trip, cursing the slow-moving vehicles that crossed his path. Helenka met him at the door. Her very presence touched something deep inside him, something that burst open, sending its infection throughout his being like a lava flow. Ignoring her protests, he grabbed her roughly and forced her into submission on the hallway floor. His fury crested as he thrust himself into the ignorant, innocent peasant woman.

Afterward, Helenka cried for half an hour. "You hurt me. You've never hurt me before," she whimpered. Yegeni was stricken; he hadn't meant to abuse her. He comforted her as best he could.

"I'm not myself, Helushka. Forgive me. I . . . I lost control of myself."

Helenka sulked. He couldn't begin to explain that he was trying to forget—forget his life, what he had done to his friend, and that he was responsible not only for his death, but for the desecration of his body.

"Please, Helushka, don't cry. I'm sorry," he said.

"I didn't know you could be so cruel."

"We never know what we're capable of." He rocked her tenderly in his arms, stroking her coarse, brown hair. "I'm sorry . . . I'm sorry . . . I'm sorry. . . ."

CHAPTER FIVE

It was warmer than usual for August. Peter Barnsworth sat in his shirt sleeves in his London office, feet propped on his big, ugly desk. His attention was focused on the Signac painting on the wall. The painting was his latest indulgence, the result of an unexpected inheritance, a month ago, from an ancient, nearly forgotten uncle. It was incongruous amidst the drab surroundings, but that didn't bother Peter. Pointillist technique fascinated him: that each individual dab of pure color, a dot meaningless in itself, could complement its neighbor to give the illusion of form and substance, was a lesson in creative thinking not unuseful in the intelligence business. Peter accorded it the rapt attention of a devoted pupil.

The buzz of the intercom bored its way into his concentration. Annoyed, he swiveled his chair away from the luminous colors and punched the offending button.

"Yes?"

"Your call to America, sir. It's finally come through."

"Put it on 6, Betty."

She obediently patched the line into the scrambler, which shut out her ability to listen, as well as any other attempt, human or electronic, to monitor the call. Secrets were becoming increasingly amusing to her. Before the day was out, she would probably have a report on this private conversation to type for the files. With a wry smile, she turned back to her typewriter.

Betty Cowdrick had her secrets, too. She paused, fingers splayed above the keyboard. Unable to resist temptation, she pulled out the gold chain hung round her neck that disappeared into the amplitude of her bosom. The full carat diamond ring swung from the end of the chain, rising from her cleavage like a phoenix, its fiery sparkle catching the light. The mere sight of it sent a visceral thrill through her body. Soon that full carat would be joined by a gold band studded with more diamonds; the set had been chosen nearly six months ago. And soon she would be able to wear both on the fourth finger of her left hand.

Betty was a woman who had recognized early that her only fulfillment in life would come through devotion to her work. Accordingly, she had set up housekeeping with a sickly, demanding mother in Islington and poured all her energies into rising through the secretarial ranks in British Intelligence. She had been Peter Barnsworth's personal secretary for fifteen years. Peter admired her diligence and loyalty and only occasionally took advantage of her time, but she gave more than willingly of both time and energy; she had nothing else to live for.

Until she met Dudley Thurston.

She was thirty-five when romance beckoned for the first time in her life. Dudley was a recently widowed shoe salesman who recognized in Betty all the attention and mothering he had lost upon the death of his wife. It was a whirlwind courtship during which Betty soon discovered that a typewriter and a classified document or two could never be replacements for sex. Betty and Dudley announced their engagement. British Intelligence was quick to respond: Her Majesty's government wanted to know every detail of Mr. Thurston's life. The security of the Empire rested upon his answers. Dudley fled. Betty's heart broke.

She returned to Islington and the pouting wrath of a mother scorned. For ten years she pined, threw herself into her work, and assembled a startling collection of erotic literature.

It was sheer chance that she had attended a British Embassy "do" a year and a half ago with Peter, when his wife came down with appendicitis. There she met a handsome, slightly younger American who found himself drawn to the warm, womanly qualities she possessed. Before long they were sharing the bounty of her library shelves.

But Betty had learned her lesson. She kept this lover to herself, hidden even from her mother, and this time Her Majesty's government was denied the key to her bedroom. She gazed at the winking diamond in her cupped hand. After twenty-three years at MI6, she was tired of security and its demands. As soon as her fiancé completed the book he was writing, they would be married. Two weeks before the wedding, she would give Peter Barnsworth notice. Until then, MI6 wouldn't even know she had a suitor. And then it would be too late: she would no longer be in the intelligence business. Meanwhile, she wore her ring nestled between her breasts and kept her own delicious secret.

In his office, Peter, oblivious to his secretary's private life, was growling into the telephone. "Don't you people get messages? I've had a call into you for three hours!"

The voice on the other end chuckled. "You've had a call in to your operator for three hours, but they just sent it under the Atlantic. Can't you people learn to run a phone system?"

Peter let the remark go by. Carter Sloan was hardly the ideal colleague, but he had been David Payne's assistant and in the wake of Payne's accident two months ago, Carter had inherited the liaison desk in Washington. Peter was obliged to deal with him—at least temporarily. How an American had ever been recruited into the British Secret Service still mystified him, despite Sloan's half-British, half-American ancestry and dual citizenship, even despite two decades of acceptable performance. Peter gritted his teeth.

"Carter, I need Jessica Autland."

"David Payne's daughter?"

"Yes."

"What do you mean, you need her?" The belligerence in Carter's voice was undiminished by the distance it had to travel.

"I mean," said Peter pointedly, "I want you to send her over here. Fast."

"Oh?"

"When I spoke to her on the telephone, I indicated there were some . . . unfinished matters . . . regarding her father's work for us. Bureaucratic procedures. Unfortunately, I was unable to persuade her as to their urgency."

"I'm not surprised."

"Perhaps you can do better in person. She knows you. She might listen."

"I don't know. She's taking David's death very hard. I think in some crazy way she's blaming herself for letting him go off on that hiking trip alone. It's only been two months; give her a little time."

"I wish I could." Peter wanted to add that he also blamed himself for Payne's death, but he refused to give Carter the satisfaction.

"I'm beginning to think you know more than I do. . . ."

"Yes, Carter, I've always been quite certain of that."

Carter was not amused by British pomposity. "Am I getting the picture that there was more to David's trip than a mountain hike?"

"You're getting no picture, Carter. You're getting Jessica."

"No go. I smell a rat. Whatever you have cooking, may I remind you that she's a freelance journalist by profession. She doesn't work for us. She's out of your jurisdiction."

"But you're not."

"She's one of those Freedom of Information Act supporters, for Christ's sake! A power to the people liberal. It drove her crazy that David worked for us; they had an ongoing argument about intelligence. She's a woman of strong opinions and I don't think . . ."

"The subject is not open for discussion."

"This isn't a family business, Peter. The children are not required to follow their father's footsteps. Especially a father killed in the line of duty."

"This is an order, Carter. I don't care how you do it, just get her over here."

"You know something? You're the most callous bastard I've ever known."

Carter banged the telephone down, not caring to subject himself to the response. What the hell did Peter think he was doing?

When, after two years of marriage, David Payne had refused to give up his career with MI6, his wife filed for divorce without telling him she was pregnant. Five months later, she married Jim Autland, an American sheep rancher, and moved to the States with him, making the child legally his. Jessica grew up in Colorado without any knowledge of her real father. It was her mother's way, Carter supposed, of protecting herself and her child. It was no life with a husband in covert work: risks were high, hours uncertain, and there could be no sharing of office troubles at home. Agents shouldn't marry, thought Carter wearily.

With Payne's assignment to a desk in Washington, Jessica's mother finally told her the truth, whether out of deep-seated guilt or on the assumption that Jessica was now safe, Carter wasn't sure. At any rate, he'd been in the office the day an eager, coltish woman in her early twenties had arrived at the gate at Langley demanding to see David Payne on a matter of life or death. David had not been forewarned; he arrived at the gate ready for any number of crises, but hardly ready to meet a daughter he never knew he had. It was an awkward meeting between two strangers who bore a striking resemblance. And to their mutual delight, they found they liked one another. In a short time they had formed a strong bond.

It was extraordinary, mused Carter, how the father-daughter relationship had blossomed in six years. Yet, although Jessica practically idolized her father, she was outspokenly critical of his career. A product of her generation, thought Carter angrily. All those kids so righteous about the government not interfering in foreign politics. How the hell did they think the world was run?

He shook his head sadly as he reached for the telephone. Maybe they were right. Here the Service had gobbled up another life, and now Peter wanted the daughter, too. What the hell was happening? Despite a twenty-year career, the intelligence business sometimes turned Carter's stomach.

Three thousand miles away, Peter Barnsworth was thinking the same thought.

Jessica Autland moaned slightly in her sleep, dream images receding as she was pierced by a brilliant light. She was a raindrop with the sun shining on it, suffused, engorged with light. She opened her eyes. The sunlight was lancing through her hotel window. She looked at the travel clock on the bedside table: 2:00 p.m., an hour and a half before her appointment with Peter Barnsworth.

Smashing the pillow behind her, she propped herself up in bed.

"London," she muttered. The buzzing of a saw sounded outside her window. She rubbed her eyes and adjusted the pillow away from the light. What on earth was she doing in London?

Carter Sloan had harangued her all afternoon about the necessity for this trip. Only half convinced, but finally responding to his sense of urgency, she had rushed to get to the airport on time, only to find herself on an earthbound plane for an hour before being transferred to one capable of flight. Two hours later, when the Washington-to-London flight took off at last, the three toddlers sitting with the tired-looking woman in front of her had made sleep impossible.

Jessica admitted that the trip would have been more comfortable had she accepted Carter's offer of a first class ticket, but the less she was beholden to the Service, the better she liked it. The price of her pride was total exhaustion when she reached her hotel.

As Carter instructed, she took a taxi from her hotel in Albemarle Street to Harrods department store, where she purchased a box of stationery, then strolled down the Brompton Road. At precisely 3:30, she turned into a residential side street flanked by stately row houses. Number 37 was the fourth from the corner. Lace curtains at the tall windows, wide steps with a curve of iron railing, and an ornate front door bestowed a Victorian graciousness to the old stone.

A maid in a black uniform with white apron and cap answered the bell instantly. The maid ushered her wordlessly into a paneled drawing room.

It was a comfortable, upper middle class room with two chesterfields and several wing-backed chairs clustered about a Chinese carpet in shades of muted rose. A marble fireplace dominated the room.

Almost immediately, the sliding doors at the far end opened, admitting a man in his mid-fifties with a dense crop of dark hair veined with gray. He closed the doors behind him.

"Good afternoon, Miss Autland. I'm Peter Barnsworth." He gave her a firm handshake. Fierce blue eyes bored into her, then softened as he smiled. He was dressed in pressed tweeds and carried a Meerschaum pipe. He looked, to her American eyes, as if he had just finished reading the *Times* over his egg cup and was contemplating taking the Bentley for a spin. Despite her earlier peevishness, she thought she was going to like Peter Barnsworth. He motioned her to one of the wing-backed chairs and waited until she had settled herself.

"First, let me express how terribly sorry I am about your father."

Jessica murmured a thank you.

"I assure you that I feel his loss as deeply as you. He was an extraordinary man. I knew him for thirty-two years; there is no one I respected more." Unsure how to proceed, he took the moment to sit opposite her.

"Your father was . . . dedicated to intelligence work. It was the most important thing in his life. Until he found you, of course."

"We had a very special relationship, although it was rather short. I know he enjoyed working for MI6; we had a friendly disagreement on that subject. He found a desk job tedious after so many years in the field."

"Exactly. He often told me about your 'friendly disagreements.' That makes it doubly difficult for me to say this, Miss Autland." He puffed on his pipe, then stared at the ornately carved bowl as if it could help him speak. "But I think you should know the truth. Your father was working an off-the-record assignment at the time of his death."

It caught her off guard. When she could speak, her voice was a whisper. "He told me it was a spur-of-the-moment hiking trip. He wasn't working in the field any more."

"It was an extraordinary circumstance."

"But his cover was blown."

"Yes, it was a big risk. He didn't have to accept this assignment. He chose to go, knowing those risks fully. He felt the objective was worth it."

"And was it, Mr. Barnsworth?" Jessica was surprised by the intensity of the anger that surfaced. "Was the objective worth sacrificing him?"

Peter sighed. "From the outside, death always looks like a needless sacrifice. And perhaps it is. I can't be the judge of that. I do know that we do not treat any man's life lightly. And we have no direct evidence that it was not an accident. It may have had nothing to do with the mission."

"Simply coincidence. What a surprise that a blown agent gets blown away."

Peter could think of nothing to say to ease the moment for her. How could he make sense of an existence that defied sense? Despite her blazing green eyes, so like her father's, she looked soft and vulnerable, younger than her thirty years. She was wearing a silk blouse with a high neck ruffle and a cream-colored suit, but an underlying sensuality about her transformed the classically cut lines into something subtly sexier. Her glossy, auburn hair was pulled loosely into a chignon, leaving soft tendrils to curl about her face. Indignation aside, she looked utterly charming. How thrilled David must have been to have found this daughter!

He paced to the fireplace, debating how much information to reveal. Why couldn't intelligence gathering be left to electronics, to satellites? People only complicated the business! He spoke softly.

"Miss Autland, I know this is a shock, and I'm truly sorry."

"Why? Why would he do it?"

"Perhaps I can explain the background of your father's work for us. Some of the facts that were shielded from you in the past."

He sketched, briefly, the details of David Payne's years of service, ending with the close relationship between Thespian and Lark and the strange personal request the Russian had made two short months ago.

"Suddenly, Lark was afraid to trust anyone but your father. Based upon their relationship, David felt compelled to make the contact. In a cable sent to me after the meeting, he indicated that Lark had firm intelligence on Russian penetration into the Secret Service. If we are dealing with moles, as we call them, this information is of the highest priority. You must not think, Miss Autland, that your father was called into service and sacrificed for nothing."

The blaze was gone from her eyes. Something precious had been snatched from her life and her instinct was to fight, to lay blame, to pass judgment. And to seek retribution. But how could she judge this man? He and her father had shared the same code. Their values were not hers, but she could not condemn Peter Barnsworth without also condemning her father. And David Payne had chosen to accept the risks. It was his life; he had the right to live, and perhaps even die, as he chose. Anger was replaced by an overwhelming sadness.

"Thank you for trying to put it in perspective for me, Mr. Barnsworth. . . ."

"Call me Peter."

"Peter. It is ironic though, isn't it?" She shook her head.

"It was impossible for this . . . Lark . . . to trust anyone except my father. But now that he's gone, someone else will have to be trusted after all."

"Well, actually," replied Peter, clearing his throat, "I am hoping that will not be true. Lark made another request a few days ago; he asked for the only other person he feels is absolutely above suspicion. I'll admit it's a bit out of the ordinary; perhaps he sees this mission as a legacy of some kind." A long silence. "Lark asked for you, Miss Autland."

Somewhere behind Jessica, a clock, hitherto unnoticed, tick-tocked like a time bomb. Jessica found herself breathing in rhythm to the ponderous ticking.

"Really, Mr. . . . Peter . . . I'm not in your business. Why on earth would a Russian I've never even met ask to pass this kind of information to me?"

"Apparently he met you several years ago at an international conference. You, of course, were unaware of his identity, or of his special link to you."

"But. . ."

"Unfortunately, I don't read minds, my dear, so I can't tell you his motivation. I'm sure it has to do with his tie to your father, but also the fact that he would recognize you."

"It's ridiculous! I'm not in the same business as my father. If he needs to hang on to some sort of sentimental link to his past, I'm afraid I don't. . ."

"It's unusual, but from Lark's viewpoint, it's not totally ridiculous. And I assure you, he is far from sentimental. He's feeling vulnerable in the wake of your father's death; he's afraid to trust anyone here at MI6. You may be the one person he feels won't betray him."

"You must see that this is absurd. What makes him think I'd do it? I'm not a trained agent."

"It should be a simple task, nothing more than a brush contact in a neutral city; a piece of microfilm would be slipped into your pocket or hand. The danger to you would be minimal, precisely because you are not an agent; no one would suspect that you were making a contact. And you have an excellent cover for traveling as a freelance journalist. It's actually not a bad idea."

"If you know anything about me from my father, surely you know that I've never approved of. . ."

"We're not talking about meddling in another country's

affairs, Miss Autland. We're talking about another country meddling in *ours.*"

"I don't think. . ."

"Think of yourself as a lifeline to a drowning man. He has nowhere else to turn. You may be the only person he is absolutely certain is not working for the Russians. How simple to slip you a bit of microfilm without arousing suspicion or exposing himself to a double agent. I'm familiar with your disapproval of clandestine operations, but surely you would help to unmask Russian spies in the midst of Her Majesty's government." Peter gave her his most sincere smile.

"You're making it sound as if I am the only hope."

"No, of course not. We have a very capable Service. It would expedite a difficult problem, however. And it may save this man's life."

Jessica leaned back, resting her head against the wing of the chair. Peter took a long draw on his pipe.

"We would give you a crash training course for your protection," he continued. "But even on the outside chance the KGB knows the information is going to be passed, you still would be safe: As a civilian, you would be a totally unexpected target. A brush contact is the simplest technique to master. If I thought you were in any danger, I would not even suggest it."

"I still don't understand why an agent whom *you* trust couldn't handle this."

"Frankly, until I receive Lark's information, I don't know whom to trust. Lark made it rather clear he would not contact anyone from MI6. I thought, because you were so close to your father, and knowing that he considered this a crucial mission, you might be persuaded to finish it for him, to accept Lark's request." He was going for the jugular, but he had no choice.

Jessica pushed a lock of hair from her forehead. She was too tired to wade through the jumble of emotions that were bubbling just beneath the surface. The whole thing was preposterous!

"Think it over," said Peter. "Come back tomorrow morning at 10:30 and tell me your decision."

Jessica nodded. What she really needed was sleep, then perhaps she could sort out her feelings and think clearly.

She stood, picked up her purse, and reached for the package from Harrods.

"Better leave that here," said Peter. "It was a gift. And tomorrow morning, stop in Piccadilly at Fortnum and Mason. Pick up a tin of biscuits, or marmalade or such."

Jessica gave him a skeptical look.

"One must play little games in our business, my dear."

"And what game am I playing?"

His smile was genuine; she could see he enjoyed the subterfuge. "First, you're being sociable: you're bringing Miss Harcourt, the lady of the house, a little breakfast treat. Secondly, you're giving MI6 the opportunity to make certain you are not being followed." He pulled a braided cord hanging near the sliding doors. The maid appeared.

"Thank you for coming," said Peter.

The evening air felt pleasantly cool as Jessica turned into Brompton Road, now filled with the tangle of rush hour traffic. Impulsively, she decided to walk the mile and a half back to her hotel. There was comfort in joining the flow of people streaming home for the evening meal, comfort in the mundane routine of ordinary existence where spies and microfilm and death were the stuff of novels read before bedtime.

She gave herself to the solace of the evening, to its promise of rest and renewal.

At Wellington Arch, coming up from the underground walkway, comfort gave way to depression as she was confronted by the marble and bronze war memorials, tribute to the thousands who had been asked to die for their country in war. And were still being asked, she reflected, in a time of peace. The evening no longer promised respite. She quickened her pace, anxious to reach the hotel.

Room service delivered an uncommonly good dinner, but she hardly tasted it. For the first time in her life, she honestly didn't know where she stood.

As much as she was repelled by the thought of working for a covert organization, she was intrigued by the importance Peter had placed upon her participation. It was a bit heady to think, even for a flash of history, that she might be involved in the fate of the free world. Heady and frightening. She admitted that she was scared. This microfilm had cost her father his life, despite years of experience and expertise; she was being asked to rely on luck and anonymity. Lightweight qualifications at best. Besides, intelligence gathering was hardly the life she had chosen for herself. It was foolhardy, and she would tell Peter in the morning that her answer was no. Let someone trained for risk do the job.

Of course, Peter had said the risk was minimal. Why did she feel this sense of excitement? Had her father felt it as well? She could picture him arguing with her over the importance of MI6, and suddenly she understood him better. Of course he had felt it! He was a link in a chain, however delicate, that affected the balance of world power. She hated herself for being intrigued.

She crossed to the window, looking out at the deserted skeleton of the building going up across the street as she explored every cubbyhole of her mind. Her feelings were in direct opposition to all the arguments she had used in the past. She paced the floor as the decision rippled into huge, philosophical questions about the nature of life itself. She was trapped in the conundrum. Finally, weary with self-examination, she drifted to sleep, her unconscious gleefully taking charge of a dream world filled with obscure images and encoded truths.

The next morning was gray, low heavy clouds portending rain. Suitable, thought Jessica, pulling her raincoat more tightly around her as she walked over to Fortnum and Mason. The mechanical clock over the entrance read exactly ten o'clock. She looked right and left for some shadowy presence of MI6. If Peter were so certain that no one would suspect her, why was he checking for surveillance? Spooks! Paranoia went with the business. She forced her mind away from the thought. She had made her decision —no point in dwelling on it.

But it gave her a peculiar feeling to know that unknown eyes watched her every move. As she paid for the tin of Patterson's Shortbread she had selected, she was skittish and dropped the 50 pence the clerk gave her in change. It was foolish to be nervous; supposedly she was being followed by the good guys.

Outside, the burden of moisture finally overpowered the air suspending it and a light drizzle began to fall. Jessica hailed a taxi and debated the virtues of a female Prime

Minister with the driver all the way to Brompton Road. He was relieved to drop her in front of Harrods. She entered, then emerged from a side door and walked to the row house around the corner.

In the drawing room, Peter was standing by the fireplace. He extended his hand with a welcoming smile.

"Good morning, Miss Autland. Feeling more rested?" He took the Fortnum and Mason package from her and set it on the table.

"Yes, thank you."

The maid brought in a tray of coffee. She cast sidelong glances at the two people in the room, then withdrew without a word. Peter poured the coffee from the delicate blue Wedgwood pot.

"Cream?"

"Black, please."

He unwrapped the package and his eyes kindled as he saw the red plaid tin with the Scotsman on top. "Ah, Patterson's! Excellent choice!" He held out the opened box, but she shook her head.

"No harm in enjoying the byproducts of the game, Miss Autland." He selected a piece of shortbread and munched it with his coffee.

They sipped in silence, an awkward tension building.

"I hope you didn't have too difficult an evening," said Peter.

Jessica smiled for the first time. Peter noticed that her whole face seemed to come alive.

"Thank you, I had a terrible evening, as I'm sure you were hoping I would."

Peter looked slightly abashed, started to protest, but Jessica put up her hand.

"One of the disadvantages of being a Libra is the ability to see both sides of a question. I'm an awful fence-sitter. I no sooner convince myself of one side, than I make an equal case for the other." Her eyes teased him. "But you probably have all that in your file on me."

Peter's smile was noncommittal. "And on which side of the fence have you landed?"

Jessica took a deep breath and gazed at the ceiling.

"I'm a journalist," she began. "I write about people: how they cope, what they think about the way life treats them, their hopes for themselves and the world. I've never liked politics except as it directly affects people's lives. But it occurred to me last night that I'm passive. I report on how we adjust after things have happened. I got to thinking last night, what will they put on my tombstone? 'Here Lies a Recording Secretary'?"

Her earnestness was appealing. Peter felt a stab of envy that David had such a daughter.

"Why are you smiling?" she challenged.

"I was thinking how like your father you are."

"Am I? My father hated the Washington job because he wasn't in the action any more. But I stay out of the action, sitting at my typewriter. Perhaps a person should take an active role once in a while."

"It can be rewarding."

She regarded him thoughtfully. "I don't know whether it's a latent desire for adventure, or the feeling that I'm making a contribution to the world. Maybe it's a connection to my father, and I need that. I don't know." She sighed. "It was a long night, but you can be pleased: you hooked me. I landed on your side of the fence."

"Thank you, Miss Autland. Thank you *very* much!" Peter thrust the tin of shortbread at her. "Do try one, they're first-rate!"

She couldn't help laughing; they were allies now. She took a piece of shortbread.

He paced in front of the veined marble fireplace, detailing the plans for her training at the MI6 "estate," a country house in the Cotswolds, a few hours drive from London. It would take a week. She would live there for immersion training in self-defense, fitness, surveillance evasion, communications, the types of contact Lark might use, and firearms. In all probability, none of it would be necessary, but he wanted to ensure her safety.

"My stepfather tried to teach me to shoot when I was growing up on the ranch," said Jessica. "Probably why I retreated to the safety of the written word. I don't believe in guns, Peter. I won't shoot anyone; I absolutely refuse to do that."

"You won't have to shoot anyone, I'm sure," soothed Peter.

"I did an article, several years ago, about a family—a family of hunters, all experts on guns. 'Never point a gun at anything you don't intend to shoot' was the father's motto. He shot himself in the head in his own living room, demonstrating to his daughter that the gun wasn't loaded. Two months later, the son shot his best friend: an accident in the woods. The son's body was found not far away with a bullet in his head from his own gun." She shook her head. "I am haunted by that family. Guns invite death; I won't carry one."

"For your own protection, a few sessions of target practice will be included in the curriculum," said Peter. The authority in his voice was not lost on Jessica.

"The training is for your safety; we aren't anticipating trouble," continued Peter. "Lark will be contacted when you are ready, then the ball will be in his court." He pulled twice on the braided cord by the door, then outlined the rest of her day. She would go shopping with a woman who would leave the house with her. They would return to her hotel for lunch at one o'clock, after which she would pack her bags, leaving them in her room. Then she and the woman would continue shopping. At some point, a car would pick her up and drive her to the country.

"Remember," he concluded, "we are operating with maximum security. Not even your instructors will know what your assignment is. Don't drop even the slightest hint. This is our private project, Miss Autland: just you and I together."

For better or worse, till death do us part, she thought. Aloud she said, "You'd better start calling me Jessica."

The drawing room doors opened to admit a dowdy woman of indeterminate age, wearing an unfashionable but serviceable gray suit. There was something oddly familiar about her.

"I'm Betty," she said, offering her hand with a smile. Although her clothing, hair, and even manner were altered, Jessica was certain this was the same woman who had been the maid.

"Betty has several duties around here, as you'll discover," said Peter, in response to her quizzical look. "At the moment, she is Miss Isabel Harcourt, the lady of the house and your shopping companion. An old friend of your mother's."

Jessica looked astonished. "But mother *does* have an old friend named Isabel Harcourt who lives in London!"

"Of course. This is her house. We arranged for her to embark on a short holiday. Are you ready?"

Jessica could feel her last independent breath being squeezed out of her as the tentacles of MI6 closed tightly.

Peter led them to the door. "Your father would be proud of you," he said, helping her on with her raincoat. He retreated to the parlor to watch them from behind the curtain as they descended the steps. How long would it be, he wondered, before he could stop hating himself?

CHAPTER SIX

Sitting in the small, dingy outer office above Oxford Street, Kosov couldn't help overhearing snatches of the telephone conversation taking place behind the closed door of the inner room. He wasn't trying to listen. There was simply no other place for him to go except into the corridor. The trouble was, try as he might, he couldn't hear enough to understand what the conversation was about.

He gave up, busied himself with staring at the jumble of files and papers strewn on every conceivable surface in the room. Two desks, three file cabinets, several side tables; all were stacked high. The papers had no relationship to the actual activities that transpired within these four walls, but he knew they supported the claim on the door that this was the office of the Bonmar Trading Company. Their sheer volume and disorder would discourage all but the most diligent from searching the premises. And if it came to that, his boss would be long gone.

A throaty laugh erupted from the inner office.

Odd, thought Kosov, how many sides a man's personality can have. Although he couldn't discern the drift of the conversation, he noted a silky quality to the Major's voice that was totally unfamiliar to him. He treated his boss with the utmost circumspection; Nikolayev was demanding, his temper volatile and harsh. Kosov had seen it at its worst. Yet the soft tones coming from the other side of the closed door gave no indication of the darker side of the personality.

The sound of a key in the lock turned his attention to the door leading to the hallway, and he rose quickly as the door swung open. Yuri entered, wiping his forehead on the short sleeve of his shirt. His sandy hair was damp and left a wet splotch on the cotton fabric.

"It's too hot," he complained. "The lift was out; I had to

climb the stairs." Carefully he unhooked his wire-rimmed glasses, took a handkerchief from his back pocket and wiped his temples where the glasses pressed a permanent, thin indentation.

Kosov nodded. "It was out yesterday, too."

"He here?" said Yuri with a toss of his head toward the inner office.

"On the phone."

"He still in a sweat about that Italian Alps thing?"

Kosov raised his eyes to the ceiling and shrugged.

Both men sat down on the padded bench against the wall. Yuri cleaned his glasses with his handkerchief, shaking his head.

"It's always us little guys who get blamed for the failures." He looked at Kosov sympathetically. Technically, Kosov was his boss, the leader of the field team. Nikolayev told Kosov what he wanted, and Kosov figured out how to do it with Yuri's help. But in reality, although he'd only been working with Kosov for a year, he felt more like an equal. When Kosov's tour of duty ended, Yuri would take his place. Still, at the moment, Kosov was in charge, and the Major had skewered him for this mistake. Yuri tried to prop him up with sympathy.

The door to the inner office was flung open, and Nikolayev's tall frame filled the doorway. He motioned both men inside.

"Well, Comrades, we're moving at last, despite your blunder in the mountains." Nikolayev settled himself behind the desk.

Kosov and Yuri sat, at Nikolayev's sign, in the straight-back chairs opposite him.

"I'm giving you both another chance," said Nikolayev. "Of course, Kosov, I had to make a notation in your dossier about an unauthorized wet action. . . ."

Kosov flinched at the KGB euphemism for murder. Yuri was right: the little guys got the blame. It wasn't his fault the English agent had died; he'd followed his orders exactly. But mistakes had a way of dribbling down the chain of command. Now the blot on his record would shadow him forever.

"But," Nikolayev continued, "I'm certain you can overcome one error. You've done excellent work in the past. I'm relying on both of you. This operation is extremely important. Your job will be surveillance. Surveillance only. That is a direct order; I want no violence. Any more violence and you're washed up, understood?"

"Yes, Comrade-Major," said Kosov.

"You do your best for me, and I'll do my best to get you back to your wife."

Kosov nodded, a glimmer of hope in his eyes. He was trying to make a good life for himself and his new little bride, Raya. She had been a translator at the Russian Embassy in London. They had been married for four months when a complicated pregnancy forced her back to Russia where her mother could care for her. Then, two months ago, the baby had been born dead and Raya had fallen apart. Now she refused to leave Moscow. He needed to be at her side, but his tour of duty in Europe had three months to run. Possibly Nikolayev could get him sent home early.

The lecture over, Nikolayev allowed himself a smile, pressing his fingertips together in front of him, unable to hide an almost schoolboy delight. "This will be an interesting assignment. We have the upper hand from the outset. And I will be your field director."

Kosov sat up straighter in his chair. He was going to have the Major on his neck for the whole job. He was already nervous.

"This is to be a flawless operation," continued Nikolayev. "Requisition three transceivers with earphones from the Embassy here in London. We'll keep in touch by radio once we're active. And pack a bag. We don't have a destination yet, but it will probably be the Continent."

Kosov and Yuri exchanged glances. They would be glad to escape the dreariness of London.

"It shouldn't take long," said Nikolayev. He leaned forward. "The target is a woman: American, auburn hair, green eyes, 5'6", about 30. Name: Autland. Jessica Autland. Be ready to begin work in a week."

CHAPTER SEVEN

A week later, Jessica was in Dover. The chalk white cliffs of Dover Beach were dazzling in the sunlight, not glimmering in moonlight as Mathew Arnold had eulogized them, and no flotilla of small boats escaping from Dunkirk bobbed on the waves. But as Jessica stood in line to board the Hovercraft to Boulogne-sur-Mer, she was singing under her breath:

> There'll be bluebirds over
> The White Cliffs of Dover . . .

She couldn't remember the next line and the phrase kept repeating itself in her head; it brought tears to her eyes.

The Channel crossing was a luxury after a tiring, intensive seven days of training in the English countryside. The Hovercraft lived up to her expectations. It rose from the cement beach in Dover, gray rubber flaps huffing at its sides, ungainly propellers whipping above it, like some monster of the future. It took forty minutes to cross the Channel, skipping above the waves, occasionally bumping the crests—a roaring, heaving behemoth. It bellowed onto French soil and deflated with a mighty sigh. Transportation as entertainment.

Jessica joined the stream of travelers boarding the train to Paris. Settling into her seat, she let her inner monologue follow its own pattern.

Training at the country estate for the past week: she hadn't exactly resented it, but she had been impatient with the secrecy surrounding even mundane activities. She had no classmates; she had seen no one during her stay except instructors, yet she had known there were others—footsteps heard outside a closed door, a glimpse of a car pulling into the drive before she was whisked away.

Who were they? Where would they go and what would they do?

Target practice was particularly ironic in the verdant summer countryside. She was forced to shoot various weapons for an hour each day to the accompaniment of enthusiastic praise when she placed a tiny hole in a paper target shaped like a man. The targets were never shaped like a woman. Perhaps the English thought that ungentlemanly. In any case, she had refused to carry the small, pearl-handled automatic that Peter ordered her to put in the lining of her suitcase. Political advantage could never justify the taking of human life, she told him. There was no point in carrying a gun if she adamantly refused to use it, and she might be in more danger if it were discovered. He had acquiesced grimly.

The meadows and wheat fields of France rolled by. She glanced away from the window and caught the man sitting opposite her staring at her hands as her fingers twisted nervously in her lap. Self-consciously, she held them still. His eyes moved up to meet hers, held a moment, then turned back to the copy of *Le Monde* lying on his lap. Suspicion! Who was he? Was he watching her? The paranoia had already begun.

Her father once said that one could learn to live with constant fear, that it became a welcome companion, trusted to sharpen the wits and give impetus to action. She had been full of doubt then, but now she sensed fear as a looming presence, possibly a companion, she admitted, but hardly welcome.

Her cover as a freelance journalist was comfortable because it was true. She was writing a series of articles on Paris for *Around the World,* an English travel magazine published by Rutford Publishing. If anyone took the trouble to check, the company was prepared to acknowledge that she had been given a contract. Peter had even arranged that, if she produced an article, it would appear in the magazine. But her contact telephone number for Rutford rang on a special line in Peter's office, and during off hours, he carried a beeper. He was her "editor," using the name George Wheeler. She could maintain communication simply by picking up the telephone. The connection wouldn't go through a scrambler, as she was always to call from a public phone, but information could be couched in innocent trade talk, the meaning clear between them. She was to report to Peter when and where Lark set up the contact.

Spurred by the thought of her cover story, or perhaps by the spike of fear, she extracted from her handbag a notebook and the blue fountain pen Peter had given her. An ordinary pen, except that the top was hollow, with a space large enough to hold a piece of microfilm. Rather deliberately, she made a few notes; the pen worked perfectly. A furtive glance at the man opposite her proved him to be engrossed in his newspaper. Jessica sighed. Was she excited or depressed? Had her father felt this ambivalence at the beginning of a mission?

Her train arrived at Gare du Nord exactly on time, depositing her in the midst of hundreds of other summer travelers. She concentrated on finding the man from the train, but he had vanished; it seemed a good omen.

As her taxi scuttled in and out of traffic, the wide boulevards and graceful architecture swept her back through time: elegant carriages and plumed horses replaced the snarl of modern, honking automobiles. What a beautiful city, Paris!

"Quelle bonne après-midi!" she called out as she caught the driver's eye in the mirror. He held her glance for a moment, then returned his concentration to the swarming traffic. *"Oui,"* he said flatly.

The afternoon was indeed appealing. It had rained in the morning, but now the sun was sparkling on the remaining puddles; the city looked freshly washed, proud of itself. The taxi came to a halt at the entrance to the Hotel LaPorte tucked into a corner of the Seventh Arrondissement on Boulevard Raspail. It was an ideal location, a short walk to the cafés of St. Germain des Prés, yet only three or four stops on the métro from Madeleine and l'Opéra in the heart of the Right Bank. It would be easy to get around the city.

The hotel hadn't changed since the last time she had stayed here, almost ten years earlier, fresh out of Columbia University and weary from an intense, undergraduate relationship that had fallen apart. Eight weeks in Paris had been a glorious tonic then. She warmed at the memory of a torrid affair with a dark-haired Adonis who turned out to be an American studying at the Sorbonne. Too bad they had lost touch after she returned to the States. The trip had even provided her with her first sale as a writer: an article for an American magazine on student life in Paris. All in all, a productive eight weeks. She was smiling as the doorman took her suitcase.

Hotel LaPorte was a modest establishment, neat, clean, but far from fancy. Although it catered to middle income travelers, it preserved a certain graciousness not uncommon in older European hotels. The lobby was as she remembered it: no more than a dozen comfortable leather chairs were grouped around small tables and the tiny restaurant off to the side was accessible only through the hotel. Sentiment aside, it would be easy to spot surveillance here.

A thin man with a drooping moustache was sorting receipts at the front desk. Reluctantly, he put them aside, pushed the registration form toward her.

"Autland? *Mais oui*, we have your reservation, Mademoiselle. May I have your passport, please?" His voice sounded like a recording, his eyes were blank. "Amal," he said, handing the bellman a key as Jessica finished signing the register. "512 for Mademoiselle."

Room 512 was directly across from the elevator. The French windows were open, letting the warm afternoon breeze freshen the usual stale hotel room odor. Stepping to the window, Jessica looked down into a narrow side street where a bakery and greengrocer provided neighborhood amenities. She turned to the private bathroom, a concession to her Americanism. Same old fixtures, but clean. She tipped the bellman, then sank down onto the bed. The bedspread hid a lumpy mattress.

Unpacking was an abbreviated ritual, a few things for the closet, the rest remaining in the suitcase. She would be in a hurry once she received the microfilm. She plopped into the velvet tub chair. Street sounds floated up to her open windows. She was here; now all she had to do was wait.

The minutes crawled by, punctuated only by an occasional loud voice or automobile horn rising from the hum of life outside. "Biding Time" was the one class missing from the curriculum in the English countryside. At last, she crossed to the desk, opened her typewriter, and laid out her notes on the Hovercraft crossing. A writer writes.

She worked steadily and was stunned, as she typed the

last period, to discover it was nearly dinner time. The article was fairly respectable; her concentration was so compartmentalized from professional experience that even thoughts of Lark had failed to break the barrier. Unfortunately, that also meant that he had not tried to contact her.

Jessica used the telephone booth on the corner, down the block from the hotel. The connection to London went through quickly; she recognized Betty's singsong coming from across the Channel.

"Rutford Publishing."

"Jessica Autland for George Wheeler."

"One moment, please."

It was the ritual they had pre-established. Betty sounded utterly convincing as a switchboard operator. Peter was right about her versatility. Peter's voice came on the line.

"It was a lovely crossing," said Jessica. "Paris is *très gai*. And I've written my first article, just to let you know you're getting your money's worth. But I'm terribly lonely."

"Industriousness is good for the soul; that's your Puritan ethic. Chin up, you won't be lonely for long."

"It's good to have a friendly voice as near as my telephone."

"At your service, my dear. Enjoy your dinner."

"Thank you. I'm interpreting that as carte blanche for at least a one-star, one-fork rating."

"We'll try to sneak it through the Treasury."

The next morning was hazy and hot. She ate breakfast by the open French windows in her room and sat at the typewriter to polish the Hovercraft article. By noon, the phone had not rung and she decided upon a quick lunch in the hotel dining room. At the desk, the blonde who worked the early shift assured her that she could be paged in the restaurant. The meal was uninterrupted.

The afternoon dragged by. She rewrote the article, peered into the apartment opposite her window, and memorized the street map of Paris she had brought with her. Waiting was agony.

The next day she read two popular paperbacks, but later couldn't remember the name of either. She took to eating rushed meals in the hotel dining room, then racing back upstairs.

She called Peter, using the public telephone in the lobby this time.

"Rutford Publishing." Betty's singsong never varied.

Peter was unperturbed. "Patience, patience, my dear," he soothed. "These things take time. Interviews are always subject to last-minute schedule changes."

By the end of the third day, cabin fever struck. She slept badly; dark smudges appeared under her eyes. What had gone wrong? She should have been back in London by now.

On the fourth day, instructing the desk to take messages, she burst from the hotel like a rabbit sprung from a trap. Paris enveloped her.

The Left Bank held her memories of ten years ago. She walked the streets, amazed by the new, delighted by the familiar. Some businesses were closed, observing the Parisian penchant for the August *grandes vacances,* but tourism was making inroads on the old customs and many shops were doing a brisk business.

In the Rue Bonaparte, at L'Oiseau Doré, the small boutique where ten years earlier she had run amok, Madame Picarde remembered her and gave her a fond welcome, enticing her yet again with a dazzling collection of clothing. She bought a dress for old time's sake, then lunched at Lipp, not too proud to trudge up the twisting iron stairs to eat with the common folk.

By late afternoon, she had called the hotel six times to ask for messages, even called twice, disguising her voice, to leave word for herself to be certain the desk was attending to its obligation. She felt ridiculous hearing her own words read back. There were no other messages.

Absorbed in frustration and thankful to be free of the confines of her room, she didn't notice the gray Citroën that clung to the curb a half-block behind her, or the stocky man with the narrow face who sometimes walked along the sidewalk on the opposite side of the street. Boredom had replaced fear, that companion who kept the wits sharp.

The most difficult part of life, she mused over briny Bélon oysters in a charming café, is that one has to live every second of it consecutively. There are no fast cuts, as in a film, where the waiting can be reduced to one terse scene, then on with the plot. No, life served up the minutes one at a time, the next not offered until the first had been completely devoured. Life was relentless. She gobbled up a rich chocolate mousse and took a wrapped napoleon back to the hotel.

The lobby was deserted and she glanced wearily at the desk as she entered. Drooping Moustache was poring over a magazine, but he straightened with a grunt as she approached. From a box behind him, he extracted a paper, tossed it on the counter, then returned to his magazine. Jessica tried not to snatch it off the counter. She affected an indifferent *"merci"* as she headed for the elevator. The note read: "Jonathan Meunier from *Fine Arts Magazine* wants your article by Friday, August 23."

At last! The code placed the meeting a day before the stated day, so that would make it Thursday. Tomorrow. The time was determined by adding the two numbers of the date together, which made it five o'clock. It was finally happening.

She had never heard of Jonathan Meunier or of *Fine Arts Magazine*. The telephone directory yielded no listing for *Fine Arts*. She switched to the I-Z volume, found four columns of Meuniers, but no Jonathan or even J. Puzzled, she looked at the message again. Had the desk clerk made an error? She went back to the directory; there was a Meunier Boutique, but that didn't fit. Lots of first names and initials. Where did *Fine Arts* fit in? Then she had it and she grabbed the A-H volume again. Art gallery. Galerie Meunier was listed on Rue des Saints-Pères. So, tomorrow, Meunier Gallery, five o'clock. She fell into her first deep sleep since her arrival.

Before breakfast the next morning, Jessica was in the phone booth in the lobby.

"Rutford Publishing." Betty's voice had become slightly bored. Jessica played through the scenario.

"Jessica Autland for George Wheeler."

"Hold on, please."

Peter's voice was cheerful. "Yes, Jessica?"

"Just wanted you to know I've decided to include an interview in this piece."

"Excellent. First person encounters make for crisp writing."

"Ah, pithy advice from the editor." Her laugh tinkled, tinged with excitement. "I may have a rough draft by this afternoon. And the Galerie Meunier has a show you would enjoy, if you could spare the time."

"You'll have to tell me about it."

"You can count on it. Every graphic detail!"

Now that the waiting was over, her mood was lighthearted. A simple brush contact while browsing in an art gallery, and she would be on her way back to London. If one had patience, the spy business wasn't so bad.

It was eight hours to rendezvous, eight sunlit hours to enjoy the city. Her interest had become professional again: if she could get another article out of this trip to sell to Rutford, it would make the lost time of the past few days worthwhile.

By three o'clock, exhausted from observation and weighed down with notes, she returned to the hotel to rest. She had begun the day warily, looking over her shoulder for a suspicious presence. But later, free of shadows, she began to relax. After all, the entire basis for her presence in this mission was as the unexpected link. Who was going to follow a writer touring Paris on assignment?

At 4:15 she crossed the street to the small sidewalk café facing the hotel and ordered a Verveine. Half an hour later she paid her bill and sauntered toward Rue des Saints-Pères. Now she was conscientiously checking for a tail as she had been taught: watching store windows for reflections; turning into a street, then abruptly switching direction; ducking into doorways to emerge seconds later to confront those behind her. She was enjoying the game, was certain she had not been followed.

A gray Citroën was only one of several cars already parked along the street as she turned into Rue des Saints-Pères. She barely glanced at any of them, her attention on the moving cars and pedestrians. At exactly five o'clock, excited and a little cocky, she stood on the sidewalk evaluating a painting in the window of Galerie Meunier.

The small gallery was deserted as Jessica entered. The buzzer in the floor mat brought a smiling woman from behind a screen at the back of the room.

"May I help you?"

"I . . . I'd like to look, thank you."

The woman waved her hand around the room. "Help yourself. I'll be in the back if you need anything."

Jessica made a brief inspection of the work on the walls. It was morbidly silent in the room; her heels echoed on the hard waxed wood. She faced each painting in turn, hardly aware of what was directly in front of her, focusing her attention on her peripheral vision. It was 5:05. She glanced through the big window into the street. Several figures passed; no one looked in.

She moved to the file of unframed lithos in a stand in the corner, positioning herself so she could be seen from the street. She leafed through the file slowly, pulling some pieces out to look while stealing glances outside. It was 5:10.

The woman padded out from behind the screen.

"Were you looking for anything in particular?"

Jessica gave a nervous laugh at the choice of words. "No, I'm a slow looker. May I browse?"

"Certainly. There are some lithos by our featured artist, Berton Allard." She waved a hand toward the painting on the walls. "But we've other artists also. If you're interested in posters, I have some rather good ones of shows this year in local galleries."

"Thank you. I'll have a look."

It was 5:15. She took another tour of the room, then returned to the file of prints. How long should she wait? Had she misinterpreted the message? What if she were in the wrong place? She pawed, unseeing, through the pictures. It was 5:20.

"I'm sorry to trouble you," she called out, looking toward the screen. The woman stuck her head out. "May . . . may I have a glass of water, please? I feel a little faint." Jessica put a hand to her face.

"Of course." The woman brought her a glass of mineral water and motioned her to the narrow, white bench in the center of the room. Jessica gulped down the liquid. It was 5:25.

"Feeling better?" asked the woman as she retrieved the glass.

"Thank you. Yes. I'm sorry."

"Did you see anything you liked?"

Jessica looked at the bright colors ranged around the room. "Well, uh, I'm very drawn to Allard's use of color, the fluidity of the movement, but a painting might be out of my range. I'll browse through the lithos."

The woman nodded and retreated.

It was 5:30. Where was Lark? She'd wait until six o'clock. With a sigh, she plunged into the pictures in the stand.

The buzzer under the mat sounded the minute she turned her back. She jumped. A young man, well dressed, dark hair combed flatly to his head, entered, smiled briefly, and glanced sweepingly at the paintings. His appearance was not even close to the photograph she had seen of Lark. Was he an intermediary? Had Lark been detained and sent this man in his place? She watched him from the corner of her eye as the woman came from behind the screen.

"Ah, Louis," she said, wagging a finger. "You are early. But it is ready." From the back room she brought a painting framed in ornate ormolu.

"Yes, yes, it's exactly right," said the young man.

"I'll wrap it." The woman turned and Jessica caught Louis's eye.

"It's a very handsome frame."

"Thank you." His eyes played over her body. "Are you an Allard fan?"

Jessica flushed under the frankness of his gaze. "Actually, I've never seen his work before." She looked cautiously toward the screen, then back to Louis. He had both hands in the pockets of his denim pants. Did he have something for her? A message? Had Lark sent him? Her confusion registered on her face.

"I'm investing now," he said. "He'll be valuable one day. I suggest you buy one."

"Thank you, I'll keep that in mind."

His smile was warm. "If you like, I could help you choose."

"Here you are," said the woman, appearing with the painting wrapped in brown paper. He took it, then looked at Jessica.

"Join me for a drink? I'll tell you about Allard, and then we can come back. The gallery is open till nine."

Was this a signal? Was she supposed to go somewhere with him? But in the few moments they had been alone, he'd made no attempt to give her anything. "I'm sorry. I'm busy this evening," she said.

"Another time?" His look was inviting.

Jessica wanted to laugh. She was playing superspy, and this man was only trying to pick her up.

"No, I'm leaving Paris tomorrow. Thanks anyway."

With a shrug, Louis hoisted his painting. "You should buy a painting as an investment, though. Allard is going to be hot," he said over his shoulder as he walked out the door.

The woman turned to Jessica, palms up. "Louis always has to try."

Jessica nodded. The woman looked at her expectantly. It was nearly six o'clock. Desperately, Jessica turned back to the lithos.

The woman made a final attempt at a sale. "How are you doing?"

Jessica looked at her, grabbed at the print in the file before her and thrust it at the woman. "I'll take this one."

The woman beamed. "Good choice. That's one of my favorites. I'll tell Louis you bought something. He'll be pleased." She leaned forward and spoke softly. "He's Berton Allard's younger brother."

Miserably clutching her artwork, Jessica stood in the doorway, looked up and down the street. As she turned right and started back toward the hotel, two men came out of a café, climbed into the gray Citroën, and slowly pulled away from the curb.

In the hotel lobby, Jessica's hopeful glance at Drooping Moustache brought a bored, empty look in return. She shuffled into the elevator. Upstairs, depositing the artwork on the dresser, she seized the scrap of paper and re-read the message. "Jonathan Meunier from *Fine Arts Magazine* wants your article by Friday, August 23." She couldn't have made a mistake; what else could it mean? Had the desk mixed up the date? She used the telephone in the hotel lobby to call Peter.

"Articles never go as one plans," she complained as soon as Betty had put her through to Peter.

"What happened?"

"I wasn't able to get the interview. It was a no-show."

"I forgot to warn you that research is often dull."

"I've learned that several times over, thank you!" Jessica laughed.

"No other problems? You don't think anyone is trying to scoop you, do you?"

"Not that I know of. I was careful today."

"Good. Keep on your toes."

"Thanks." Peter seemed calm enough; perhaps this was normal procedure for contacts to be missed. But she would be glad when the whole thing was over.

The Michelin Guide lay open on her dresser upstairs. Food! She deserved at least a two-star, two-fork rating. She glanced ruefully at the rolled lithograph. Would MI6 rather pay for an expensive gourmet meal or an abstract expressionist lithograph? They probably wouldn't pay for either if she couldn't make contact with Lark.

CHAPTER EIGHT

A cool, leisurely bubble bath had done wonders to restore her spirits. Jessica decided upon a well-known restaurant near the river for dinner, and further indulged herself by dressing in the soft, green silk dress she had bought from Madame Picarde. The color exactly matched her eyes, giving them a deeper, luminous cast.

She was relaxed as she descended in the elevator, but bedlam greeted her as the doors parted to reveal at least seventy-five Japanese tourists milling about the lobby snapping pictures while two harried bellmen tried to clear a pathway through mountains of luggage. Apparently a tour bus had deposited this horde a few minutes earlier, but the desk did not have enough rooms reserved. Drooping Moustache was clearly losing the skirmish as his frantic instructions in French and English were met only with smiles and slight bows from an indignant tour leader who brandished a reservation confirmation from his travel agent like a battle standard.

Jessica picked her way through the melee, ducking out of camera shots. Suddenly she felt a hand on her arm. Turning, she discovered its owner to be an attractive man with velvety brown eyes and a strong, straight nose. His black, curly hair leaned more toward tousled than unkempt; his six-foot frame was solid and tapered in a fashionably cut summer suit. He towered over the teeming Japanese like a skyscraper over traffic. She stared in astonishment as he spoke.

"Jessica? My God, it is! Jessica Autland!"

The voice sent a ripple of excitement through her.

"Gordon?"

Then she was swept into his bear hug and swung around. The maneuver usurped more than their allotted space, unleashing a torrent of Asian invective accompanied by polite smiles and bows. The offenders returned bows and smiles with apologies, then held each other at arm's length as best they could in the crush of bodies, eyes devouring each other like children seeing the tree on Christmas morning.

"What are you doing in Paris?"

"I was going to ask you the same question."

"I can't believe it!"

"How are you? You look fantastic!"

"How long has it been?"

"Ten years, I'd say."

"You . . ."

"Let's get out of here!" They elbowed their way through the throng and escaped, breathless, to the relative serenity of the sidewalk.

"Magnificent!" said Gordon, with a lingering appraisal. "You were a beautiful girl ten years ago, but now—a magnificent woman."

Jessica blushed. "Thank you. You look rather dashing yourself."

"What are you doing in Paris?"

"A business trip."

"And you returned to the Hotel LaPorte. May I flatter myself that it was in memory of me?"

"It has certain fond memories, I will admit. This is my first trip back to Paris since we. . . ." She gestured vaguely in the air. "But I certainly didn't expect to find you here." She lowered her voice. "You aren't working this hotel, are you? Hitting on traveling American ladies?"

"I have forsworn such sordid occupations. But if this American lady will allow herself to be hit upon, I'm free for dinner. Were you on your way somewhere?"

"Your timing is perfect; I could use a pleasant diversion."

"Business is bad?" he asked, taking her arm and propelling her down the street.

"Business is all right. I needed a friendly face." The pressure of his arm against her body sent a bolt of lightning through her.

"That's something I specialize in, a friendly face for all occasions. I shall wine and dine you under the starry Parisian night—just like old times. And then. . . ."

"You haven't changed a bit. Ten years and you are exactly the same. Aren't you married yet?"

"Nope. I never found anyone to match the first girl I gave my heart to. Any more excuses?" He looked pointedly at the bare fourth finger of her left hand.

"Where shall we have dinner?" she said quickly.

"Is there a choice?"

There wasn't, of course. The tiny restaurant on the Quai des Grands-Augustins had been the romantic setting of their last dinner together, ten years earlier. It had left them practically penniless then. Michelin had bestowed only one star, but the three-fork decor reduced the food to a mere accessory. The room was exquisite: crystal sconces on the wall twinkled in the glow of candlelight; a deep vermilion rosebud graced each table; vases of fresh lilies in huge sprays perfumed the air. They settled into a secluded banquette.

"And just what is the business that has brought you back to me?" asked Gordon, as the waiter handed them menus.

"I'm a journalist," replied Jessica. "I'm doing some travel articles on Paris." She glanced at the menu. Madame was not burdened with a price list. "And you? What are you doing here?"

"NATO," said Gordon, signaling to the waiter. "I divide my time between Brussels and Paris. Shall we order?"

The meal decided upon, they tried to account for the passage of a decade.

"I had nearly finished my work at the Sorbonne," Gordon was saying over an awesome pâté de fois gras, "when my mother became ill and I had to return to the States. I couldn't go back to Europe—her health was failing. So I took my Ph.D. at Georgetown. I tried to find you several times in New York, but you weren't there. Disappeared completely."

"I had finished Columbia, and the *New York Times* had enough reporters, so I went to visit a friend in California. I got a job on the *San Francisco Chronicle*. The letter I wrote to you in Paris came back stamped 'No such person.' I thought maybe I invented you!"

He gave her a slow, steady smile that reached out and engulfed her. "We did have a sensational eight weeks back then, didn't we?" he said.

"The best."

"I missed you."

"It's probably good we lost track of each other." Jessica kept her tone light. "We might have discovered we hated each other in the humdrum world."

"You can't really imagine that!" He had a way of making his eyes dance that she had forgotten.

"It's hard to keep up that level of romance."

"Not when the prince has just rediscovered his fairy-tale princess."

Jessica laughed. "You may be the exception. I'd forgotten what a smooth talker you are. What were you doing at the hotel tonight?"

"Saying goodbye to a friend. He's going home to New York tomorrow. I tell all my friends to stay at the LaPorte, for old time's sake. And it finally paid off."

Dinner arrived. The kitchen managed to pull off a coup, clearly indicating that a reassessment of its one-star rating was in order. The duck was impeccably roasted with peaches; the ris de veau in sherry sauce was impressive. A mellow Bordeaux rounded out the meal perfectly.

"You look very successful," said Jessica as she sipped the wine. "NATO must agree with you."

"It's interesting, challenging . . . and gives me a amount of status." His eyes twinkled. "But tell me about you. What do you write?"

"Nothing important, yet. I worked as a reporter for a couple of newspapers, then I started freelancing. It's harder, but I love it. I get a byline now. Human interest stuff, mostly. Kind of the offbeat angle on current events."

"I'll bet you're good at it."

"I keep selling." She held up crossed fingers. "Eventually, I'd like to have a regular column. I'm very interested in women's issues."

"Does that mean you're a libber?"

Jessica laughed at the horrified look on his face. "If you mean that in a pejorative sense, no. I'm not militant. But, on the other hand, I don't always wear a bra." His eyes slid down to the green silk curve of her breast.

"My problem," she continued, flushing, "is that I'm uncomfortable with aggression. I don't like to lead the fight. So I'm a great supporter with my typewriter."

"Ah, the safe choice."

"I do my share. I wrote a long piece for the *New York Times Magazine* exploring discrimination against women in corporate structure and other professions considered to be male bastions. And *Forbes* published my article on equalizing pension benefits—for both sexes."

Gordon smiled. "Touché."

After the dishes were cleared, the waiter arrived with a dessert tray. Gordon chose a napoleon that, Waterloo notwithstanding, could have conquered the world; Jessica settled on a saintly *mousse au chocolat*. The conversation flowed easily. Jessica had forgotten the sheer animal magnetism of this man, the charm, the warmth. Any thoughts of Lark were completely driven from her head. Over a brandy, she told him about finding her real father.

"And you had no idea?" said Gordon, swirling his brandy in the delicate snifter.

"None. Jim Autland had known my mother before she married my father. As soon as she was divorced, he married her, and presto—I was born into the Autland family. A very premature baby, I might add. I never knew she had been married before."

"It must have been a shock when you found out. Why did your mother tell you, after all those years?"

Jessica shrugged. "I don't know. Maybe she was tired of the lies, wanted to set the record straight. Or maybe she wanted David to know he had a daughter. . . ." She smiled self-consciously. "I call him David. I think of him as my father, but I called Jim 'Dad' for so long. . . ."

"Are you close with him now?"

Jessica stared into her brandy, then took the last swallow.

"He died this past spring in an automobile accident while on vacation."

His eyes shared her pain; he looked away. "I'm sorry," he said.

The night was fragrant as they emerged from the restaurant. The Seine made gentle slapping sounds against the cement embankment where a passing boat ruffled its waters. As they leaned on the parapet, the mood of old friends sharing the past was charged by the present magic growing between them.

"How is it you never married?" asked Gordon, tracing the line of her jaw with the back of a finger.

"I did." They continued their walk, arm in arm, along

the water. "For three years. I wanted a career; he wanted a *hausfrau*. I came home from a writing assignment one day to find he'd taken up housekeeping with my next door neighbor. It was a grade B movie. I can laugh about it now, but it changes you. Why didn't you marry?"

"I was always terribly wrapped up with my job. I suppose the women knew they were in second place." He stopped walking, pulled her to him. "Or perhaps the right woman had come and gone from my life."

Ten years melted away with a single kiss. A taxi took them to Passy. As it turned into the Rue Raynouard, Gordon played tour guide. "An historic street, my darling. Number 66." He pointed as they passed. "Ben Franklin lived here with his lightning rod. Behind this garden, number 47, leered old Balzac. Rousseau lived in this street and . . . so do I." The taxi stopped in front of a graceful building with cupolas and grillwork.

Gordon's flat was on the fourth floor, spacious and elegant, but Jessica had only fleeting impressions as she sipped the brandy he offered. The air between them was electric, conversation superfluous. Gordon knew how to let the fire smolder as he proceeded slowly, oh so very slowly, to touch, then to kiss her closed eyes, the tip of her nose, then found his way more urgently to her mouth.

She was greedy for the touch of him, the taut muscles of his body, the texture of his skin. Her body undulated under his exploring hands. He undressed her slowly, smiling as he folded each garment with care, then turned to admire and caress his latest revelation. She was trembling with desire as he cupped his hands over her breasts and bent to kiss the mole nestled in the valley between them.

"A mole not easily forgotten," he said. Jessica held his head against her breasts, burying her face in the sweet scent of his black curls.

She had not forgotten the things that pleased him and was rewarded with sighs of pleasure. They touched with the memory of past caresses, yet with the urgency of new discovery, the years of separation fading away, yet adding mystery and newness to their togetherness. He led her into the bedroom. Even there, entwined on the cool sheets, he did not hurry, but let her draw him deeper and deeper as they moved together, pleasure building upon pleasure, exquisite and unbearable, until the universe exploded.

Afterward, they lay silent for a long time, her head resting in the crook of his arm, their bodies reluctant to draw apart. Jessica had one threadlike thought of messages and microfilm and missed meetings, all highly improbable and unimportant. Gordon was stroking her hair.

"How long are you staying in Paris?" he asked.

"Is it time to talk already?"

"Not if there's something you'd rather do."

She answered him with her hands, taking the lead this time. Her joy in touching him aroused him as much as her caresses. Their passion rekindled quickly, demanding urgent, swift release.

Finally spent, no words left to say, they slept, naked bodies still entwined.

The howl of the telephone woke Jessica. She blinked, adjusting to the unfamiliar surroundings. At the window, closed blinds parried the intruding thrusts of morning light. The bedroom, like the living room, was elegantly furnished with Art Deco overtones in a masculine slant. Two etched flamingos in an extended stance flanked the curved mirror above the dresser, where a chrome clock read 8:00 a.m. Jessica stretched luxuriously as she heard Gordon's voice on the telephone in the living room. Snuggling into his pillow, she buried herself in his lingering scent. The bedroom door opened.

"Ah, sleeping beauty, up at last." He tweaked her toe from the foot of the bed.

She folded her arms under her head. "How long have you been up?" He was smartly dressed in a tan suit and blue shirt.

"A while. Your morning meal awaits you in the breakfast room."

"Very impressive!"

He went to the bathroom and returned with a deep red silk robe, holding it for her as she got up. As he wrapped it around her, he kissed the nape of her neck; she reached for him in response, but he took her hands in his. "Oh no, I have an important meeting this morning. You'll have to be content with breakfast."

"Killjoy."

They ate breakfast in the kitchen, the Eiffel Tower across the river framed like a painting by the window.

"You never answered my question," said Gordon. "How long are you staying in Paris?"

"I'm not sure," replied Jessica as responsibilities edged back to produce a twinge of guilt. "I . . . have some research to do for these articles."

"What are you looking for?"

"Some offbeat places to go, things to do."

"Well, my love, you are in luck. I happen to know a great deal about Paris. Ask me anything."

"I thought you had a meeting."

"I do. We'll discuss it over dinner tonight." He kissed the top of her head. "Make yourself comfortable here."

"But. . ."

"There's an extra key in the cookie jar."

She followed him into the living room, balancing her coffee mug, and watched as he flipped on the telephone answering machine.

"You don't have to worry about the telephone," he said. "Pretend you live here." He raised her chin with his forefinger and gave her another quick kiss. "See you tonight."

"Have a nice day at the office, honey," said Jessica, straightfaced as she watched him stride out the front door. His laughter floated back down the hallway.

She dressed hurriedly. Playtime was over. Better get back to work.

CHAPTER NINE

A gray Citroën swung into Rue Raynouard as Jessica settled herself into the back of a taxi. It hung back in traffic. Half a block from Hotel LaPorte, as the Citroën eased to the curb, it was barely a flicker of interest in Jessica's peripheral vision. She paid her fare and entered the lobby.

"Ah, Mademoiselle," called the woman desk clerk. She looked distressed. "But you have just missed your friend by no more than that!" She snapped her fingers. "Ah, *c'est dommage.* He said he couldn't wait." But he left some brochures. Places to go till he returns. Ha, ha, ha. *Les hommes, n'est-ce pas?*" She winked at Jessica.

Jessica smiled uncomfortably in return. Had Lark been here in person? God, how could she have been so irresponsible? She'd had no right to run off with Gordon; she was here on business. Taking the folders the woman handed her, she turned quickly to the elevator, berating herself. She would have to forget Gordon until this business was over.

Upstairs, she spread the brochures across the bed. They were full of pictures and blurbs detailing most of the tourist attractions around Paris. She was confused; there had to be a message somewhere. Then she saw the light pencil line under the section marked "Rodin Museum."

"Rodin Museum," she read. "Open 10 a.m. to 6 p.m., closed Tuesday. 7F admission—Sunday 3.50 F." Too many numbers and days to work the code. There had to be more information. The rest of the pamphlet yielded nothing. She leafed through the remaining folders. On the back page of the last one, she saw the cramped, slanted scrawl: "Enjoy Paris. The museums are best on Saturday when you avoid the reduced rate crowds. I'll be back on the 3rd. L."

So it was the Rodin Museum, Friday at three o'clock. Today! Jessica was smiling as she changed into a cool dress and put on her walking sandals. Lark must have sent someone to deliver the pamphlets. Peter was right: she shouldn't have worried. She would call to let him know the game was still on.

The blue pen still lay safely in her purse, and she tucked her notebook under her arm. The Rodin Museum would be the last stop on a ramble through Paris again today. The writer on reconnaissance. Halfway out the door she remembered Gordon and turned back to the telephone. The answering machine recorded the information that she wasn't free this evening and that she would see him tomorrow. She didn't bother to mention that she was planning a quick trip to London.

Downstairs, she went directly to the public booth on the street corner to call Peter.

"Rutford Publishing." Betty was still on duty. She must be tired of this, too, thought Jessica.

"Jessica Autland for George Wheeler."

"I'm sorry, he's not in at the moment. I can get a message to him if it's urgent."

"No. Tell him I've arranged another interview. That will make three. And tell him that Auguste Rodin is considered a master sculptor, not just another chiseler." Jessica enjoyed this part of the game.

"I'll tell him." Betty was laughing.

Jessica emerged from the telephone booth and looked around, logging every pedestrian and automobile in the entire block in front of the hotel. As she walked toward the Métro station, the gray Citroën slid away from the curb. Had she seen it before? It slithered on through traffic as she descended the steps. She dismissed it from her mind.

The hours passed quickly. Having decided to include a section on small hotels in her article, she traipsed through a dozen lobbies and jotted down notes on rooms and rates. By two o'clock, although not far from the Rodin Museum, she was ready to begin evasive action to get there. She followed an erratic route through crowded halls in the Louvre, ducked through the teeming Lazare train station, hopped on and off metro cars, grabbed bus rides and hailed taxis. By the time she reached Rue de Varenne 77, the Hôtel Biron, which housed the Rodin Museum, she felt like a professional. She wondered if anyone had been following her anyway.

After paying admission and purchasing the museum guide booklet, she passed into the large, walled garden, heavy with the scent of roses in full bloom. The Hôtel Biron resembled a gracious private mansion, except that the statue in the garden to her right was Rodin's "The Thinker."

Jessica walked purposefully toward the entrance. Assuming Lark was inside, she would get the film, then fly to London immediately. After handing Peter the film, she could turn around and fly back to Paris, devote her attention to Gordon. But first, business.

Jessica entered the right rotunda first. It was swarming with visitors, but none of the faces matched the photo of Lark. She glanced at the full-sized, bronze Eve, head bowed, arms wrapped around herself in shame. We never had a chance, thought Jessica: Women were made to bear the shame of sex from the very beginning.

In the center gallery she thought she saw him—a broad back and balding head bent over the entwined figures of "The Kiss." She moved alongside, her attention distracted by the satiny marble of the figures rising from the rough-hewn rock. Passion celebrated—in spite of the cloud of Eve's shame that endured in men's minds. But as the man straightened, she saw that she had made a mistake. She drifted through the doorway.

The left rotunda was less crowded. While seemingly absorbed by the dark, carved paneling, she scanned the faces. Lark was not there.

As Jessica climbed the eighteenth-century staircase, a group of teenagers paraded past her on the way down, jostling each other and laughing loudly. One of the boys whistled softly as she caught his eye. It was flattering to know that thirty was not yet considered over the hill.

Fewer people roamed upstairs. She found him in the second room. Her mouth went dry. He was here! It was going to happen!

He looked very like his picture, a bit older, perhaps. But it was definitely Lark. He wore a short-sleeved, plaid shirt tucked into tan pants—not very Russian. She smiled, unable to stop herself, but he turned away abruptly, examining the nude study of Balzac before him. Holding her nerves in check, Jessica walked stiffly to the other side of the statue. Balzac's legs straddled a rough tree-trunk-like form, from which his bulging stomach rose majestically.

Jessica rubbed her damp palms on her skirt. She was nervous. She surveyed the other people in the room: an older couple stood by a tall, carved cabinet behind Lark; a young boy, near the study of Balzac draped in a monk's robe, was writing in a notebook; two young women chatted quietly by one of the huge, arched windows; a professorial type peered closely at each sculpture through thick glasses; and a blond bulldozer of a man in a shapeless suit sweated over a glass display case. Jessica moved to the right, behind the nude of Balzac. Lark remained where he was, consulting his guidebook.

A stocky man with a curiously narrow, sloping face and pointed chin entered from the passage, absorbed in his brochure. His eyes tracked the room once, then he moved toward the several headless studies ranged against the wall. He returned to the printed page.

Jessica maneuvered into a position about three feet from Lark. No one seemed interested in either of them. Lark stepped sideways in her direction as he thoughtfully considered Balzac's bulk. He nodded, as if deep in thought. Jessica brought her hand up to brush a strand of hair away from her face, moving her arm so that her notebook, then her handbag slipped from her grasp and fell, the contents spilling across the polished parquet floor. Lark stooped to retrieve the small canvas makeup case that had landed at his feet. Kneeling, Jessica gathered her belongings, but as she reached to take the case from Lark's outstretched hand, she became aware of a third presence between them. She followed the trousers up to the shapeless jacket, then to the broad face. It was the blond primate who had been hovering over the display case behind them.

"May I help you?" he said. His forehead shone with perspiration. He crouched at her side with a flickering glance toward Lark. Shifting the case from his left hand to his right, Lark stood quickly, proffered it again. The man reached up and swept it from Lark's grasp. He examined it.

"Thank you," said Jessica, glaring, putting out her hand.

Her sharp look was met with a thin smile. He turned the case over in his hand. "I wanted to see if the clasp had

88

broken," he said. His eyes darted to Lark, then back to Jessica.

"I don't think so," she said, hand still extended, eyes boring into his. *"Thank you."* Her voice was glacial. He hesitated, glanced from Lark to the case, then dropped it into her outstretched palm.

Jessica knelt to retrieve the remaining articles on the floor, wanting to look up at Lark, but not daring. Had he tried to pass the microfilm with the case the first time? Damn! Who was this man. His voice held only the barest trace of an accent, impossible to identify. Stuffing her belongings back into her handbag, she stood, looked around. Three new people had drifted in. The stocky man apparently had taken a photograph of Balzac; he was winding a camera as he crossed to the window. Lark was already at the threshold on his way out of the room; the hulking interloper was looking after him.

Jessica hesitated, looking at Lark's retreating back, wondering if she should follow, but the blond man was already in motion. One of the young women approached her.

"Here, I think you dropped this, too."

Jessica looked down at her outstretched hand. The girl was holding the blue fountain pen. She hadn't even realized that it was missing from the items she had put back into her purse.

"Thank you very much!" God, was she totally incompetent? Wildly, she looked back at the doorway. Lark and the hulk were both gone.

Jessica stood still, filled with resentment. Another failure. This time she was angry. She turned. The pugnacious, spread-leg stance and folded arms of the nude Balzac rose before her, mirroring her feelings of belligerence and vulnerability. She took some deep, calming breaths. Right here, at Balzac's feet, she was playing her own version of his most famous work: *La comédie humaine.*

CHAPTER TEN

Yegeni Vassilovitch Alexiekov knew he was in trouble as he turned his back on Balzac and strode from the room. How much trouble, he wasn't certain, but he was going to have to find out. The idea was distinctly unappealing. Who was this man who had insinuated himself at Jessica's side the very moment she reached for the microfilm? It shocked him that he had no idea. The man's sudden presence, even his face, were a complete surprise, and that meant that Yegeni had made a mistake. Until now, he'd been playing a game, certain he was in control. Clearly he was not. As he crossed the passage, he could feel the new shadow behind him like a coal car behind the engine.

Yegeni had successfully covered his trip to retrieve the microfilm from Thespian's body two months ago. But after a few weeks back in Moscow, he became aware of a subtle change in status. He and Natasha were suddenly bombarded with social invitations: theatre, ballet, cocktails, dinner. The company was always KGB or KVD, the talk always political, slyly probing under a veneer of comradeship. He had played the paragon of a KGB colonel with more than usual care, affecting a straight Party line, monitoring his comments even to his wife. It was exhausting. His charge to draw out Denisenko only made him more aware of his own subtle examination.

At first, he thought it might be part of the general, periodic probes the KGB mounted against its own personnel. Then, during two short trips on legitimate Party business to Germany, and one to Paris, he had been aware of surveillance. Not that they were clumsy—far from it. But he had spotted the tail immediately. Of course, it was possible that the surveillance was MI6, in which case he was in even deeper trouble. But the tags hardly looked like natty Brits.

He had allowed himself to be followed while traveling in each city, pretending to be oblivious, always careful to keep himself meticulously clean. He had not even allowed himself to think about MI6, had kept the microfilm safe in its hiding place inside Russia to foil any surprise searches of his luggage or his person. Only once, his patience wearing thin, had he granted himself a small rebellion: he spent an entire afternoon "sightseeing" in Bonn, zigzagging through the city like a marble through a maze. The poor tail had to use every technique in the book to keep up with him. Yegeni had been careful not to lose the man, and he made no contacts with foreigners. It was a meaningless triumph, but it made Yegeni feel better when, after a harried day, the shadow was forced to file a lily-white report. He had hoped they would tire of the game.

The fact that the surveillance was surreptitious was what worried him the most. If someone had realized, from the archives tapes, that he had photographed the documents, then he would have been accused. He didn't know why else they would be watching him. The surveillance didn't follow standard KGB procedure: they weren't trying to frighten him or let him know they suspected him, weren't probing his friends, hadn't restricted his movements. It was rather as if his guilt were presumed and they were waiting to catch him in a mistake. And he had nearly made one.

He was willing to play for time, but two weeks ago, a Russian agent had been uncovered in Britain's electronic intelligence center in Cheltenham. Suddenly the microfilm, with its list of spies within MI6, was very urgent: certain parties with secrets to protect would muddy the evidence against the spy, conceal his true contacts, perhaps even indict innocent persons. Yegeni had to let Peter Barnsworth know whom he could not trust in his organization.

And so the game had changed. Yegeni's hand was forced; he had requested Jessica Autland out of desperation, and he could no longer afford a shadow. Now it was he who used every technique in the book.

The bird dogs had changed often, but he was getting used to two regulars. Number One Regular, a nondescript, bureaucratic-looking man with glasses, had been on him yesterday. The man must have taken his vitamins and had a restful night, because he was extra sharp: Yegeni had been unable to shake him in time to make his rendezvous with Jessica at Galerie Meunier. It infuriated him. Regular Number Two, a thin man with black hair who was nervously jumping on and off Métro cars, had been easy to lose earlier this afternoon. That was probably why Yegeni had failed to spot this new man who had queered his drop to Jessica: he'd let down his guard in the wake of success. Or the KGB was gearing up, he acknowledged grimly.

Now, as Yegeni threaded his way through the visitors in the passage, he planned his strategy. He still held the microfilm concealed in his left hand. With a swift, easy motion, he brought his hand up to the waistband of his pants. It took less than a second to slide his hand down inside, as if tucking in his shirt. The movement was hidden from the man behind him. He could feel the snap of elastic as the microfilm slid into his briefs, held securely by the elastic legbands. He smiled to himself, blessing yet another sign of his Western decadence: he wore the skimpy, Parisian bikini briefs advertised by muscular, sexy Continental types in posters on the Métro. It was a secret paean to his fantasies. Why shouldn't that abbreviated cotton pouch hold secrets of state as well as secret pleasures?

The first item disposed of, he turned his attention to the second. It rankled him that the primate in the business suit, with his broad Slavic face, had managed to escape his notice until too late. He had to do something about it: it was time he learned who was interested in his movements. But first, he had to protect Jessica.

He strode toward the staircase. A serious young woman wearing glasses had just reached the landing in front of him. With the coal car bearing down behind him, Yegeni approached the woman, patting his shirt pocket. Yes, the guidebook was still there, and the package of True cigarettes. The guidebook would be the best choice.

He planted himself in the woman's path. "Excuse me, have you the time?" he asked. The tail paused, suddenly taken by a small bust on a pedestal against the wall.

"Three-thirty," said the woman, looking at her watch.

"Lovely museum, isn't it?" pursued Yegeni. "Would you like my guidebook? I'm leaving." He removed the pamphlet from his shirt pocket and thrust it at her. The tail whirled, looking startled.

"Why thank you," said the woman in surprise as she looked at the brochure. "But. . . ."

It was whisked from her hand by the man who suddenly appeared at her side. Yegeni had already fled down the stairs. The man bounded after him, pamphlet waving in his hand, leaving the astonished woman to gape over the balustrade.

Yegeni's next encounter was a choreographed ballet worthy of his Russian blood. The elderly gentleman standing near the foot of the staircase wiping his glasses never even saw him coming, but as their bodies crashed together, Yegeni was prepared for the impact. His left arm extended to steady the old man, while with his right, he deftly caught his eyeglasses as they flipped into the air.

"I'm terribly sorry," said Yegeni, as he propelled the octogenarian to a bench near the entrance. "I hope you're not hurt."

"Imbécile! Imbécile!" croaked the old man as he fumbled for his glasses, which rested safely in Yegeni's hand. *"Je ne parle pas anglais. Imbécile!"*

Yegeni sat next to the man. He whipped the package of True cigarettes from his pocket and slid them on the bench. The old man was too preoccupied to notice the soft pack that was tucked under his right thigh, but the KGB man, hanging back at the foot of the staircase, was clearly confused as he saw the deliberate placement of the cigarettes. He looked uncertainly at the pamphlet in his hand.

Yegeni returned the spectacles to the old man, walked past the tail without a glance, then bounded out the door. He broke into a trot through the garden and out the gate, then darted around the corner into Boulevard des Invalides.

The tail swooped like a falcon, clawing at the pack of cigarettes under the old man's leg.

"Imbécile!" shouted the old man, who was putting on his spectacles and found himself newly disarranged by yet another unexpected contact.

But the man had already moved to the doorway. There, a perplexed guard, with barely enough time to react to the fleeing man who had thrust a matchbook into his hand, was confronted by a second man who snatched it away. He stood in the doorway, scratching his head, as he watched the second man sprint down the steps and through the garden.

"Imbéciles!" the old man behind him was muttering to himself. *"Tout le monde est imbécile!"*

Friday afternoon traffic was heavy with country-bound Parisians leaving for the weekend. Yegeni plunged into the street, dodging the fast-moving vehicles, ignoring the shouts and raised fists his unauthorized presence provoked. Safely on the other side, he looked back over his shoulder. The KGB man was past the gate, almost to the curb, ready to pit himself against the roaring traffic.

Yegeni sprinted around a corner and flattened himself against the wall. He had less than a minute to wait. As the tail drew abreast of him, legs pumping, Yegeni shot out and poked his knuckle into the man's back. The man stiffened in surprise. This time Yegeni spoke Russian.

"Now, Comrade, who told you to spy on me?" he hissed, keeping one hand on the man's arm and his body close enough to act as a shield for the finger he pressed into his back. He faced away from the street and sidewalk; a passing pedestrian saw only two men talking in the shade of the building.

"Speak!"

"I only follow my orders."

"Whose orders?" Yegeni jabbed harder with his knuckle.

"Please, I. . ." the man shrugged his shoulders, but the shrug was preparation for movement. He wheeled sharply to the right, his own right arm coming back to knock Yegeni's arm up into his own face with a slam. The sweet taste of blood trickled into Yegeni's mouth as his lip split against his teeth. Before he could react, the man had gripped his wrist and jerked it violently behind his back. Yegeni's involuntary yelp brought an increase in pressure on his arm. His opponent had a smile on his face as he leaned forward and pulled a Graz-Bura automatic from his jacket, pressing it into Yegeni's side. Again, anyone passing would have seen two men in conversation, their positions only slightly altered from a few moments ago.

"This works better than a knuckle, Comrade," said the man as he clicked off the safety catch. "But it was a good try. I'll keep it here, where we both know where it is." He slipped the hand holding the gun into his jacket pocket, where a flick of the wrist would bring it into firing position; the shot would leave only a small hole in the fabric. He did not release the pressure on Yegeni's arm.

"But forgive me, I did not answer your question. We shall have to take a little ride." He guided Yegeni toward the street and hailed a taxi, arranging his beefy body in the cramped back seat before giving the driver an address in Montparnasse. Then he settled back, produced a silencer from his other jacket pocket and fitted it carefully onto the barrel of the gun. With a satisfied smile, he placed the gun in his lap, the bore toward Yegeni, his hand resting lightly on the grip.

Neither man spoke. Yegeni dabbed at his cut lip with his handkerchief until the bleeding stopped. The lip was beginning to swell; he had trouble keeping his tongue from exploring it. The neighborhoods of Paris flashed by. Yegeni busied himself by looking out the window; they passed the fifty-six story Maine-Montparnasse tower, the sleek railroad station, then the cemetery with its sleeping giants of art and literature. Finally, the taxi stopped in a narrow street to the side of a large café with an open terrace full of tables. There were three stories of flats above it.

The thug motioned Yegeni to the sidewalk.

"Your treat, my friend," he said, motioning Yegeni to pay the fare. Yegeni obediently handed the driver several francs.

The café was crowded as befitted a warm, late afternoon in August, but the two men attracted little attention from the patrons, intent upon conversation and *café au lait*. The gun was back in the man's pocket. He surveyed the area casually, keeping his body close to Yegeni's side. They entered the building to the left of the restaurant.

In the vestibule, Yegeni said hello to a little boy who crashed past them with a ball, but the prod of the gun in his back wiped the smile from his face. The man indicated the stairway with a flick of his head. Their footsteps were silenced by the rubber treads as they climbed the stairs.

On the first landing, a door opened onto a long corridor, freshly painted. The building was obviously well cared for. Halfway down the hall, the man stopped at a black door marked with the number twelve. He knocked once, then three short knocks, then once again. The door opened a crack, the chain visible across the opening, but no face appeared.

"It's Vdovin," said the man in a low voice into the void.

The door closed briefly as the chain dropped, then opened wide. Vdovin pushed Yegeni into the center of the room. The thin, black-haired man who had opened the door looked contemptuously at Yegeni, then walked out, closing the door behind him. Yegeni recognized him as Regular Tail Number Two. Vdovin turned to put the chain back on.

Yegeni looked around. The room was small: a narrow hallway immediately to the right led past a bathroom to another room. The blinds were tightly drawn, making it necessary to have the bare bulb in the ceiling fixture turned on. The closed windows blocked any ventilation; cigarette smoke hung in heavy, bluish layers and the odor of stale tobacco mixed with sweat was strong. Although the corridor was well tended, it was obvious that the apartment had received little attention. Sections of paint peeled from the ceiling, hanging like limp streamers from a forgotten party.

A daybed on the right, with a small club chair at its foot, and a worn, dirty rug comprised the living area; a table with two paint-chipped chairs served as a dining area. Sitting at the table was a man in blue pants and a knit shirt. He coughed. Yegeni sat in the chair opposite him, face to face with an old friend.

"Comrade Denisenko! What brings you out of the People's Republic?" He tried to sound hearty.

Denisenko looked at him with tired eyes. His jowly face revealed nothing. When he spoke, it was to Vdovin.

"What happened?"

"What happened," interjected Yegeni, "is that this ape has been following me. I asked him to take me to his boss." He reached for the single cigarette remaining in the Marlboro pack on the table, lit it and added his plume of smoke to the foul air of the room.

Denisenko's eyes assessed him, then returned to Vdovin. "You, Vdovin. What happened?"

With a disdainful look at Yegeni, the thug told his story of the Rodin Museum. Comrade Alexiekov had contact with four people: a woman who conveniently dropped her handbag near him, a woman to whom he handed a pamphlet, an old man to whom he'd tried to slip a pack of cigarettes, and a guard at the door to whom he handed a matchbook. Vdovin triumphantly deposited the props on the table. Denisenko examined the pamphlet, the matchbook, then shot Yegeni a glance as he picked up the package of True cigarettes.

"I think he was making a drop," said Vdovin.

"You *think* . . . ?" Anger, then resignation passed across Denisenko's face before the mask slammed down again.

Yegeni laughed. "Comrade, I played a little game to confuse your bird dog, here. I don't know what you think you are doing, but it is inconceivable for your department to spy upon me, to interfere in my operations!" He leaned across the table. "Dmitri, we are old friends! What are you doing?"

Denisenko waved Vdovin out of the room. With a dispirited shrug, he shambled down the hall to the bedroom, a disappointed hound that had tracked his quarry but was denied the kill. The sound of a closing door sealed his banishment. Denisenko spoke quietly.

"I must ask you the same question," he said. "When we were at the Institute together, you once said there was no higher calling than serving the Party for Mother Russia." He slammed his fist down on the table, sending cigarette butts like popping corn out of the ashtrays. "Are you serving the Party? Or are you serving someone else, Yegeni Vassilovitch?" He spat out the patronymic with contempt.

"You are doubting me?" cried Yegeni. "A leak in English operations, *your* area, with employees in *your* department? How dare you even suggest I would betray my country. I'm Russian to my marrow." Russian, yes. He avoided any mention of the Party.

"Whom were you contacting at the Rodin Museum?" Denisenko was unmoved by Yegeni's outburst.

"No, Dmitri," said Yegeni, his voice patient now, explaining to a recalcitrant child. "The question is, who was contacting me? I've been working on a developmental project and was expecting an important piece of information. Information which is confidential to my department. My contact had not yet arrived when I became aware that I was not alone." He gestured toward the bedroom. "I didn't know who had sent him, or why. I certainly never expected you. What are you doing in the middle of my operation?"

"As you mentioned earlier, there's been a leak."

"Then I suggest you check your own people before you point the finger at an old friend. Go back to Moscow, Dmitri. Clean your own house; you may be surprised at what you learn."

"I'm monitoring people in my department. But also looking into those who have access to our records. You may remember, we were logged into Archives at the same time."

Yegeni laughed. "It is now a crime to meet accidentally in Archives?"

"Barakov suggested you may have taken advantage of a situation."

Yegeni didn't miss a beat. "Ah, Barakov. Not the most comfortable ally. If you must know, Dmitri, Barakov came to me also. He asked for assistance in an inquiry into *your* loyalties." He waited for some reaction. There was none.

Denisenko plunged on. "Let us not play games, old friend. I studied the security tapes from Archives. At first, I didn't believe it."

"And what was it that so strained your credulity?" Yegeni gave a mirthless laugh; now he was nervous.

"The papers on the floor. . . ."

This time Yegeni's laugh was a bit more forced. "You couldn't believe that I dropped my papers? Or you couldn't believe I picked them up? Which?"

"My papers were on the floor also!"

"Yes, and superspy that I am, I voodooed you into a coughing fit, then cannily forced you to drop them when you went for water. Can't you see the absurdity? Your papers were right where you dropped them when you returned. Were you missing anything from your file? Dmitri, Dmitri, the KGB sows suspicion, but still, we must try to be reasonable men. How could I have stolen them?"

"No, you didn't steal them. Barakov was correct; you took advantage of a situation. You photographed them, Yegeni Vassilovitch."

A fraction of a pause. "That would be impossible," said Yegeni quietly.

"It was cleverly done; on the tapes it was impossible to

see exactly. Your body was bent forward, hiding the movements of your hands. . . ."

"I don't know how to pick up anything from the floor without bending over. I never thought to hold my hands up to the camera."

"Suspicious," continued Denisenko, ignoring the interruption, "but not conclusive, although there was a flash of metal reflected in the shiny floor. As I said, suspicious. That's why Barakov came to me. Until I saw the tapes, I never connected your movements as I came into the room. You were sliding something into your pocket, Comrade. Was it a microfilm camera?"

"This is outrageous! I shall go directly to Chebrikov. We will have an investigation!"

"We are having an investigation! When Barakov came to me, he said he had two prime suspects: you and me. I know it isn't me, Yegeni. So I must prove to him it is you."

He shouted for Vdovin, which brought on a short spasm of coughing. The man plodded down the hall, arms loose at his side, the gun still in his right hand. His bland eyes held a splinter of interest.

"My men have been keeping track of you, Yegeni," said Denisenko. "But today, when you lost the regular surveillance, we expected something unusual. Fortunately, Vdovin was working backup and was able to pick you up. His orders were to stay tight on you; if you contacted any foreigners, or if he suspected a drop, he was to intercept, retrieve the information, and bring both you and it back here." He gestured to the items Vdovin had dumped on the table. "You were passing a lot of things. Were they decoys for the real drop?" He turned to Vdovin. "Search him. If he was trying to pass something, maybe he still has it on him." He looked at Yegeni with a shrug. "I'm sorry, it is necessary."

Vdovin moved to Yegeni's side. "I find it easier to search if I have cooperation," he said. "Would you stand, please?"

As Yegeni rose, mouth open in protest, Vdovin struck, the trigger guard of the gun landing precisely on its mark below the ear. Yegeni melted to the floor.

Denisenko shook his head. "You must learn to use the physical as a last resort, not a first."

Vdovin knelt and began removing Yegeni's clothing,

handing each piece up to Denisenko, still sitting at the table. "I prefer not to waste time," he answered.

Denisenko went through each article of clothing, minutely examining pockets, hems, and seams. Finally, Yegeni lay clad only in his Parisian briefs. With a sigh, Denisenko nodded to Vdovin, who rolled Yegeni's body to the side and tugged at the black cotton. As the elastic rolled down, something flipped onto the floor. Vdovin scrambled after it, then triumphantly handed the microfilm to his chief.

The light bulb overhead slowly seeped into Yegeni's consciousness, forced him to rise through layers of discomfort to open his eyes. He had a massive headache; the light bulb seared into the back of his skull, obliging him to close his eyes again. It seemed like a good idea to try to sleep, but somewhere in the back of his mind, unfinished business nagged him awake. He raised his eyelids delicately.

He was lying on the daybed in his underwear. Under him, the slipcover was rumpled and soaked with his sweat. His clothes were piled in a heap on the floor. Vdovin sat in the club chair at his feet, the gun resting in his lap. Yegeni turned his head slightly. The movement produced an explosion of pain. When he could focus again, he saw Denisenko sitting at the table fingering a small object. It was a tiny roll of film. Yegeni moved his eyes to his wrist; his watch indicated he had been out for over an hour.

Denisenko saw the movement of Yegeni's head and looked up. "So," he said. He held up the microfilm. "My six networks in London? Why, my old friend?" His jowly face was filled with sadness rather than rage.

Yegeni said nothing. His head pounded. He raised his arm to rub the back of his neck; Vdovin tensed in response, the gun shifting slightly in his lap as his hand closed over the trigger.

"I need some water," said Yegeni.

Denisenko motioned to Vdovin, who went into the kitchen, returning with the gun in one hand, aimed unwaveringly at Yegeni, and a glass of water in the other. He stood at the side of the bed, looking more apelike than ever, and offered the glass. Yegeni tried to sit up, but fell back with a moan, clutching his head. Vdovin leaned over to bring the glass within Yegeni's reach, the gun still pointing unerringly at his target.

Yegeni nodded a thanks as his fingers closed on the glass and he took a deep breath, tightening the muscles of his stomach to give power to his arm. With an upward thrust, he sent the water flying into Vdovin's face. Automatic reaction threw Vdovin's blond head back as the water sloshed over him. In that instant of surprise, his grip on the gun loosened. Yegeni anticipated the move, had his hand ready to wrench the automatic from his opponent's hold with a twist.

Vdovin recovered quickly and professionally, reaching out to recapture the weapon, but Yegeni was already in motion. Holding the barrel where he had grabbed it, he lunged forward, smashing the handle into Vdovin's groin. The man grunted with a sharp expulsion of air as he folded in agony, but he was a man used to pain. His left hand jabbed blindly for Yegeni's head, contacted the glass still in Yegeni's hand, and slammed it under his chin, pressing against the larynx. Yegeni's body jerked convulsively as his air passage was blocked. Using his sudden advantage, Vdovin kept the pressure of the glass steady and strong as he groped for the gun, his body still bent from the pain in his crotch.

Yegeni's face was suffused with blood, his eyes wide. With all the strength he had left, he brought his knees up, crashed them into Vdovin's side. The blow shifted Vdovin's weight just enough to force him to relieve the pressure on the glass at Yegeni's throat. Reprieved, Yegeni tucked his chin and rolled sideways. They both had their hands on the gun now, struggling for possession. In his peripheral vision, Yegeni saw Denisenko hurtling toward them like a tank.

Rolling onto his back, Yegeni twisted, knees bent under his chin, so that Vdovin was now at his feet. He thrust his legs forward, straightening them to act like a battering ram. The impact jolted his body as his heels slammed into Vdovin's massive chest and sent the man flying backward in a kind of comic reverse leap, arms akimbo. His body crashed into the oncoming bulk of Denisenko, who grunted as the breath was knocked out of him. The gun flipped into the air as both men thudded to the floor on their backs.

Yegeni dove off the side of the daybed, his arm sweeping across the rug for the gun. His fingers had just found the handle when Vdovin's shoulder hammered into his ribcage. They were locked together, rolling and twisting, sweaty hands slipping, clawing to keep possession of the weapon. Denisenko, still huffing for breath, crawled toward them on his hands and knees. Yegeni slashed a foot at his face, but only succeeded in swinging him sideways. Denisenko roared, enraged, and reared, ready to lunge.

The explosion, muffled by the silencer, took them all by surprise. There followed a choked scream; blood spurted over the three bodies. Vdovin arched upward, fell sideways, hit his head on the daybed, then slid to the floor, an ugly red mess where his neck had been.

For a stunned second, the other two men remained motionless. Then Denisenko charged. But Yegeni had the gun firmly in his grasp. He plunged the barrel into Denisenko's soft belly. Denisenko froze, his face only inches away.

Slowly, shakily, Yegeni stood, forced to take several deep breaths to regain his equilibrium. His head ached hellishly. The heat and exertion made him nauseous. Denisenko eyed him warily; he coughed.

"I got tired of the lies, Dmitri," said Yegeni, in answer to the earlier question. He motioned Denisenko to the chair by the table. The roll of microfilm lay amid the rubble of cigarette butts and spilled coffee. Yegeni scooped it up, stood before his seated friend.

Denisenko rubbed his face where Yegeni's foot had struck. He slumped in the chair, the fear in his face like a raw wound, his eyes glued to the gun pointed at him. "What are you going to do now?"

"I would like to say, 'give me twenty-four hours before you do anything, for old times' sake.' But that wouldn't be practical, would it Comrade? As you have demonstrated, your loyalty is to the Party, not to me."

"You don't have to continue with it. We could work something out," pleaded Denisenko.

"No, there's nothing to work out. I made my choice long ago. I must get this film to London."

Denisenko's tongue darted nervously between his lips; his Adam's apple jerked in his throat. "You would expose all of my people there?"

"I have no choice, Dmitri. I'm sorry." Would he ever stop having to say those dreadful words?

"Wait," cried Denisenko. "Not in cold blood! Not you, Yegeni. I know you. Remember when we were young, remember how you cried when your papa's horse was shot because he'd gone lame? You're not a machine. Our ideologies may differ, but you're not a murderer!"

Yegeni blinked at the word.

"You miss the point. The film must go to London." His voice was choked. "What would you do in my place?"

"I wouldn't shoot you, Yegeni Vassilovitch."

"Yes, Dmitri, you would."

It seemed odd to Yegeni that the simple act of crooking his finger—and the little spit of sound that came out—should make Denisenko's body jump, causing a red stain to erupt on his chest and spread slowly into the knit of his shirt. He fired twice more, so that it would be as fast and painless as possible. Then he had to look away.

His boyhood rushed in upon him: snowball fights in Sokolniki Park with his best friend, Dmitri; marching proudly in Red Square in the ranks of the Komsomol, doing imitations of old Petricoff, the stern English professor at the Institute. A sob escaped him; then the memory of another body, a torn body lying in cold storage in a morgue, made his juices flow again and his brain could focus on the concept of purpose. There *was* a purpose. He had to get the film to London. Friendship and personal feeling had to be put aside for the greater good; that was one of the precepts of Party doctrine. But it took its toll. I'm sorry . . . I'm sorry . . . I'm sorry. . . .

CHAPTER ELEVEN

In addition to the regular population of elderly pigeon feeders, the Jardin du Luxembourg was alive with strolling, hand-holding couples, mothers pushing prams with small children in tow, and students in eager, earnest conversation on the lawn. In the less formally designed area of the park, near the Rue Auguste Comte, Major Nikolayev sat on a bench under the trees looking at a photograph. Over the music of children's laughter, he heard someone nearby playing a flute obligato, while from the tennis courts the thwack of ball against racquet provided a rhythmic base. But his eyes were riveted to the photograph before him. The plump man sitting next to him pointed to the figures in the photo.

"The man standing—there—picked up the case first. The other one, the one crouching in the middle there, took it from him and looked at it before handing it back to her. I figure he must be the tail, except that he blew his cover." Kosov was proud of his work this time.

"Yegeni Vassilovitch Alexiekov!" said Nikolayev. He could hardly believe he was looking at a picture of a contact between an amateur American spy and a high-ranking KGB officer. He had only met Alexiekov once, in London, while working on a liaison project with the Disinformation Department. So Alexiekov was working for the British! And he was using Jessica Autland in place of her dead father, David Payne. Not a bad touch. Russians were sometimes overly emotional.

"You don't think Alexiekov passed the microfilm with the makeup case?" asked Nikolayev.

"No, the tail scared him off."

"Where did this other man come from?"

"He was a tight tail coming in to the museum. Alexiekov seemed unaware of him until the drop. The man followed him out. I don't know after that; I had to stick with the woman. Yuri was in the car; he saw them both head towards the Invalides."

Barakov was working fast, thought Nikolayev. His surveillance from the Russian side had already turned up Alexiekov. Nikolayev's own surveillance from the London angle had turned up Jessica Autland. Between the marks and their tails, the Rodin Museum must have been crowded today!

"You're improving, Kosov. She went straight back to the hotel?"

"Yes. She made a call from the phone booth on the corner, but didn't speak to anyone else. I left Yuri there. I thought you'd like to see the photo."

"Yes. Stay on her. I'm sure he'll try another contact. He's got something all right. And we're going to get it. We'll follow the usual procedure this evening. You keep it very loose."

Kosov nodded and trotted off down the walk. Nikolayev cracked his knuckles. The operation was going well; he had it covered from every angle. But if Barakov had identified Alexiekov as the traitor and had him under surveillance already, he was going to have to play it shrewdly to get his promotion. Next time, he'd get both the microfilm and Alexiekov. That would impress Barakov. He was already ahead: Barakov probably didn't know about Jessica Autland. He smiled as the scented breeze filled his nostrils. Yes, he was ahead by quite a lot, and he was closing in fast. In his trap tomorrow, he'd catch two foxes instead of one. He could smell more than nature in the air: there was a sweet whiff of success.

CHAPTER TWELVE

Jessica stepped out of the shower, toweled herself briskly, then dusted her body neck to toe with the Chanel bath powder she found on the shelf in Gordon's bathroom. She wondered briefly whose powder it was; the apartment offered no other evidence of a female presence. Catching a glimpse of her floured form in the mirror on the back of the bathroom door, she critically assessed the indentation of her waist and the smooth swell of her hips. Still within the permissible limits, but she would have to go easy on the chocolate mousse. She wrapped herself in the fluffy blue bathsheet hanging on the hook next to the sink, opened the bathroom door quietly. Gordon was still asleep, snoring gently. The chrome clock on the dresser said 10 a.m.

She eyed the telephone on the night table by the bed; its silence was becoming oppressive. She had instructed the hotel to give out Gordon's number to anyone who called or arrived. That was last night, after the fiasco at the Rodin Museum.

She had watched from the upstairs window as Lark bolted through the garden, casting a hurried look over his shoulder. It was no surprise, a few moments later, to see the bland-faced bull who had intervened when she dropped her handbag charge after him. The garden wall had obscured her view beyond the museum grounds, but not her anxiety, which had blossomed like a hot-house rose. Peter was wrong: this was not going to be a casual brush drop. There had been a new edge to her voice when she stopped at the phone booth outside the hotel to report this latest complication. Betty had connected her without delay; Peter listened in silence.

"Your friend is a professional, my dear," he had said when her tale was finished. "He'll use extreme caution."

She could hear concern in his voice, even as his words sought to reassure her.

"I feel as if I'm in quicksand, sinking fast."

"Not at all. Professionals have to trust one another."

"You once called me an amateur."

"That is still your salvation—and ours."

It had been an unsatisfying exchange, but at least he knew the rules had changed. He had seemed so genuine when talking of his feelings for her father. Was he really concerned for her safety, or more interested in obtaining the microfilm? It was an unsettling question.

For the remainder of the afternoon and into the early evening she had sat by the telephone in her hotel room. At last, she had surrendered to her own rationalization: it was doubtful that Lark would summon her in the night and her sanity demanded a respite. Still, she had run her hand back and forth over the top of the telephone for a long time before dialing Gordon's number.

He was delighted that her plans had changed and had lived up to his promise; he did, indeed, know a great deal about Paris and had showed her a large part of it, from the Folies Bergère (which he described as the quintessential Parisian experience) to several offbeat little *caveaux* on the Left Bank. He had an unsuspected flair for nightlife that had remained untapped ten years earlier, probably through lack of funds. He made up for it last night. Jessica's troubles faded like old memories in the glow of his presence. She had dutifully taken notes and promised him an advance copy of her article.

When they returned to his flat at 4 a.m., the tiny red light on his telephone answering machine had glowed forlornly, indicating no calls had come in. Jessica was relieved she hadn't spent an hysterical night alone in her hotel room.

She smiled now, as Gordon mumbled in his sleep. His curly hair and the slightly pouting lips gave his face an impish quality, at once innocent and mischievous. It was difficult not to be bowled over by this man, she thought as she bent down to lightly stroke his cheek. His eyes fluttered open, looking startled, then gleamed with that peculiar dancing quality as he recognized her.

"I was having a delicious dream."

"Oh?"

He reached up for her, hand sliding under the towel, stroking her. The towel slipped to the floor unheeded. "Want to make my dream come true?"

He pulled her down, nuzzling her neck, nibbling her ear lobe. "Mmmmm, you smell good," he breathed into her ear. She slithered into bed next to him, letting his hands roam over her body. Her nipples became taut at his touch and he grew hard as he moved against her. It was a good way to begin the day.

Their lovemaking was playful, more inventive than before, a teasing game punctuated by an exuberance that brought its own kind of arousal. Their bodies were still on the downward slope of release when the jangle of the telephone intruded.

"The reviews are coming in already," said Gordon, rolling away from her to reach the instrument. Jessica watched him, delicious, sensuous languor replaced by instant alertness, tightening her body like a compressed coil.

"Hello," said Gordon, his voice thick. He turned back to look at her, then extended the receiver, hand over the mouthpiece. "Why are you receiving calls in my bed from strange men?" he asked.

"I tell the normal ones to call when I'm in the kitchen," she replied, wiggling her eyebrows at him as she took the phone.

"Mademoiselle Autland?" It was the sandpapery voice of an old man.

"Speaking."

"La Petite Horlogerie here. Your watch is finished. 57 francs."

"Thank you." She handed the receiver back to Gordon.

"Well?" he said.

"Well, I have a hot date—with a little old watchmaker. I had my watch repaired and it's finished." She kept her tone bantering as she crossed to the dresser and, her back toward him, slipped her watch, lying on the dresser top, into her handbag.

"I hope you took it to Jean Pierre," said Gordon from the bed behind her. "He's the best in the city."

"No, I didn't know." She extracted a small bottle of vitamins from her bag to cover her movements.

"You should have asked me first. Where did you take it?"

"Some place the hotel recommended. It was before our fortuitous meeting." She flashed him a smile over her shoulder. "But in the future, I shall defer to your expertise." She turned away. La Petite Horlogerie. She'd have to look up the address in the directory. Five and seven were twelve: she was due at noon. The hedonistic interlude was over, replaced by the familiar, terrier-like grip of anxiety. Halfway to the bathroom, she realized Gordon was speaking.

"Sorry. What did you say? Keep talking, I can hear you." She closed the bathroom door.

"I said, we can pick up your watch on the way." Gordon raised his voice as he addressed the closed door. "I have nothing scheduled today. We'll have a picnic in the Bois, browse through the Marché aux Puces, and have dinner on the bateaux-mouches cruising the Seine. That should be plenty of information for your article."

"Sounds lovely." He heard the water running, then the door opened. "But I can't." Jessica came back into the bedroom, screwing the lid on the bottle of vitamins, then plopped it back into her handbag.

"What do you mean, you can't?"

"I'm sorry, Gordon, today is the only day I could see the travel agent who's helping me. She's putting together a package—airfare, hotels, restaurants—that I'm using in the article. I'll call you as soon as I've finished." She leaned over and kissed the top of his head. "You can't have me all to yourself; I'm a working woman."

"You worked yesterday. Today is Saturday. Even NATO takes a day off."

"Woman's work is never done."

"Well, it can't take long, I'm sure. I'll come with you and wait outside. Then we. . . ."

"Gordon, work is work. I don't know how long it will take and I can't concentrate when someone is waiting outside. I'll *call* you!"

They dressed in silence.

"I have time to make you breakfast," said Jessica, as she put the finishing touches on her mascara. "Daddy's old-fashioned pancakes. Uh, Daddy Autland, that is."

"Sounds positively folksy." He conceded a small smile.

She left him to put on his socks and went into the kitchen. The telephone directories were under the phone on the counter. She found La Petite Horlogerie, keeping an ear cocked for Gordon's movements in the bedroom, memorized the address near the Gare St. Lazare, then rummaged through the cupboards and drawers, looking for the utensils and ingredients she needed.

Gordon had evolved into a better humor by the time they ate breakfast. Avoiding the topic of the day's activities, they chatted about Jessica's childhood on the ranch in Colorado, the differences between Jim Autland and David Payne, and the difficulty of discovering one had two fathers when childhood was over. As Jessica was going out the door, Gordon made one more effort to salvage the day he had planned.

"Can I pick up your watch for you? You could go directly to your travel agent. It might save time."

"You are impossible!" replied Jessica with a laugh. "We will have a picnic in the Bois and ride the bateauxmouches, I promise. There's always tomorrow! And here's something to remember me by." She kissed him fully and lingeringly, then ran down the hall to the elevator.

"I don't need tomorrow, I can live on my memories," he called after her.

La Petite Horlogerie was no more than a narrow window and a door set between a camera store and a tailor's shop, all part of the same building, with two floors above the commercial space. Its dingy window was filled with dusty watches and clocks, more jumbled together than displayed. An "OPEN" sign, hand lettered in black ink, nestled against the smudgy glass pane in the door, the only evidence that the shop might still be in business.

Jessica strolled past the entrance, stopping before the window of the camera store next door, using the glass as a reflector. After calling Peter from a public phone, she had taken a circuitous route to the clock shop to check for surveillance. A gray Citroën had swung behind her cab as it turned out of the Rue Raynouard, setting up a resonance in her memory that put her on guard, but it became lost in the crush of traffic in the Place de la Concorde, where she had abruptly switched to the métro. Coming above ground at St. Lazare, she saw a gray car turning the corner ahead of her, but it was gone before she could determine the make. Besides, she reasoned, it would have been impossible to track her progress on the métro. Still, she filed the Citroën away in her mind. She was doing the best she could with her abbreviated training. Next time she would remember to look at the license plate.

The camera store glass reflected a picture post card street. She looked up and down, then sauntered back to La Petite Horlogerie. It was close to noon. The overhead bell tinkled as she opened the door and stepped inside.

It took a moment to adjust her eyes to the pervading gloom of the interior; the only source of light came from the not-too-effective window. The sandpapery voice she had heard on the telephone called out at the sound of the bell.

"*Un moment, s'il vous plaît.*" The voice emerged from a curtained doorway at the back.

The wall on the left was hung with dozens of clocks of various sizes and shapes, all producing a cacophony of ticking. The effect was unsettling, as if here, in the time factory, each second was accorded exaggerated importance, each instant measured and recorded many times over. Tick—time wasted; tock—time ill used.

The tinkle of the brass bell over the door made Jessica jump. A plumpish man stood uncertainly in the shadows, waiting to regain his sight. The brown beret pulled tightly over his head emphasized his ski-slope nose and pointed chin, and despite the dim light, he kept his black framed dark glasses in place. His gray pants bagged around short legs; his blue work shirt was wrinkled. As his eyes adjusted to the murkiness, he immediately turned his back on Jessica and stood peering into the grimy display case which ran the length of the room.

The curtain at the back of the room parted and the owner of the voice appeared, a wizened figure in a worn, black suit with an incongruous red plaid tie. He shuffled to the man standing at the counter, ignoring Jessica.

"*Que vous faut-il?*" he said.

The man looked at him uncertainly, then into the case. "The lady was here first," he replied in English, not looking at Jessica. She couldn't place the accent exactly, but it sounded Eastern European.

"I'm waiting for some work to be done. Please go ahead." She tried to see his face again, but he kept his body angled away from her. The first glimpse of him had seemed familiar, the memory slightly out of focus.

The old man shot her a glance, then devoted his full attention to the customer.

"I want an antique clock," said the man.

"I'm sorry, on Saturday we are only open for repairs. Could you come back on Monday? The owner will be here then."

"I'll look while you take care of the lady."

"But monsieur," replied the old man, indicating the merchandise hidden behind the dirty glass, "you cannot see unless someone shows! I have much repair work today. Please come back on Monday." Despite his frailty, his scratchy voice was firm, authoritarian. He opened the front door and stood aside, a smile on his wrinkle-pleated face. "Selling days are Monday through Friday. *Bonjour,*" he said pleasantly with a gesture toward the sidewalk. The customer nodded and walked out of the shop.

The old man stood motionless behind the closed door, frowning. He flipped the cardboard sign so that the neat, black letters reading "CLOSED" faced the street, clicked the lock, then swooped around to face Jessica.

"If you ever come here again, see to it that you are alone. We have no room for mistakes in our business, mademoiselle. Now, you have five minutes for your meeting." He crooked a finger and disappeared behind the curtain in the rear. Jessica took a deep breath. The dust permeated her lungs; she coughed as she followed him into the rear of the shop.

Behind the curtain was a small workroom. Scattered clock parts covered a counter with a high stool next to it. A chest with small, square drawers held supplies neatly labeled: hairspring, mainspring, crystal. A tall glassfront display case hugged the wall opposite the work counter.

With a grunt of exertion, the old man rolled the case away from the wall, revealing a rough wooden door about five feet high. He opened it with a key from his pocket, then vanished into the blackness with a gesture for Jessica to follow. Feeling a bit like Alice in Wonderland, Jessica stooped low and climbed through the opening. She could barely make out the first step of the stairs directly in front of her and she groped along in the dark, following the wheezing, labored sound of breathing as it rose ahead of her.

She nearly ran into him on the landing when he stopped. Then she heard a click and the stairway was flooded with light. The old man turned. With a resigned gesture, he motioned her to step into what looked like a closet, then without a word, he swung the door closed, leaving her alone.

The single electric light bulb hanging overhead was overpowering after the darkness on the stairs, causing Jessica to blink rapidly. She was in what looked like a supply closet, with shelves on three sides, including the swinging side through which she had entered. Stacks of office forms, small office supplies, bottles of fluid, and other paraphernalia lined the shelves. She stood bewildered, then listened at the door in front of her. There was no sound. Cautiously, she eased the door open.

It was a narrow, windowless room, painted white. A series of charts depicting front and back views of the human body covered the walls. Small dots, superimposed on the forms, were annotated in Chinese. Another chart showed close-up drawings of an ear, a hand, and a foot, all similarly annotated. This was the treatment room of an acupuncturist. Apparently the stairway led from the watch shop through to the adjoining building behind it, which faced the next street. In the center of the room was a reclining chair with a stool beside it. Someone was sitting in the patient's chair, in the fully reclined position, facing away from her. He didn't acknowledge her presence. She moved to the front of the chair.

Again, she recognized him from the photograph. He was wearing the same shirt and pants he'd worn yesterday at the Rodin Museum. Lark was sound asleep.

She hesitated, then gently touched his hand. He awoke with a start.

"Forgive me, I must have drifted. I didn't get much sleep last night." He spoke in a ragged voice, rubbed a hand over his stubbled cheeks, then manipulated the lever on the side of the chair to bring it into an upright position.

"We don't have much time," Jessica said. "The man downstairs. . . ."

"Yes, we must hurry." He pulled the small roll of microfilm from his pocket. "Here it is. The price goes up every day. Please get it to London as soon as you can."

Jessica took the film, cradling it in her palm. It seemed too small an object to have claimed the life of her father. Lark broke into her thoughts.

"Thank you for agreeing to do this. I know it was . . . an imposition."

"Peter said you had no one else to trust." She was embarrassed by his obvious sincerity.

Lark nodded. "That is how I must live now, and so must you. Trust *no one*. Since we can't identify our enemies, we must work alone. Deliver this microfilm personally to Peter Barnsworth—from your hands to his hands. It will reveal to him exactly how far KGB penetrations have gone in British Intelligence."

His eyes searched Jessica's face. "You look like your father," he said.

"Thank you." She smiled, resisting the urge to pat his hand. There was something enormously likable about him, a vulnerability. He wasn't the steeled, remorseless professional she had expected. She could understand her father's fondness for him.

"I feel responsible . . ." he gestured helplessly. "I seem to be responsible for a great many things lately." With a sigh, he looked away. "I hope I haven't put you in danger. At the inception, this seemed the most workable plan. Perhaps I made a mistake."

"Peter seemed to think I would be safe," said Jessica. She wanted to reassure this exhausted, defeated man.

"I thought I had shaken my surveillance," he said, rubbing his hand over his face again. "But the man who took your case from me. . . ."

"I know. I saw him run through the garden after you."

"I've taken care of that problem. I don't think you were identified. But I didn't want you to be seen in public anywhere near me again. Were you followed here?"

"No." Jessica stopped. "I'm not sure," she amended. "I was careful, but someone came into the shop just after I arrived. The man downstairs was very angry."

Lark pursed his lips. "I thought we would be safe here; the old man is a friend. It's not a regular MI6 safe house, but your father and I used it many times. Well, let's hope we have a little luck on our side. You leave through the clock shop. I need to sleep for an hour or so. I can't think clearly. If there's a security problem, the old man downstairs can signal me and I can get out through the doctor's office. Get back to London as quickly as possible. Can you get a message to Barnsworth before you leave Paris?"

"Yes, I'm sure I can."

"Tell him I need to come out, code red." Lark spoke without inflection, his voice tired. "I can no longer go back to Russia."

"I'll tell him."

"He won't be able to contact me, I have to keep moving. Call the shop downstairs and leave a message for Raymonde as soon as you have spoken to him."

"I'll contact him right away. Is there anything else I can do?"

"We'll leave it to him. Make sure you're not followed. If you get the film to London, it will be enough."

Jessica opened her handbag. She extracted the blue fountain pen, unscrewed the top to slip the microfilm into the compartment, then reassembled it.

"I'll get it there."

"Those green eyes." He gazed at her until she looked down shyly. "Just like your father's. He was an extraordinary man: intelligent, full of humanity." His hands were clenched into fists in his lap.

Impulsively, Jessica reached out, covered his hands with hers. "London," she said. "We'll have lunch one day when you get there; I'd like to talk to you about my father."

He nodded. With a great effort, he heaved himself out of the chair. The shelf in the closet swung forward easily after he released the hidden mechanism.

"Be careful," said Lark as Jessica stepped into the stairway. "And thank you."

He swung the shelf again. Jessica was left in total blackness at the top of the stairs. She descended, testing each step while keeping her hand against the wall. When she reached the bottom, the little door was closed tightly; it did not yield to the pressure of her hand. Groping in the dark, she felt for some kind of release mechanism. The wall was smooth. She thought something furry brushed her foot and she gasped, fighting panic, wondering if the old man were trying to punish her. She rapped against the wood; there was no sound from the other side. If the man in the beret had come back. . . . She banged on the door with the heel of her palm. At last, there was a scraping sound, the rattle of a key in the lock, and the door swung inward. The old man presided at the door like a haughty butler.

"Thank you," she said shakily as she stepped through the opening. The man said nothing as he shoved the display case back into position, then motioned her to follow him to the front door. Meekly, she obeyed, shamed by the scorn in his eyes. As she stepped onto the sidewalk, the door closed firmly behind her, the sign reading "CLOSED" still in place.

In the outside world, a golden afternoon was bustling with life. She saw no one watching the shop, and there was no sign of the man in the beret. With the now precious handbag containing the blue pen clutched protectively under her arm, Jessica strolled toward Rue St. Lazare, all nerve endings on intense alert. She would telephone Peter from the nearest pay box, then take a taxi directly to the airport without even checking out of her hotel; she would come back to Paris tonight or tomorrow. A smile of accomplishment touched her lips and her step was jaunty as she walked up the street.

Suddenly she stopped. A gray Citroën was parked on the opposite side of the street. The sun glinted off the windows, masking its interior. It was one Citroën too many. Without waiting to see the license plate, Jessica whirled and walked swiftly back past the clock shop to the far corner. The smile was gone from her lips, replaced by that old companion, fear. As soon as she cleared the corner, she broke into a run.

CHAPTER THIRTEEN

The occupants of the gray Citroën, faces hidden behind dark glasses, slouched low as they watched Jessica's exit from the clock shop and her progress up the opposite side of the street. As she abruptly reversed direction, the three of them sat up in unison, like a chorus on cue.

"Follow her, Yuri," said the man in the front passenger seat to the driver. "We know she won't be making a drop; she's supposed to deliver it to London herself. But don't let her leave the country. You'll have to think of a way to keep her in Paris without any violence. I'll be in touch by radio."

Yuri patted the cigarette-case sized transceiver in his shirt pocket, clicked the switch from the audible call signal to a silent vibration receiver which he would feel against his chest. He ejected himself from the car and hit the sidewalk in a dead run as Jessica turned the corner toward Rue Havre.

The remaining two men leaped from the car and rushed toward La Petite Horlogerie. Kosov reached the front door first, Nikolayev hard on his heels. The "CLOSED" sign was displayed, the door firmly locked.

Turning, Nikolayev faced the street, hands in his pockets as he watched the traffic. Behind him, partially shielded by his body, Kosov bent over the lock and extracted a small tool from his pocket. In less than a minute, the door was open. Both men entered to the merry tinkle of the overhead bell, removing their dark glasses to accommodate the lack of light.

The old watchmaker, bent over his work table in the back room, barely had time to straighten before the two men were upon him. The taller man grabbed the watchmaker's arms, twisting them behind his back violently; he grasped the man like a ventriloquist holding a dummy.

The pinch-faced man, the same one who had followed the woman into the shop, grinned at the old man in recognition, then aimed the blow. There was no cushion of soft belly flesh in the fragile body to absorb the punch; it compressed the old man's midsection nearly to his backbone and he folded in half.

"Where is her contact?" said Nikolayev behind him.

The old man said nothing as he wheezed and gasped for air. His body suddenly convulsed, sending a spatter of vomit onto Kosov's scuffed shoes. With a grunt of disgust, Kosov raised his arm for another blow, stayed only by a shake from the head of his boss. Nikolayev pulled his arms upward, forcing the old man's body to straighten, legs dangling awkwardly, saliva sliding down his chin. Kosov leaned forward with a sneer, thrusting his face close to the frightened old man.

"Where?" he bellowed. "I don't want to have to kill you for such an insignificant piece of information."

The old man smelled of vomit. Kosov grimaced and pulled back, jerked the lolling head upright by the hair. Despite his distress, the old man's eyes met his with a spark of defiance. His throat rasped as he gathered his saliva.

"I'm old, I'm not afraid to die." He spat into Kosov's face.

Eyes ablaze, Kosov drew his sleeve slowly across his cheek to wipe away the spittle. "Ah, but you're not going to die. We know how to keep you alive. You'll only wish you could die." He struck again. The old man doubled over with a sound like a collapsing balloon. At the same time, Kosov brought his knee up to the man's groin. Nikolayev released his arms and the man slithered to the floor, writhing, breathing convulsively, face contorted.

Kosov rolled him over with a kick. "Where?"

The old man winced, futilely scrambling away from Kosov's foot to protect his vital parts. Kosov bent down, ready for another blow.

"Up . . . upstairs," croaked the old man.

"How do we get there?" said Nikolayev on the other side of him.

The old man was gasping, a gravelly, shuddering sound.

"Don't make us ask twice," said Kosov, prodding his ribs with his foot.

"The . . . the cabinet. Be . . . behind the ca . . . cabinet." The stuttering voice was barely audible.

Nikolayev and Kosov rolled the cabinet aside. The small door would not yield.

"The key!" barked Nikolayev, swinging back to the old man.

"I don't have it! It's locked from the inside."

He fell silent, eyes wide, as Kosov seized his right arm, forcing the hand flat on the floor, palm down. Holding the hand in position with his left foot, heel resting on the floor, Kosov raised his right leg slightly, then crashed the heel down. The man screamed. Kosov's laughter filled the room.

"Next time your fingers will be under my heel. One by one. Give me the key!" He raised his foot again.

With a nod, the old man pulled his hand back, cradling it against his chest. Kosov's heel had missed his little finger by a hair's breadth. Shaking, he fumbled in his jacket pocket and produced the key. Kosov tossed it to Nikolayev, turned back just as the old man lunged toward the curtained doorway. His hand pressed a tiny black button on the wall a second before Kosov's blow to his head crumpled him into the corner. But he had managed to warn the man upstairs.

Nikolayev was through the doorway, climbing in the dark like an animal with hands and feet on the steps. Kosov felt his way behind. Once they located the latch, the wall of shelves swung open easily, admitting them to the supply closet. They barely paused before opening the door to the treatment room. It was empty.

Nikolayev charged into the hall, opening and slamming doors on his way to the stairway. He reached the waiting room just as Yegeni Alexiekov, his back to them, opened the door to the street. The strong sunlight framed his body in the doorway, edging his silhouette in a golden aura.

They reached him at the same time. Pressing on either side, taking him by surprise, they gripped his arms and propelled him across the threshold onto the sidewalk.

"Hello, Comrade Alexiekov," said Nikolayev pleasantly in his ear as soon as they reached the sidewalk. He purposely used the more familiar "comrade" and omitted Alexiekov's superior rank

Yegeni's shoulders drooped, but his face betrayed no

emotion. "I don't believe I've had the pleasure," he replied, with a sidelong glance to the left. The fashionably casual clothes and sculpted features of the speaker beside him didn't fit with the more typical Russian heavy on his right. They made an odd pair.

"You must remember me," said Nikolayev. "We met during a little KGB-inspired bombing escapade in London a few years ago. I'm Major Nikolayev."

Yegeni grunted. "I work with so many, it's easy to forget a face."

"This time, Comrade, you'll remember my face." He looked up and down the street, hoping to spot one or two of Barakov's men on Alexiekov's tail. They were either very good, or Alexiekov had lost them. He hoped it was the former; he wanted Barakov to know that he had Alexiekov under control. It would be another rung on the ladder to his promotion.

Yegeni was held in a vise-like grip between the two men as they began to walk down the sidewalk. "Would you mind telling me what this is all about?" He didn't stuggle: Nikolayev was taller than he, the other man outweighed him by at least fifty pounds. Sandwiched between the two men, Yegeni received a few curious looks from passers-by, but nothing more. The rule on Parisian streets, as in any big city, was to mind your own business.

"In due time," said Nikolayev. "To encourage your cooperation, I would like to point out that the man on your right has a gun in his pocket."

Yegeni glanced down.

"We're taking the long way around to the clock shop," said Nikolayev, still hoping to gain a point by parading his catch. "We have some common interests to discuss."

"I cannot imagine what we could have to discuss, Major Nikolayev," said Yegeni, keeping his voice polite, but putting a slight accent on the inferior rank of "major." "I know nothing about a clock shop; you are intruding into my work for the Party, which has nothing to do with you. I'm not impressed with strong-arm tactics from my own people, especially those of inferior rank. I think you owe me an explanation."

"Very good, Comrade." A smile played about Nikolayev's mouth. "I respect coolheadedness in a crisis."

Yegeni felt anything but coolheaded. Fatigue was nibbling at the edge of his alertness, dulling his mind, and he had to force himself to concentrate. How had these men found him? There were two possibilities. Number one, the bodies of Denisenko and Vdovin had been found, probably by the third man who had left the apartment as Vdovin had shoved him inside. Whoever he was, he would know that Yegeni had killed both men. But how could he have traced Yegeni's movements through the night to this house? He had never told MI6 about the old man's stairway in the clock shop. Could Thespian have told Barnsworth, and Barnsworth put it in his damned computer? Which moles at MI6 would have access to that information? He had broken his own rule of safety by trusting the old man. Had he walked into a trap? But they wouldn't be able to identify Jessica—she would still have a chance to reach London.

That brought him to possibility number two, infinitely more terrifying. Denisenko's body may not have been found; Barakov may not even be aware of the confrontation. But Jessica may have been followed. Despite his attempt at total secrecy, someone else in London besides Peter Barnsworth knew about the microfilm. How could he protect Jessica now? It was more important than ever that she succeed, that the traitor be exposed. Whoever tipped the Russians knew his name was on the film and would stop at nothing to destroy it.

He had been walking, unseeing, between the two men. His shoulder muscles inadvertently flexed in response to his thoughts; the two men responded instantly by tightening their hold on him. It brought Yegeni back to an awareness of his surroundings. Whatever happened now, he had to protect Jessica.

They reached the corner and turned right. Rue St. Lazare was busier than the side street, but there was no help in the flow of people, only the potential for innocent victims. It was futile to expect assistance from the outside world. He tried again as they turned at the next corner. The clock shop was halfway down the block.

"I think you're making a mistake, Major. It would be a shame to ruin your career. I am a superior officer from an autonomous department. I shall have to report this assault to Security."

Nikolayev remained unfazed, still host to a small smile.

They hurried Yegeni the few remaining yards to the shop. The overhead bell sang out, but Yegeni noted with despair that the old man did not appear in response. Kosov pushed him roughly against the wall, sweeping three clocks to the floor with a crash. The ticking of the remaining clocks sounded like a time bomb measuring the last seconds of his life. The longer he could keep them here, he thought, the longer Jessica had to leave the country. If she had managed to get away from the shop. He clenched his teeth.

Kosov prodded his jaw with the barrel of the snub-nose Smith and Wesson he'd had in his pocket. American handguns, thought Yegeni, so cheap and easy to get that even the Russians used them, even in Europe. Democracy for all.

"I'm sure we won't need that," said Nikolayev as he waved Kosov aside. "Comrade Alexiekov knows when to cooperate."

"I fail to see the need for cooperation, Major. Or have you been transferred to my department? I am working on an assignment from Department A, which has nothing to do with you."

Nikolayev's laugh was hearty. "Let's get right to the bare bones, Comrade. We know about the microfilm. We know about the woman. My associates are taking her into custody now." He shrugged. "There is no point in not cooperating."

"I don't know what woman. . ."

Nikolayev pulled a photograph from his pocket. Yegeni saw himself kneeling at the foot of Balzac's statue, handing the canvas makeup case to Jessica, Vdovin planted between them with his mouth open.

"I want to know how you got the film," said Nikolayev. "What else you know about London operations. Who your contacts are. What information you've passed. Kosov will take charge of your interrogation. He was well trained at Lubyanka Prison, so I suggest you tell us everything."

Nikolayev crossed to the front door, clicked the lock. Yegeni shifted his eyes to Kosov, leaning against the counter, but the gun didn't move from its target. Nikolayev returned to Yegeni's side and with a jerk, he pulled the winding chain from a cuckoo clock on the wall, tearing it from its innards with a protest of failing metal and wood.

The heartbeat tick was silenced. He looped the chain around Yegeni's hands, behind his back, pulling it until the links bit into his flesh, then he tore the chain from the cuckoo mechanism and bound Yegeni's feet. He pushed him down into a sitting position, his back against the wall and nodded to Kosov.

"Do you know how to play KGB roulette, Comrade?" asked Kosov as he stood over his prisoner. Yegeni looked up without answering; he could tell by Kosov's tone that he enjoyed his work. Nikolayev retreated to the counter in the shadows on the other side of the room.

There was just enough light for Yegeni to follow Kosov's movements as he emptied the chamber of the Smith and Wesson and placed three bullets in his pocket, reloading the remaining two back into the chamber. He slapped the cylinder into position. Yegeni could see the gun, but it was impossible to discern bullet from shadow in the protruding cylinder on either side of the barrel.

"Only I know which chambers are live," said Kosov. "For every wrong answer, I get a free shot. Perhaps in the knee. Or the elbow." He moved the gun, aiming as he spoke. "Maybe in the hand, or the foot. Shall we begin?"

"Your Major has made a mistake, Kosov," said Yegeni. "As your superior officer, I order you to release me. I will put in a good word for you; there's no need to suffer because of another man's error. The KGB does not take kindly to assaults against its own agents. We're on the same side, remember?"

"That's the wrong answer," barked Kosov. The Smith and Wesson moved to his right knee. Yegeni tensed, not taking his eyes from Kosov. A sneer curled the pinched features. The hammer clicked.

The little room exploded with sound. The watchmaker was a craftsman: every clock kept perfect time. One o'clock was announced with cuckoos, chimes, music, gongs, and bells, simultaneously bursting from every corner. Yegeni felt no pain, but couldn't look at his knee. He had never been shot before; he wondered briefly if the mind played tricks to compensate for the trauma.

Kosov was laughing. "A celebration!" he crowed. "The first shot for free and you get a celebration!" The smile disappeared as quickly as it had come. "That means we have two empty chambers and two full ones. The question is: shall we begin?"

"Certainly," said Yegeni. He was past fatigue now.

"Where did you get the information on the microfilm?" Nikolayev's voice floated from the other side of the room.

"Comrade," replied Yegeni, "I planted the microfilm as part of a disinformation operation to discredit some highly placed people in London. If you think it's authentic, if our moles in London think it's authentic, then that means I have also fooled MI6. It is a delicate plan, but quite effective, don't you think?" He thought of mentioning Denisenko, but decided to save that for later in case he had to produce a traitor: Denisenko wouldn't be able to defend himself. "Would you mind telling me who gave you the authority to interfere?"

Kosov looked at Nikolayev uncertainly.

"Comrade Alexiekov," said Nikolayev icily, "Kosov has explained to you that he has two live chambers and two empty chambers in his weapon. It is immaterial to me how much pain you are willing to suffer before you tell me what I want to know. Kosov was forced to kill your friend, David Payne, because he wouldn't cooperate. So you can see we're serious." He ignored Kosov's surprised glance.

Yegeni could taste his hatred, but he kept his face blank. He wanted to kill this major with his bare hands. Nikolayev's voice continued through the gloom. "We know Payne's daughter came from London to pick up the microfilm from you. Now, I want to know where you got it and what you know about London moles." Nikolayev put his fingertips together and pushed; the popping sounds were audible above the ticking that filled the room. Kosov lowered the gun, the barrel three inches from Yegeni's left knee. At that distance, it would make a hell of a hole, thought Yegeni as his eyes followed the snub nose in the dim light. He still couldn't see which chambers were loaded; he had a fifty-fifty chance. He had no choice but to go for it.

"Of course she came to pick it up, Major," he snapped. "That's what is giving the operation credibility in their eyes. The fact that one agent has already died makes them think the information is hot. London won't have any doubts about the authenticity of the film. And you are trying to wreck the entire plan."

The telephone shrilled from the back room, causing all three men to jump. Nikolayev motioned to Kosov, who backed toward the curtained doorway, gun still pointed at Yegeni. As he lifted the fabric, Yegeni could see the crumpled form of the old man in the corner. They're not going to win, he vowed. He felt as if his heart were pumping pure hate instead of blood, could almost feel the tingle of it in his veins.

With the curtain draped over his right shoulder, Kosov looked to his left briefly, located the ringing instrument, then reached with his left hand to answer it. He kept the gun in his right hand trained on Yegeni. Yegeni made a mental note that Nikolayev must be unarmed.

"La Petite Horlogerie," said Kosov into the phone in terribly accented French. Yegeni listened to the ticking clocks, his eyes on Nikolayev.

"Yes, go ahead," said Kosov. He listened a moment. "Very good. Thank you." He crossed to Nikolayev, held a whispered conference. Yegeni could not make out the words.

"I'll tell you what, Comrade Alexiekov," said Nikolayev, crossing to stand above him. "Kosov will stay with you. I'm sure you will be able to fill him in on a great many more details of your delicate operation. Meanwhile, I'll view the film. I'm sure I won't have any trouble getting it from the woman." He smiled. "A simple way to verify your story, isn't it? If it is truly a disinformation film, she will be allowed to deliver it to London. I will then tender my most abject apologies to you. If it is not a disinformation film . . . then we have caught a traitor, haven't we?"

Nikolayev opened the front door. A shaft of sunlight lanced the gloom, alive with dancing dust particles.

"Break his story," he said to Kosov. The door slammed behind him.

Kosov looked down at Yegeni. He spoke in a singsong, as one would address a child.

"Now Comrade, we have two empty chambers and two full chambers. . . ."

CHAPTER FOURTEEN

Jessica had started to run the moment she was out of sight of the Citroën. She leap-frogged from rational thought—had the man in the shop arrived in the Citroën?—to pure instinctive flight as she pushed her way into Au Printemps, the department store on Boulevard Haussmann. She elbowed through the shoppers in the book and housewares departments on the main floor while turning to look wildly behind her every few paces.

On the second floor, she took the connecting bridge over Rue de Caumartin and headed for the racks of women's clothing. She pulled several skirts and blouses from the display and darted into the fitting room. The saleswoman poked her head into the cubicle to ask if she needed assistance.

"I'll take these," replied Jessica, indicating the rose-colored skirt and print blouse she had put on. "But I'd like to wear them. Can you remove the tags?" She reached into her purse, handed the woman a wad of francs.

With a snip, the woman deftly removed the tags, accepted her money, and withdrew. Jessica loosened her chignon and shook out her hair, letting it fall freely to her shoulders. She didn't look completely different, but the color and silhouette were altered; it might work. The woman returned with her change and a bag for Jessica's own clothes.

Reluctantly, Jessica left the bag on the stool, returned to the selling floor and hurried directly to the exit. Emerging again onto the boulevard, she joined the stream of shoppers heading toward Galeries Lafayette, then abruptly crossed the street, turning into Rue Scribe. As she ran along the sidewalk, she formulated the message to Peter in her mind.

The line of people waiting for mail at the counter of

American Express was noisy. Jessica went directly to the bank of telephones. Animated talkers in the booths, sound cut off, gave the impression of a silent movie. She slipped into an unoccupied booth. Betty's voice came on the line after two rings. She wondered if the woman ever got a day off. They went through the Rutford Publishing ritual. Peter's voice sounded solid, secure. She relaxed a little.

"I'm coming home," she crowed softly, her hand cupped to the mouthpiece.

"With everything?"

"Everything and more. My friend wants to come too. He has a little red dog with a wagging tail. He's afraid to travel with it."

"Where did he get it?"

"I don't know. He recommended a book: Thomas Wolfe's *You Can't Go Home Again.*"

"Where is he now?"

"Traveling. I can get a message to him. I do have a problem, however."

"Yes?"

"Someone else wants my story."

"Do they know you've completed it?"

"It's possible."

"Damn!" In the pause, Jessica could hear him breathing. "All right, listen to me. I think it best that you and your friend come together. Have you been to Versailles? It would be a good addition to the article. The Water Mirror Basin in the gardens is lovely. We can rush publication by the 22nd if you can get a rough draft by Sunday."

Jessica calculated quickly. He wanted them both at the Water Mirror Basin at four o'clock this afternoon.

"That's fine."

"My friend Jack will meet you. He'll have the firm's plane for you; it's more reliable than a public airline."

"How will I know him?"

"He has a red handkerchief to match his wife's red coat. Tell him about the Grand Trianon."

"That should be easy."

"I have confidence in you. Stay with the tourists; they know the best attractions. And remember everything you've learned."

"Thanks."

She replaced the receiver, frowning. There had been a

subtle change in Peter's tone, but at least he was going to get them home; she was no longer working alone. She thumbed through the directory in front of her, marked her place with a forefinger as she dialed the number.

"La Petite Horlogerie." It was not the familiar, sandpapery voice, but a younger, thicker voice with a terrible French accent. Jessica hesitated, but if she didn't leave the message, how could she help Lark?

"I'd like to leave a message for Raymonde," she said.

"Yes, go ahead."

Her eyes swept the American Express lobby before she spoke. No one was looking at her.

"Tell him we've got a ride to the airport, from the Water Mirror Basin at the Versailles gardens, four o'clock today."

"Very good. Thank you."

Jessica leaned back, resting her head against the wall of the booth. This would soon be over. She was mindful of Peter's warning to stay with the tourists. He was right; she was safer in a crowd. She looked at her watch; plenty of time before the meeting. She'd get something to eat at one of the crowded cafés. Nothing could happen to her there.

She tucked the handbag firmly into the crook of her elbow, tried to quell the lump in her throat. Things were heating up. Her anonymity had been trumped; Peter had only one card left to play. It seemed reckless to think her amateur standing would take the trick.

On the sidewalk outside the American Express office, she squinted right and left for the malevolent gray Citroën. There was no sign of the car.

She marched toward Place de l'Opéra cloaking herself in the safety of passing bodies. A multitude was the order; a multitude she would join.

The rhythmic chanting was audible before the placards could be read. A small corps of shouting demonstrators, flanked by gendarmes, was parading, gawked at by motorists and pedestrians alike. Jessica infiltrated the rubbernecking crowds and slid into a seat under a green and white umbrella at Café de la Paix, from where she read the bobbing signs.

"HALTE AUX POUVOIRS NUCLÉAIRES, FOSSOYEURS DE L'HUMANITÉ!" "POUVOIR NUCLÉAIRE, NON MERCI!"

Only one banner was in English, short and succinct: "NO NUKES!" Several people were distributing flyers to onlookers. Twenty years ago the demonstrators would have been oddly dressed hippies. Today, they were well-dressed, middle-class citizens. The surprisingly orderly demonstration didn't seem to be provoking any disagreement or heckling. Apparently the cause was supported by the man in the street; only governments were interested in the engines of war and destruction.

Jessica ordered a light lunch, paying when she was served to maximize her mobility, but she was self-conscious as she ate. Keeping one hand protectively on the handbag in her lap, she watched the crowds with the intensity of a Secret Service man guarding the President, seeking the face and behavior that presaged a threat. Yet despite her apprehension, she felt the pride of accomplishment: she had the film in her possession. She'd done it! But her father had also possessed the film; it still had to be delivered to London. The *croque-monsieur* stuck in her throat had to be washed down with Evian. That old companion, fear, was back, wiping out her momentary triumph. She watched the street in front of her for the opportunity to move.

It came as a taxi drew up to the curb about twenty feet from where she was sitting and deposited its passenger. Jessica bolted between the tables and ducked into the back seat before the man could close the door.

"Driver, please drive on, I'm in a hurry." The taxi obediently edged into the tangle of cars. Jessica peered out the back window, but it was pointless to speculate on which, if any, of the milling population were interested in her movements. When she gave the driver the name of the Hotel Inter-Continental, he raised his eyebrows. It was a ridiculously short ride, but his passenger thrust a handful of francs at him, more than double what the fare would be. So he kept his mouth shut and weaved through Place Vendôme, finally coming to a halt in the Rue Castiglione. He'd been driving a taxi for twenty years; nothing surprised him anymore.

At the colonnaded entrance to the hotel, Jessica leaped from the cab and ran up the red carpet. Her choice had been correct; even in August, the lobby was swarming with people. She went directly to the concierge's desk.

"When is the next tour to Versailles, please?"

He consulted a small leather folder on the desk. "In English, Mademoiselle?"

"Yes."

He looked at his watch. "Fifteen minutes. Do you wish to purchase a ticket?"

"Please."

"The bus will be in front of the hotel." He took her francs, handed over the blue ticket.

The timetable was in her favor. She strolled into the main lounge with its raspberry carpet, sat in an empty Louis XV chair facing the door and waved away the approaching waiter.

Within ten minutes a group of tourists had gathered at the hotel entrance. Jessica joined them as a large red and chrome bus marked Gironde Tours lumbered to a halt in front of the door. A poised, sultry woman, whose figure transformed the severely tailored red uniform she was wearing, descended to announce the tour to Versailles. Standing in line, Jessica suddenly remembered Gordon. She had promised to call him, but in her panic, she'd completely forgotten. Now it was too late; the woman was herding her flock onto the bus, exchanging tickets for guide books as they boarded. Annoyed with herself, Jessica climbed the steps.

She should have told Gordon this morning that she would be busy for a day or two. Why couldn't she stay away from him until this job was finished? She only became embroiled in more lies; it was unnecessary. She would call him from Versailles, tell him she had to rush back to London for a conference and would be back in Paris tomorrow. Concentrate on one thing at a time, she told herself as she took a seat in the third row next to a pretty black woman who was engrossed in conversation with her elderly parents seated in the row ahead. The coach was already half full from pickup points at other hotels.

The woman in uniform stood at the front of the bus, picked up the microphone.

"My name is Claudine. I will be your guide this afternoon."

She paused, signaled the driver to open the door to admit a latecomer, a sloppily dressed, sandy-haired man in his thirties. He wore wire-framed glasses, which creased the temples of his fleshy face as they journeyed to his ears. A hearing aid adorned his right ear. He slumped into a seat in the rear and looked out the window as Claudine continued speaking.

"I hope you will enjoy the tour. Please feel free to ask me any questions you may have. I shall do my best to answer." She had a smoky voice and spoke English with a lilting French accent. It was obvious she had done her homework. She spoke intermittently for the forty-five minute ride to Versailles, pointing out landmarks along the twisting streets of Paris, through the Bois de Boulogne, and across the Seine into the suburbs. Her passion for all things French was infectious. Jessica pulled out notebook and pen to make notes.

In the huge Place d'Armes, in front of the Palace of Versailles, the bus disgorged its passengers, who formed a tight circle around Claudine. There were now about thirty-five people in the group; a few families with children, several couples both young and middle-aged, one young couple obviously on honeymoon who hung upon each other, and several unattached men and women of various ages. Claudine spoke with an intense fervor, proud of her French heritage. Her eyes slid over the group almost provocatively.

"A thousand nobles lived in the palace itself, with their four thousand servants. We will proceed through the wrought-iron gates to the Ministers' Court."

Jessica played the writer at work, recording impressions in her notebook. So absorbed did she become in the grandeur around her, she almost forgot that she carried microfilm in the tip of her pen. The palace was ablaze as the afternoon sun danced on endless rows of windows and cornices.

A slightly overweight woman, a blowsy fortyish, with brown hair tumbling over head and shoulders, fell into step beside Jessica. She wore a flowing orange dress and carried a garish straw bag in the shape of an enormous daisy, each petal decorated with bright orange yarn. Jessica suppressed a smile as she noticed the huge bag swinging at her side, then looked at its owner. The face was a trifle overly made up, but the smile was appealing, the eyes warm. As the group reassembled around Claudine, inside the courtyard, the woman whispered to Jessica.

"I see you're taking notes. You a teacher, getting ready to report back to the kids about your summer vacation?" She giggled at her own joke.

Jessica smiled. "No, I'm not a teacher. I'm writing an article on Versailles. I don't want to forget anything."

"Oooh, a writer," cooed the woman. "You know, honey, I always wanted to be a writer. Some of the stories I could tell! Never seem to get the time, though. Do you know De Martinos?"

"Dee Martinos?"

"It's a *waahhnderful* steak house in Chicago." She had a way of extending the vowels of words she wanted to emphasize. "I'm a waitress there. This is my first trip to Europe."

"Are you enjoying it?" Jessica was amused by the rush of instant warmth.

"I think it's *faaabulous!* Although, confidentially, there are a lot of women in my tour group. It was for singles only, I thought maybe I might meet someone, you know? *Him!* But I haven't met anyone at all interesting. Not that that's why I came," she added hastily with a toothy smile. "But you always have to be on the lookout!" She looked at Jessica's bare ring finger, then scrutinized the group around Claudine. "I think we're both in trouble with this gang, honey."

Jessica followed her gaze to the unattached males: a chubby, balding man wearing a loud print shirt was snapping pictures of everything in sight; two slightly-built young men, fashionably dressed, were holding hands; a tall, silver-haired gentleman leaned on a cane with rapt attention; the bespectacled, sandy-haired man in rumpled pants was studying the pavement; and an earnest young man in his twenties appeared unable to close his mouth as he gawked at the building before him. Jessica had to nod in agreement.

"We'll have to concentrate on the palace," she said.

"My name's Lucille, honey. What's yours?"

"Jessica."

"Oooohh, now that's a nice name. I never much liked Lucille. Well, I'm glad I found you. It's such fun to have someone to talk to on tour, don't you think?"

The elderly gentleman with the cane turned around. "If

you wouldn't mind, we could all hear the guide better if there were less conversation."

Lucille made a little pouting face as he turned his back, then winked at Jessica. The party moved on to the palace, straggling behind Claudine like cygnets behind a swan. As they climbed the circular stairway to the upper vestibule, Jessica again realized she had forgotten to call Gordon. Now she'd have to wait till the end of the tour.

"The Royal Chapel, in white and gold," Claudine was saying as they clustered around her again, "is Hardouin-Mansart's masterpiece. Here Louis the Sixteenth, as the teen-age dauphin, married Marie Antoinette."

"Let them eat cake!" sang out Lucille. The silver-haired gentleman gave her an icy stare. She winked at him.

As they moved through room after room, each more splendid than the last, Lucille remained firmly entrenched at Jessica's side.

"You know, I'm glad I came today. The tour I'm with, from Chicago, came here yesterday, but this *deevine* man I met at the Louvre (she pronounced it Loo-ver to rhyme with the vacuum) wanted to take me to lunch yesterday afternoon. Well, I couldn't very well turn that down, now could I, honey?" Her laugh was a whinny. She lowered her voice. "He turned out to be married. His wife was even traveling with him. He told her he was going to the barber shop when he met me for lunch!" The disappointment in her voice was touching. "But you have to keep trying. Tomorrow we have the Champs Elysées, the Eiffel Tower, then Notre Dame (when she said it, it rhymed with fame). It's just too bad there are so many women!"

Jessica's response to this monologue was a pleasant nod. She wanted to concentrate on what Claudine was saying, but she couldn't bring herself to hurt such an earnest, lonely woman. Instead, she moved closer to the guide as the group trailed into an ornate hall. The vaulted ceiling was painted lavishly with nymphs, animals and flowers.

"The seventeen mirrors on your left," said Claudine, "were the first mirrors in France; they were a gift from Italy. They reflect the magnificent view of the gardens from the opposite windows. This Hall of Mirrors is one of the most famous halls in Europe. In Louis the Fourteenth's time, the hall was used for balls, receptions and official occasions."

"What a *waaahhnderful* room for a ball," tittered Lucille. The silver-haired gentleman stalked past her with a glare. She blew him a kiss.

Jessica was becoming desperate to escape the constant chatter of her newfound companion. "I believe you have an admirer," she whispered.

"Where?" Lucille's head whipped around.

Jessica nodded in the direction of the sandy-haired man with the hearing aid. "He's had his eye on you ever since we came inside."

Lucille cocked her head, appraising him in a new light. "Not my type at all. Look at those pants and shirt. Looks like he slept in them!" She wrinkled her nose. "Has he really been looking at me?"

Jessica nodded.

"I think I'll just say hi," said Lucille as she sidled over to him.

Jessica breathed with relief. For the next hour, as she traipsed through the richly ornamental rooms behind Claudine, she received only occasional glances and winks from Lucille, indefatigably stalking her prey, albeit without the least sign of encouragement.

Jessica gave herself to the glory of the Sun King's reign. She kept the pen firmly in her grip as she jotted notes, only occasionally thinking of the redezvous at the Water Mirror Basin.

At 3:30, Claudine brought them to the south terrace. The gardens extended on all sides as far as the eye could see, a vista of forests, fountains, flowers, statues and pools. Jessica was stunned by the immensity and beauty.

"You will have an hour to roam the gardens. We will meet back at the bus at 4:30."

Jessica immediately dashed for the steps beyond the huge pools of the terrace which led to the perfection of the gardens. She had made it only to the top step when she felt a hand on her arm.

"Whew, I'm glad I caught you," said Lucille, panting.

Jessica looked at her in dismay. "I thought you were otherwise occupied."

"Well, honey, it turned out to be a waste of time. He was the rudest man! Told me he'd been married six times and hated women."

Jessica hooted in spite of herself. "With that kind of record, you can't blame him."

"I just told him the right woman would make all the difference. Men are impossible. Where shall we go now? We could use a good chat."

Trapped, Jessica continued down the steps. "I'd like to see it all. Let's start with the Petite Trianon." She started posthaste down the mall, Lucille trotting to keep pace as she struggled to read her map. By the time they reached the fountains of the Latona Basin, Lucille was huffing a protest.

"The Petite Trianon is so far," she wailed. "I thought we could find a nice spot to sit, but if you're going to race along like this, I'm too bushed to keep up." She began fanning herself with the folded map.

"I'm sorry," replied Jessica. "I need to see as much as possible. For my article." She tapped the notebook, then clipped the blue pen to the binding with what she hoped looked like a professional flourish. "Why don't I meet you back at the bus?"

Lucille gave her a reproachful look, but nodded. Like a disgruntled schoolgirl, she flung the fat, orange, flower-shaped straw bag over her shoulder—no mean feat, for it was stuffed to the tips of its yarn petals and reached from the back of her neck to her waist.

The sandy-haired man was strolling toward them, about thirty yards away, buried in his guidebook. With a little squeak and a wink at Jessica, Lucille turned on the personality full force and steamed over to him.

"Honey," she cooed, "let's you and I go 'round this old garden together. The seventh time's the charm!" She linked her arm through his possessively.

A storm of protest followed, but Jessica was down the mall and soon out of earshot. In a few minutes she reached the Water Mirror Basin.

The front side of the basin curved, thrusting forward, flanked by statues. Five walkways, including the one she had come down, radiated from the rounded side, and led through the trees. Behind the pool, the Jardin du Roi was a mass of spectacular color and scent from thousands of flowers in full bloom. It was possible to believe that nothing existed but art and nature.

Jessica sat on the edge of the basin, trailing her hand in

the cool water, enjoying the solitude and quiet. In the peace of this balmy afternoon, the machinations of spies chasing about for a strip of microfilm seemed improbable. The morning anxiety hazed in her memory; she felt buoyed with optimism. In three hours she would be in London, film safe in Peter's hands, Lark delivered to freedom.

Sensing rather than seeing the intrusion, she looked up, startled to see a man hurrying in her direction down the path on her left. She recognized his wrinkled clothing and sandy hair. Apparently he had extricated himself from Lucille. He was wearing the same tan shirt, but Jessica's eyes were riveted to the red handkerchief that now spilled from his shirt pocket. Puffing, he slowed, then sat on the edge of the pool, about three feet from her. He swiveled his head in all directions before he spoke, then addressed the gravel at his feet.

"Have you seen a woman wearing a red coat? I can't find my wife." He delivered the words without inflection, like a bad actor reciting from a script. His English was slightly accented, but good.

Jessica stared at him, dumbfounded.

"A woman in a red coat?" he repeated, leaning toward her, adjusting his glasses, still out of breath. Jessica could see a thin wire running from his hearing aid into his collar.

"She . . . she probably went to the Grand Trianon."

"Please, would you show me the way?"

Jessica looked at her watch; it was only 3:45. Lark had not even arrived yet. She rose uncertainly. "It's that direction," she said, pointing. "But you were on the tour!"

"Yes. I had to be sure you were not followed." The man stood. He was about two inches shorter than she. He pulled the red handkerchief from his pocket and mopped his wet brow, then, leaning down to dip the fabric into the water, he wrung it out and patted the back of his neck. "Aaahhhh." The sigh of relief brought a smile to his flushed face.

Jessica chuckled, shaking her head. "And I thought you were watching . . . oh, poor Lucille!"

The man looked uncomfortable. "Yes," he said. A bond was forged between them.

"You're early," said Jessica. "Lark hasn't arrived yet."

The man motioned her forward. They walked in silence around the basin and followed the path into the next section of trees. Two women approached from the opposite direction, nodded pleasantly as they passed. Farther down the path, the man pulled her aside into a slight recess amongst the growth, where they were hidden from view.

"There's been a change in plans," he whispered.

"What happened?" The beauty of a summer afternoon faded into fear.

"Barnsworth decided it is too dangerous to bring you both out together. He wants you to go back to the hotel. Wait for him to contact you."

"What about Lark?"

"He'll be taken care of. You're to give the film to me, and we'll get it out with Lark. It's much safer for you, this way."

"But why aren't I going with him?" asked Jessica. The air felt very hot, in spite of the shade. She pushed a strand of hair off her face. There was something wrong. Peter was going to contact her? She was uneasy, didn't know what to do.

"Will Lark be safe?"

"Yes, don't worry. But we want no connection between you and him. He's being followed. We can get the film to London faster this way. And we don't want you hurt. It would be better for you to simply drop out of the picture."

"But what happened?"

The man shrugged. "They don't give me the details, just my instructions. I was told to pick up the film from you."

There was no question she should obey Peter's instructions, yet she heard the echo of Lark's voice telling her to trust no one. Lark had said the film was to go directly from her hands into Peter's. Had things changed? Was that instruction no longer valid?

"You're right, of course," she said, pressing damp palms against her skirt. "The only problem is, I don't have the film."

"What do you mean, you don't have it?" The man looked alarmed.

"Since Lark was coming with me, he decided to bring it himself." Lark would know better how to handle this new situation, she thought.

The man looked at her doubtfully. "I was told you had it."

Jessica shrugged. "Another change in plans."

He looked at the ground, thinking. "Very well. Go back to your hotel, wait for Barnsworth to contact you. You can't reach him now, he's making arrangements for Lark. We'll have Lark in London by this evening."

He stepped out of the foliage, scanned the path right and left. It was clear in both directions.

"You continue on toward the Trianon," he said, pointing to the right. "I'll go back this way. The fewer connections between us, the better." Jessica nodded and turned her back, starting down the path, wondering why she felt so unsettled. She tucked the notebook, pen still clipped to the binding, under her arm. Had she done the right thing, or had she compounded Peter's problems? Would he be furious that she had taken matters into her own hands, ignored his contact?

Absorbed in her thoughts, she had barely gone twenty feet when suddenly an arm was thrust around her neck from behind. Thrown off balance, she sagged backward toward her attacker as he dragged her back into the trees. She thrashed helplessly, too stunned to cry out, fighting the pressure against her throat. Her head was held immobile by the strong arm of her assailant. Choking, she tried to kick backwards at him, but the dragging motion made it impossible to reach him and even her flailing arms sawed the air futilely. It was no use; the man held her solidly, head pinned in the crook of his right elbow. The only part of him she could even see was the coarse, black hairs on his beefy forearm. With a grunt, he caught her waving arms, easily pinning them behind her back, sending a bolt of pain through her shoulder.

The pain galvanized her defenses; she found her voice, started to scream. They had gone some twenty-five feet into the trees, crashing through undergrowth which snatched at them, snagging clothing and scratching skin. The foliage now screened them from the path. At Jessica's first sound, the man released her arms and slammed his hand over her mouth, but although she couldn't move her head in either direction, she had slight mobility in her jaw and she clamped her teeth together hard, catching the fleshy base of his finger. He cursed, a guttural, foreign sound, but the words were unintelligible to her. Expertly, he hooked his right foot around her right leg, sending them both lurching to the ground in a Punch and Judy fall.

His full weight landed on her, pinning her into the loose, warm earth. Her scream was muffled by dirt and lack of breath; it emerged as a series of grunts.

The man's hand probed the side of her neck, found the carotid artery and pressed. Shooting points of light exploded in her brain. With a last effort at life, she thrust upward with her elbow and caught the man in the rib cage, at the same time rolling her body from under his weight. The exposed roots of the trees made the ground feel like a bed of nails.

He was on her again in a second, before she could even sit up, his meaty palm clapped over her mouth and nose so that she could hardly breathe. With his other hand, he again probed for the carotid. This time she was lying on her side, head twisting over her shoulder, but he kept his body back, out of her line of vision as she thrashed, trying to avoid his exploring fingers. Finding his objective, he pressed the artery. Treetops and patches of sun began to whirl in a kaleidoscope pattern above her. She jerked her head frantically, forcing him to adjust his position, and in that moment, she caught a glimpse of his sandy hair and fleshy face. Incredibly, his glasses were still in place, the sides imbedded in the grooves at his temples.

Then blackness closed swiftly, like a curtain drawn across her vision. She could still hear her own feeble, animal sounds, somehow detached, no longer a part of her. Then even sound ceased, leaving her swirling in a void.

CHAPTER FIFTEEN

"Terminate the flow of blood to the brain and the body dies, deprived of its command post. But interrupt the flow briefly, by pressing one of the carotid arteries on either side of the neck, and the body suffers only a blackout of command, a period of unconsciousness." The words had begun in a low whisper, then gradually emerged more clearly, until the voice of an MI6 instructor surfaced through the layers of Jessica's consciousness. The voice droned on, floating, disembodied in the blackness. "The name for the carotid artery, which conveys blood from the aorta to the head, comes from the Greek *karoun*—to plunge into sleep or stupor."

Jessica woke from her sleep with one hell of a headache, a reproach from the command post for being poorly treated. As she opened her eyes, the voice faded and slid back to join the chorus of other voices and images on the periphery of her awareness. She sat up abruptly, but the trees around her swayed, and the headache scythed her as if she were a blade of wheat. She slumped back with a moan, gathering woolly thoughts from the pastures of her mind. Focus, damn it. Think! She rubbed her hands over her face and through her hair, reconstructing how she could possibly have arrived on the ground in the middle of a forest. Her neck felt bruised on the left side, tender to the touch. Oh, yes . . . the carotid artery . . . but there was something else. . . .

The pen! The thought sent a tremor through her. Where was the pen? She examined the ground around her. Her handbag was gone; the notebook was nowhere in sight. Shakily, she stood, but her heart now pumped more blood than she needed, and she had to grasp the tree trunk for support. *Where was the pen?*

Eyes sweeping the ground, she stumbled through the undergrowth, realized she was going in the wrong direction, and reversed, making her way back to the path this time. She emerged into the full sunlight of the gravel walk. There was no trace of notebook, handbag, or pen. Defeated, she crumpled at the edge of the path, holding her throbbing head. They had won.

Half-heartedly, she pawed at the surrounding undergrowth. The brush yielded nothing but what nature had created: tufts of grass, leaves, saplings, not even a scrap of trash from man's domination of the planet. Hopelessness turned to anger and she smashed at the foliage. At last she stood, brushing leaves and dirt from her clothes. They hadn't killed her. She wondered why she couldn't seem to take pleasure from that.

A glint of sunlight winked from the ground to her right. She scrambled through the bushes, tearing leaves aside. Screened from view, only its metal clip glittering in the sun, lay the blue pen. Silently, on all fours, the released tears streaming down her face, Jessica looked at it. It must have flipped off the binding of the notebook when the man grabbed her. He had taken the only two objects he thought she had: the notebook and her handbag. But he didn't get the pen! Jessica snatched it up and hopped along the walk in an odd little dance.

"Thank you, thank you," she repeated over and over again.

She slipped the pen into the pocket of her skirt, hands fumbling in excitement, took it out, slid it into her blouse and clipped it to her bra, then pulled it out again and put it back into her pocket. She remembered the time.

Her watch read 4:10. Probably too late to warn Lark. But she had to try. Brushing at her tear-stained face, she raced along the path, dodged past a group of people on the broad main walk, and plunged into the section of garden leading to the Water Mirror Basin.

She dodged among the trees until she could see a portion of the basin. She kept low and maneuvered as far as she dared without being seen until she had a clear view.

There was no one at the pool.

Jessica remained crouched, shifted her weight to rest against the trunk of an elm tree. All right, she told herself. Lark isn't here. That could mean he arrived at four o'clock, met the contact, and they left without her. Reluctantly, she faced the other alternative: the man who attacked her somehow disposed of the real contact and met Lark in his place. If they had Lark, they would soon discover that he did not have the film. And that meant they would come looking for her again. This time they would probably kill her.

A girlish laugh drew her attention to the left side of the pool. The honeymoon couple from the tour had strolled to the water's edge and were splashing each other lightly. Their play turned erotic, and they clung to each other for a lingering kiss, then, arm in arm, they wandered toward the Jardin du Roi, oblivious to the eyes that watched them from the trees.

The Water Mirror Basin was deserted again.

Jessica hastened up the path toward the palace. She had to get to the airport, take the first flight to London. Lark was a pro: he could take care of himself. There was nothing more she could do for him now. She started to run, then halted in the middle of the walk. She couldn't go to the airport. She had no money; it was in her absent handbag. And she couldn't get a flight to London; her passport was also in the missing bag. She would have to rejoin the tour even to get a ride back to Paris.

Most of the tour group had congregated around the bus in the Place d'Armes, although it was only 4:25. Not surprisingly, the sandy-haired man was missing. Lucille spied Jessica as she approached and flounced over to her.

"Well, honey, you look awful! What happened?"

Jessica looked down. Her blouse had come untucked and her skirt was rumpled and dirty. She hadn't even felt the sting on her knees, but both were skinned like a schoolgirl's. She noticed that her hands were scratched, little welts of blood drying along the lines. She sighed as Lucille fished in the pocket inside the orange flower bag and produced a mirror. The face staring back at her was streaked with dirt, the neck sported a blotch suffused with violet. Her hair was tangled with leaves and twigs.

"Someone stole my handbag," she offered, after a pause, picking at the leaves.

Lucille gasped. "To think Versailles is a mugger's hangout just like the public parks at home. Here, let me help you." She fumbled in her bag for a handkerchief, spat on it, and began vigorously attacking the streaks on Jessica's face.

"I can do it, thanks," said Jessica, taking the handkerchief.

"Well, we are going to let them know about this, honey!" Lucille was working herself into a righteous lather. "Americans cannot be assaulted in foreign countries!" She spoke loudly; other members of the group turned, then clustered around Jessica, expressing concern.

"Excuse me. What's happened here?" Claudine appeared at Jessica's side.

"This woman has been attacked," announced Lucille.

"Are you hurt?" asked Claudine.

"No, I'm all right. . . ."

Claudine took charge immediately. "Ladies and gentlemen, please wait here at the bus, we must make a report to the gendarmes. There will be a short delay, but we will have you back to your hotels soon." She led Jessica, Lucille flapping beside her, to the police office behind the ticket booth.

Jessica recounted the incident as a mugging, saying she hadn't seen her assailant clearly. The policeman was profusely apologetic, but admitted helplessness; the chances of finding the man without a description were nil. Claudine was filled with sympathy. After completing the proper forms, Jessica returned to the bus, Lucille still sputtering at her side. Most of the passengers were sympathetic; only the elderly gentleman grumbled about the delay.

"Trouble attracts trouble," he muttered to no one in particular as he boarded the bus. He sat stiffly in the first seat and glared at Lucille and Jessica as they passed.

Lucille kept up a running commentary as the bus fought the rush hour traffic back to Paris. "I think it's a crime! Well, of course, it *is* a crime. You know what I mean. . . ."

Jessica leaned her head against the back of the seat, tuning out constant babble. To keep her imagination under control, she made a mental inventory of the contents of her handbag. With a sharp pain, she remembered the picture she carried in her wallet, a picture of her father, taken a year ago at the Lincoln Memorial. She fought the rising lump in her throat. They had even taken his picture from her.

Lucille was still rattling on at her side, oblivious to the lack of response. To distract her, Jessica asked about the flower-shaped straw bag with its huge orange loops.

"Isn't it the cutest thing?" bubbled Lucille. "This bag is

my whole European trip. I put something in here from every place I go." She pulled the handles apart, allowing Jessica a glimpse of brochures, postcards, maps, match covers, and assorted trinkets all jammed inside. "I won't look at anything while I'm here. Then, when I get home to Chicago, on one of those blizzardy nights when it's 10 below, I'll take it out and have the whole trip over again! Or maybe I'll just throw it all away, who knows?" She patted the bag, almost affectionately.

At last the bus pulled up to the Inter-Continental Hotel, the first hotel drop for the tour.

"Honey, this has just been so much fun talking to you," said Lucille as they stepped off the bus. "I'm sorry about your purse. I know it took the edge off the afternoon for you."

"Thank you," said Jessica. "I . . . have to ask a favor of you. My wallet was in the bag. I don't have fare for the métro."

Lucille dug into her wallet and handed her five francs. "You have some money back at your hotel, honey?"

Jessica nodded. "Traveler's checks." She wasn't eager to return to the hotel. Most probably it was under surveillance, but without money she couldn't move around Paris, let alone try to leave the country. She brushed aside the thought of Gordon. He would be able to help her, but at what risk? If anything happened to him because of her . . . no, better to stay away, leave him out of it.

"Thank you so much," she said to Lucille, accepting the money. "I'll. . . ." She had turned her head casually toward the street as she spoke. She stopped in mid-sentence. A gray Citroën was turning into Rue Castiglione; the driver's eyes caught hers for a millisecond as he made the turn. Jessica's face drained of color. The driver's wire-framed glasses and sandy hair were all too familiar.

Unconsciously, she put her hand into her skirt pocket, fingering the pen. The Citroën braked, slid to the curb on the opposite side of the street.

"Are you okay? You look kind of pale," said Lucille.

"I. . . ." Jessica slid her right hand out of her pocket, grabbed Lucille's arm with her left, then let her right hand hover for an instant over the orange flower bag. The pen slipped into the jumble of its contents, unnoticed by Lucille.

"I have to go," said Jessica. She turned and fled, leaving Lucille open-mouthed on the sidewalk.

She ran into the Rue de Rivoli, the direction from which the Citroën had come. At the next block, she crossed the street, terrified that the car might be coming around the corner. One more block and she was at the Tuileries métro station. She pounded down the stairs, reached the platform just as the train careened into the station, and managed to cram herself through a turnstile and into a first class car. Her lungs were ready to burst. The train surged forward as she wiggled her hand between bodies to find a pole to hold on to, but the jam of people was too tight to tell if anyone had followed her. She closed her eyes. Things were going from bad to worse: Peter's contact was missing, she'd lost Lark, she was being followed, her passport was gone, and now she no longer even had the microfilm. She was beginning to understand what her father meant by learning to live with constant fear. She forced herself to think, one step at a time. She'd get money at the hotel, then call Peter. He would know what to do.

The late afternoon sun had a spent look about it as Jessica came above ground at the Sèvres Babylone station. She walked slowly along Boulevard Raspail. There was still plenty of movement on the streets. Her eyes searched the faces around her; she knew the features she was seeking now, the shapes. It made it easier.

On the same side of the street, but a block from her hotel, she withdrew into the recessed doorway of a dry cleaner with "M. Chantel, Le Pressing" lettered on the glass door. It was closed for the evening, but the vantage point allowed her to see diagonally through the window back out to the street. She studied the block opposite the hotel. On the far corner was a small café, tables on the sidewalk, where two days ago she had sipped Verveine in innocent anticipation of getting the film at Galerie Meunier. Only two days ago. It felt like a lifetime.

No single men lounged over coffee while watching the hotel from a sidewalk table, but she could not see the interior of the restaurant. Apartment buildings lined the rest of the street. Pedestrians passed by; there were no lingerers. No gray Citroëns were parked along the curb or cruising past. It looked too good to be true.

She crossed the street to survey the block of the hotel. It resembled a movie set for a Parisian street scene: actors entered and exited, playing their lives to the hilt. Everyone belonged. So her only problem would be the restaurant.

Jessica toured the other three sides of the block, coming up on the café from behind, along the side street. There were no tables on this side, as the entire front of the café faced the busier boulevard, but the full-length plate glass windows provided an ample view inside. By maintaining a position close to the building, she could see into the room without being seen. No more than ten patrons sat inside, all of them involved with their food or conversation; no one watched the hotel across the street.

It was now or never. She crossed the boulevard, still looking at the street as she approached the hotel entrance, and didn't see the jaunty, young man in jeans and a tee shirt who came hurtling through the door. They collided with a knock of bone on bone.

"Hey, careful," he said, grabbing her elbow to steady her. He looked her up and down with amusement, taking in her disheveled condition.

"Excuse me," said Jessica. She brushed at her skirt self-consciously. "As you can see, I'm having one of those days."

"Maybe I can help?" He flashed a practiced grin, retaining custody of her elbow as he stepped to the door and opened it with a flourish. Through the open door, Jessica could see into the lobby. She stepped back quickly, pulling away from him to lean against the side of the building. He looked nonplussed.

"Hey, I thought you were going in there. I didn't mean. . . ."

"Yes. No. I've forgotten something." She dashed back to the corner, leaving the young man looking puzzled, then braved the traffic, crossing the street against the light. She ran into the café and dropped into a chair facing the window, eyes on the hotel entrance. Had she been seen? But no one came out of the hotel.

The waiter approached, but Jessica motioned him away. "Telephone?" she asked.

He gestured to the rear. She dialed and waited, fingers drumming the side of the box.

"Hotel LaPorte," came the voice over the phone.

"Give me the front desk, please."

"Hotel LaPorte, desk." The inflection was the same as the first voice, only several notes lower.

"Is there a dark-haired, stout man sitting in the lobby, wearing gray pants and shirt? He's by himself with a newspaper." She couldn't be certain, but in the brief instant she had seen him through the open door, the clothes and the narrow face had looked vaguely familiar, the pointed nose and chin more prominent without the beret and dark glasses, but still resembling the man from the clock shop.

"One moment," said the clerk. She could hear a woman's voice in the background. Then, "Yes, he's here." The voice was that of a suffering man.

"May I speak to him, please?"

"One moment."

Jessica left the receiver swinging from its cord, brushed past waiters and patrons, and ran as fast as she could across the street, this time with the traffic light in her favor. She entered the lobby just in time to see the man turn the corner around the side of the hotel where the house phones were located. His back was to the hotel entrance as he reached for the instrument.

Drooping Moustache was at the desk in a heated argument with a fat woman holding a large calico cat in her arms.

"This is ridiculous!" the woman was screaming. "I've stayed at better hotels than this with Botticelli. He's very well behaved."

Jessica was past the desk, unnoticed. The door to the stairwell was on her right, directly in view from the bank of house phones. Reluctantly, she turned to the elevator. The arrow pointed to the third floor. She looked over her shoulder. It might not get here in time!

The man at the phone leaned around the corner, facing the desk.

"Please, I can't hear," he shouted at the woman with the cat. His face was turned away from Jessica, who stood like a statue at the elevator, holding her breath. The man had spoken in poorly accented French.

The two at the desk paid no attention to him. "Absolutely not! Impossible!" Drooping Moustache was yelling at the woman. "No cats in the hotel."

"Hello . . . Hello?" said the man into the receiver, plugging his other ear.

"I insist upon seeing the manager," brayed the woman. "I will not be treated like this!"

"I am the manager, and I'm telling you—no cats!" Drooping Moustache's face flamed with rage.

Jessica pounded the elevator button. "Please," she whispered to herself. "Please. . . ."

The man at the phone turned to the desk again, his back still toward the elevator. "There's no one on the line," he said to the desk clerk.

Drooping Moustache shot him a look and threw up his hands. The woman continued her tirade.

"You will live to regret this, monsieur!"

The man at the telephone hung up in disgust. At the moment he wheeled back toward the lobby, the elevator door opened, and Jessica hurled herself inside, shouldering past a departing couple and flattening herself against the wall of the car. She could see the man cross back to the lobby, his eyes on the hotel entrance. As the elevator doors closed, Jessica put her head in her hands.

She had tried to be so thorough, but she hadn't expected him to be *in* the hotel. What were his plans if she came through the door? It didn't matter. She was past him now, but she had to think of a way to get out of the hotel. She would call Peter and then . . . suddenly the voice with the bad French accent rang a bell: it was the same voice that had answered when she called to leave a message for Raymonde. In the clock shop, he had spoken English, but now that she heard French, she was certain it was the same voice. So she had told them exactly where to find her! But how had they known about the red scarf and the recognition words Peter had given her over the phone? She hadn't mentioned them in the message to Raymonde and she certainly hadn't seen that face at American Express. Somehow, they were privy to her contact with Peter; she couldn't risk calling him again. Her one link to safety had become a trap. She ignored the whining voice that told her to call Gordon; she would not endanger him. This was her job to do.

It wasn't until she actually stood before the door to her room that she realized her mistake. Then the absurdity struck her funny. The key was in her handbag: she couldn't get in. The more she tried to stop, the harder she laughed, until tears squeezed from the corners of her eyes and she had to lean against the wall, clutching her stomach to regain control. But the spasm released the emotion and left her clear-headed.

She tried the sixth floor first, taking the stairs at the end of the hall, but the corridor was bare, so she went down to the fourth floor, peeked through the window in the stairwell. The maid's housekeeping cart was halfway down the hall. The trick was to be certain the maid would let her into her room and not send her down to the desk. She looked around the stairwell. When she saw the window, she smiled.

Standing on tiptoe, she could just reach the bottom of the window frame on the landing at the turn of the stairs. She gave the handle a push; the pane swung open easily. Quickly she took off her blouse, rolled it into a ball, and tossed it out the window. Clad in her bra, she opened the door and rushed into the corridor. The maid came out of the room near the cart, locking the door behind her as Jessica approached.

"Pardon, Mademoiselle, I'm so embarrassed," she cried, holding her crossed arms over her breasts. "I've locked myself out of my room. Can you open it for me?"

The girl looked about eighteen, darkly pretty with enormous black eyes that widened in horror as she looked at Jessica. She produced a stream of Near Eastern language that Jessica did not understand.

Desperately looking around, then down at her bare torso, Jessica mimed her plight, pointing to the keys in the girl's hand, then gestured upstairs and motioned for the girl to follow her. As they climbed the stairs, she could hear the maid tittering behind her. They had to wait at the door for a man to step into the elevator, which further amused the maid. Then, like sneaky children, they hurried down the hall. The maid unlocked the door, accepted Jessica's profuse thanks with averted eyes, and retreated, a hand over her mouth to hide her giggles.

The slight odor in the room made no impression upon Jessica as she carefully locked the door behind her. First she went into the bathroom to wash the remnants of the gardens from her body. Then, concentrating solely upon what to take with her, she crossed directly to the suitcase on the luggage stand by the dresser and began ruffling through it. She traded her disheveled skirt for a clean skirt, blouse and jacket. She slipped the travelers checks in the silk wallet into the pocket of her jacket.

Intent upon her purpose, she didn't see him until she turned to go. He was sitting in the straight-backed chair in the corner by the bed, wearing the same clothes he had worn in the clock shop that morning. His posture was very straight in the chair, hands folded in his lap, mouth open as if about to speak; startled eyes stared straight at her. He might have been calmly waiting for her return to the hotel. The enormous amount of dried blood caked on the left side of his shirt front looked like cheap, theatrical makeup. It wasn't. There was a small, neat bullet hole in Lark's chest.

Mouth open in a voiceless cry, Jessica stood rooted, staring. Then transfixed as the mongoose by the snake, she crept forward in horrid fascination. The bullet had ploughed clear through the body; the exit aperture had blown a crater in his back, scattering blood and flesh against the wall. Apparently the bullet had lodged in the wall behind him; she could see the mark where it had been carefully scraped out.

Everything else in the room was in perfect order. From far away, she heard a gagging sound, unconsciously put her fingers to her mouth. They came away wet. She stumbled into the bathroom, heaving, and kneeled by the toilet as the heaving turned into deep, wracking sobs.

Emotion spent at last, she pulled herself to a standing position, using the edge of the sink. The numbness would not leave. A splash of cold water on the face helped somewhat. Then, standing in the middle of the bathroom, she groped for her pulse, amazed by the throb of life. They killed her father. They killed Lark. And they were going to kill her. The man downstairs was waiting for her.

Her body was in motion before she recognized the thought that propelled it. She didn't go back into the bedroom, but stepped into the hall. The maid had reached the fifth floor in her nightly rounds; her cart stood outside room 518. Jessica walked down the hall. As she entered the room, the girl was placing two foil-wrapped mints by the bed she had turned down. She gestured with a smile toward Jessica's complete ensemble. "Bonne, bonne," she said.

Jessica smiled in return. "Thank you. I need another towel to wash my hair." She mimed the use of a towel, uselessly repeating the word. The girl laughed.

"Oui, oui." She crooked a finger, grabbed a ring of keys from the second shelf of the supply cart and trotted down the hall. Jessica pocketed two books of matches with "Hotel LaPorte" printed in black script, and followed.

The maid unlocked the supply closet at the end of the corridor, disappeared inside, and returned bearing a large white towel. She held it up gleefully with a word Jessica could not understand.

"Thank you," nodded Jessica. The maid relocked the door and padded back to her cart, pushing it down the corridor to 517. As she rapped on the door, Jessica called out to her from her own doorway.

"Don't bother with my room." She shook her hands and head, pointing to the door to illustrate the meaning. The maid nodded and waved, opened the door to 517 and disappeared inside.

Swiftly, Jessica approached the cart. She could hear the maid humming as she turned down the beds. Crouching at the side of the door, Jessica reached to the second shelf, edged the keys toward her, careful not to let them jingle. Her hand closed over them and she ran down the hall to the supply closet. It took several tries before she found the right key, and even then it was difficult to unlock the door because her hands were shaking so badly. She could still hear the maid humming as she replaced the keys on the cart and fled.

The supply closet was a small, airless room, heavy with the odor of commercial laundry. Jessica closed the door silently behind her, felt for a light switch. As she flipped it, a circular fluorescent tube in the ceiling buzzed, then blinked on with a harsh glare illuminating towel-filled shelves from floor to ceiling on the right, sheets and bedding on the left. Two piles of pillows, tied with twine, were stacked at the far end, as well as several large cartons of toilet tissue.

She took a blanket from the shelf, spread it on the floor and dropped the towel the maid had given her onto it. Then, grabbing from both sides, she threw sheets and towels into a large pile, folded the corners of the blanket over the bundle. Hefting it under her arm, she tripped the light switch, then eased the door open slightly. The maid was twenty-five feet down the hall, heading in her direction. She whirled; there was no place to go.

She bounded to the two piles of pillows, but it was impossible to bury herself; the bundles were securely tied and the feather pillows in each stack made them too heavy to lift. She looked around wildly, then wrestled the nearest box of toilet tissue into the corner, behind the door, grunting with exertion as she tried to half slide, half lift it into place. Faster, get the damn box *moving!* She barely made it to the corner when she heard the key in the lock.

Crouching behind the box, she tossed her own bundle of linens on top of herself, and folded her body as tightly as possible underneath. The door opened. She shifted her arm slightly to put her mouth over the conspicuous tick of her watch. Her heart was hammering at the same rate as the ticking; it felt as if her entire body were slamming against the wall behind her. She couldn't see anything: her head was on the floor at her knees, but she had a vision of the maid standing above her, looking down. The girl was no longer humming, but Jessica could hear her breathing. The light had not yet been turned on.

There was a rattling sound, then the door closed with a slam. She dared not move, unsure whether the maid was inside or out. Then the key turned in the lock.

In slow motion, she uncurled her body, pushed off the bundle, and sprawled forward over the carton, purposefully releasing each tightly coiled muscle. A few steps led her to a bulky object now in the center of the dark room, which her exploring fingers identified as the cart. Then she was at the door, listening, all her attention focused into her ears.

Nothing.

Turning the bolt quietly, she eased the door open. The maid was gone, the corridor empty.

Bundle in tow, Jessica shot into the hall, sprinted the short distance to her room, where she dumped the linens on the bed. Lark's fixed stare bored a hole into her; she felt the shock anew, had to concentrate to keep from trembling. Turning her back, she worked quickly, dividing the linen into two piles, then paused to look around the room. Several copies of *Le Monde* lay on the table by the tub chair. Was it possible that she had once sat in this room for three days, innocent and bored, reading newspapers and waiting for an unknown man, code-named Lark, whom her father . . . stop it!

She opened the newspapers, wadded each page into a loose ball, and stuffed it into each linen pile, then tied each pile into a bundle with a sheet, tucking more newspaper loosely into the open loops around the knots. The blanket she took into the bathroom, ran the water in the tub and poked it down until it was soggy.

The hallway was still, mercifully, empty. With both bundles of linen and paper under her arms, she ran down the hall to the laundry chute, fumbled in her pocket for matches, lit one, and held it to the protruding ends of newspaper. The newsprint caught with a high, orange flame, curling into ash immediately as the fire ate its way along the trail of paper into the ball of linens. The sheets caught more slowly; the towels began to smoke. She opened the chute and sent the ball of fire and smoke hurtling into the bowels of the hotel.

The second bundle caught as quickly; she sent it tumbling down to join the first.

As she hurried back toward her room, the elevator doors opened, discharging a man and a woman, preceded by a bellboy pushing a luggage cart. Jessica slowed her pace, nodded briefly to them as they passed. At her doorway, she turned to watch them enter a room at the end of the hall. She closed her own door loudly. After counting to ten, she eased it open again. The hall was unoccupied. She chewed on a knuckle as she waited. Come on, bellboy, she whispered. The damn hotel is going to burn down if you don't hurry. Then he was in the hall, whistling as he walked to the elevator. With a sigh of relief, Jessica ran into the bathroom.

The blanket was heavy as she lifted it, dripping, from the tub. At the door, she stopped to look out. All clear. She lumbered down the hall and pitched the soggy bundle down the chute, hoping the tell-tale trail of water would dry before it was noticed. She stood a moment at the chute, shaking the water from her hands. Please let this work, she prayed.

The ring of a telephone startled her. She realized it was coming from her room, automatically ran to catch it. Her first thought was Peter. Then she stopped. As desperately as she wanted to talk to him, she was afraid. And if it weren't Peter. . . .

She was halfway to her room when the elevator opened again. A waiter with a room service tray stepped out, glanced at her uncertainly, then moved to the door of her room, knocking loudly. Jessica raced for the closing doors of the elevator, which neatly framed the waiter as he knocked a second time and announced "Room service."

At the second floor, Jessica got off the elevator and

slipped into the stairwell at the end of the corridor. If she had calculated correctly, the fiery linen would have landed in the main laundry room in the basement, which would be deserted on Saturday evening, and would ignite whatever other laundry was there. The wet blanket wouldn't stop the fire, but it would dampen it somewhat, creating plumes of smoke and making the fire look larger than it was.

The four- or five-minute wait was hell on her nerves. At last, she peeked into the hallway. It was working: small wisps of smoke were curling out of the laundry chute. Five more minutes and the chute, acting like a draft chimney, was pouring smoke into the hall.

"Fire!" screamed Jessica into the hallway. *"Fire!"*

Three doors near her remained closed; the fourth opened. A woman in a dressing gown poked her head out.

"Mon dieu!" she cried, seeing the smoke.

The fire alarm began to screech as the smoke detectors got a whiff of fumes. Jessica bolted down the stairs. At the bottom, there were two doors, one on either side of the stairwell. She opened the one marked Employees Only. A short, narrow hall, with what appeared to be storerooms on one side and a large locker room on the other, led to a closed door at the far end. A busboy, emerging from the locker room, grabbed her arm as he ran past.

"Vite! Vite!" he shouted, pushing her toward the rising babble of voices behind the closed door in front of them. The fire bell clanged furiously, all but deafening them.

They emerged into the kitchen, now crowded with panicky employees. No one paid the slightest attention to her. Spying a row of aprons hanging from hooks by the door, she grabbed one, tying it around her waist. Two chefs in toques were trying to shut down the gas stoves. A sous-chef was shouting orders to employees, while leading them to the exit door on the opposite side of the room. Smoke poured into the kitchen from the cracks around a closed door on the left which must have led down to the laundry room. People began to cough as the air became heavier, more acrid by the minute.

Jessica joined the throng moving toward the door, snatched a cloth from a cutting table as she passed and fastened it over her hair.

The kitchen door exited into a short dead-end alleyway lined with trash cans and garbage pails, which in turn led into Boulevard Raspail. Jessica stayed in the middle of the group of employees as they moved to the street, melding with the gathering crowd.

A fire truck roared to a halt in front of the hotel; the rising scream of klaxons signaled more help on the way. Firemen began hauling hoses into the lobby, hampered by the flow of guests pouring out the main entrance. To add to the confusion, the crowd of rubberneckers pressed closer, held at bay by gendarmes.

"It started in the kitchen!"

"No, in the basement."

"I was taking a bath!"

Jessica moved to the outer edges of the crowd, on the alert for the familiar face of the man in the lobby. Suddenly, she saw his pointy profile about ten paces ahead, focused on the guests flowing out of the hotel. Pulling the rag down around her face, and keeping a line of onlookers between them, she hurried past the watchdog, face averted, and continued down the block. At the first corner, she broke into a run—only heeding the need to put distance between herself and the hotel.

At the next corner, a bus was closing its doors. She ran for it, pulling off the apron and makeshift scarf with one hand, banging on the door with the other. The doors opened.

Jessica reached into her pocket, making a pretense of looking for the fare. Finally, she gave him a helpless shrug.

"I'm sorry, I have only traveler's checks," she said in English.

She pulled them from her pocket apologetically. The driver let out a stream of French, all of which Jessica understood, and which caused comment from the passengers behind him. He lurched to the curb at the next stop. Yelling and waving both arms, he ordered her off the bus.

A fire engine roared past her as she stepped onto the sidewalk. Jessica walked three blocks to Boulevard St. Germain, looking for an open shop. A restaurant ahead offered a solution to her dilemma.

She chose a table in the rear, out of the sight lines of the door. She had to order something. She settled on a spinach soufflé as the least of evils, and ordered a glass of white wine. She sipped the wine, slumped over the table, her hands tracing the grain of the polished wood. When the food came, she picked at it, but ordered a second glass of wine. She wanted to fuzz the edges of her mind a little. The waitress placed the check on the table. Jessica nodded. That's why she was here.

"May I pay with these?" asked Jessica, pulling out the traveler's checks from their silky wallet.

"Mais oui."

Jessica used a check much larger than the amount of her meal. The woman watched her sign, then took the check to the register and returned.

Change, in precious francs! At least she could move around the city.

A phone in the corner was her first stop. She got the number from information, then tapped her foot impatiently as it rang. She had to get the blue pen back from Lucille, but she had run off before getting the name of Lucille's hotel. Jessica doubted that a waitress from Chicago was paying the tariff for a super-deluxe hotel like the Inter-Continental, but it was worth a try to see if she were registered.

"Hotel Inter-Continental."

Jessica stopped, mouth open.

"Hotel Inter-Continental." the voice repeated.

Slowly, Jessica replaced the receiver. She didn't even know Lucille's last name.

Back on the street, she hailed a cab and sank low in the back seat.

"Eh, bien, mademoiselle. Where to?" asked the driver when she didn't say anything.

"London," said Jessica.

CHAPTER SIXTEEN

Nikolayev's expression did not change, but his jaw muscle jumped from the pressure as he ground his teeth. It was a miracle that the KGB managed to accomplish anything, he thought, bringing his fingertips together and bouncing them lightly before he pressed them hard. The knuckles popped in quick succession. Kosov, sitting next to him on the park bench, watched the knuckle-cracking ceremony apprehensively; if the fires of Hell existed, they would be preferable to what lay before him now.

They were in a secluded corner of the Jardin du Luxembourg. The park was still populated, but evening was drawing people away to the dinner table. No one came near the two men seated on the bench under the trees. For the first time, Kosov was afraid for his life.

"It was an accident."

Nikolayev didn't trust himself to turn in Kosov's direction, but spoke to the empty path before them, keeping his voice level only by a supreme effort of will.

"Are you totally incompetent? Have you decided you no longer want a career? Or are you trying to destroy me? Is this a personal vendetta?"

"No, Comrade-Major. I'm sorry. I . . . it really was an accident."

"I distinctly recall emphasizing there be no violence. Did I not specifically say that?"

Kosov nodded with a birdlike jerk of his head.

"I was willing to give you the benefit of the doubt about the agent in Italy. But *another* accident? So far you have killed two people. It would have been very much in our interest to keep both those people alive. Do you call that *no violence?*"

Kosov didn't respond. His pointed features looked even more pinched than usual.

"I would be interested in hearing exactly how this 'accident' occurred."

Kosov took a deep breath. "Colonel Alexiekov's story was extremely difficult to break. As you heard, he had a reasonable answer for everything. I could only frighten him, apply a little pain here and there to convince him."

"It was my impression that you had a good record of success in that department."

"Yes, at Lubyanka Prison. But that was different. We had time. With some people it can take days. Colonel Alexiekov. . . ."

"You may omit the Colonel. He has lost the right to his rank."

"Comrade . . . Alexiekov was very determined. I don't know enough about Department A to know if he could have been telling the truth. The story was tight: I couldn't find a hole. After four hours, we had made little progress. I had broken his hand and his foot, maybe his arm—it was bent funny. I squeezed his balls till he fainted. I really couldn't shoot him; we had no doctor and he might have bled to death."

"I thought your methods were more subtle than that."

"Yes, but you see, the idea is to inflict pain, then give comfort. Enemy-friend. It confuses them. You repeat it over and over until they break. But it takes time. Alexiekov was very stubborn and he endures pain."

"So you killed him."

"No! No, I got the idea to use the woman. He might not mind the pain; but if he saw her threatened, it might be the way to reach him."

"Why didn't you consult me?"

"I tried. I called you on the radio, but got no answer."

"I was at the lab at the Embassy. The radio doesn't work through the lead walls."

"I wanted to scare him, take him to her hotel, tell him he would wait for her to arrive. He was agitated. I worked him over in her room, but he passed out. I . . . I went to the bathroom. When I came out, he jumped me."

"A man you had beaten into unconsciousness jumped you?"

"He was out cold when I left the room. I don't understand what happened."

"Go on," said Nikolayev wearily. It was pitiful, but he had to hear it all.

"We fought. Then the gun went off, hit him in the chest."

Nikolayev rubbed his hand over his face, then looked up at the sun, hanging like a bronze medallion near the edge of the sky. In summer, darkness didn't settle over the city until ten o'clock or so, but the day felt worn out, and Nikolayev was tired.

"What did you do with the body?" he asked, hearing the sickening echo of another question asked in a Geneva hotel room two months ago.

"I left it in the room. Couldn't risk getting it out of the hotel."

"I think. . . ." Nikolayev stopped as a subtle, high-pitched beeping sound came from his pocket. He pulled out the tiny transceiver and attached the earphone.

"This is Sable," he said, holding the radio close to his mouth.

Yuri's voice came through the earphone.

"Fox reporting. Everything under control. I used the ring trick on the man with the red handkerchief. He'll be taking a nap for another hour or two in the bushes. I met the woman, but she doesn't have the toy."

"She doesn't have it?"

"Said your boy still has it."

Nikolayev shot Kosov a murderous glance. "Did Alexiekov have the microfilm?" he asked the man next to him.

Kosov had been shuffling his feet, concentrating on the shapes he was making on the path in front of the bench. He looked up.

"Alexiekov?"

"Yes. Yegeni Alexiekov, the man you murdered."

"I. . . ." Kosov coughed slightly. "We thought he passed it to the woman, didn't we?"

"Was there any indication, during the hours you were with him, that he might have kept it?"

"I don't know."

Nikolayev slapped his hand on the bench seat next to him. Kosov flinched, kept his eyes on the path.

Nikolayev spoke into the radio. "Fox, this is Sable. Where is she now?"

Yuri chuckled. "She won't be leaving town. I have her passport."

"Where is she?"

There was a pause.

"Sable to Fox. Where is she now?"

"Hasn't Lynx got her at the hotel?" Yuri's voice was cautious.

Nikolayev swore. He turned incredulous eyes on Kosov, who was now hunched into a ball on the seat next to him, his arms crossed over his stomach, his face approaching the shade of the foliage around him.

"It doesn't appear that Lynx has her at the hotel," he said. He could no longer sit still, but got up and paced the path, spitting out his words. "What the hell is this, a clown act? I'm working with two idiots! When was your last contact?"

The voice in his ear spoke rapidly. "The bus dropped her at the Inter-Continental. I assumed she'd go back to her hotel. I had her passport and money and had told her Uncle Pete would contact her there. I spoke to Lynx on the radio; he said he was at the hotel and would wait for her."

"Then what did you do?"

Yuri's tone was sheepish. "I went to get something to eat—I hadn't eaten all day."

Nikolayev ripped the earphone from his ear, stuffed the radio into his pocket. He descended upon Kosov like a vulture, his hands at the man's throat. "If you killed her, so help me, I'll murder you with my bare hands."

"No, please, Comrade. I didn't. I didn't touch her."

"Where is she?" Nikolayev straightened, stood towering over the bench.

Kosov put his hands delicately to his neck, spoke directly into Nikolayev's belt buckle. "I was waiting at the hotel. She hadn't arrived. Then there was a fire."

Nikolayev felt as if he had lost all touch with reality. "A fire?"

"At the hotel. She didn't come out, and she didn't arrive...." His hands were on his stomach again; his face had gone puce.

A woman came jogging along the path and both men fell silent until she was out of view.

"Get out of here," said Nikolayev. "Contact me on the radio in an hour."

Kosov jumped up like a frightened rabbit and bounded down the walkway without so much as a backward glance.

Nikolayev put his head in his hands. His carefully planned operation was in a shambles. It had seemed foolproof at the outset. But without the answers Alexiekov would have provided, Nikolayev had no way to assess his exposure, to determine where the information had come from, or who else might be involved in Moscow. And now, without the microfilm . . . what was he going to tell Barakov?

He sighed. A promotion was out of the question now. He would be lucky to keep his rank. He had to find that film! Perhaps he could sidetrack Barakov by hinting at the plan he had formed this morning. He put his hand in his pocket and fingered the small roll of microfilm he had made at the lab. It was an excellent disinformation plan, direct from the local branch of Department A—Alexiekov himself.

He stood and started slowly out of the park. If he managed to reestablish contact, he would take over himself, leave nothing to chance. It wouldn't be easy, but he would find a way to do it. His only hope now was that she may have returned to the hotel and found the body in her room. At least Kosov had left it there; that may have been his first piece of luck. Assuming the hotel hadn't burned down. She would be frightened. Badly frightened. He looked at his watch. He had to hurry.

CHAPTER SEVENTEEN

The Parisian evening had its own special rhythm as the lingering daylight of summer invited natives and visitors alike to enjoy the streets. The Rive Gauche and the blooming parks were a carnival of activity.

For Jessica, the extended hours of light turned the city into a gigantic goldfish bowl, and she was the fish. Innumerable anonymous eyes peered at her, following her every move.

She instructed the taxi driver to drive anywhere, buying time to collect herself, but he interpreted the instruction as a request for a tour of the city. She sat slumped in the back seat, seeing little and hardly hearing his comments as they wound from quarter to quarter. Without a passport, she was a prisoner, every light an enemy, every corner merely part of the maze within her prison cell. Her silence dampened the driver's enthusiasm. He turned into the Champs Elysées with a sigh. Tourists, he thought; if they didn't like his city, they could go home.

Abruptly, in front of a cinéma Jessica ordered him to stop and thanked him profusely as she paid the fare. She couldn't afford to ride forever; she would have to do her thinking somewhere else.

The woman in the ticket booth informed her that the film had been running for half an hour, but Jessica bought a ticket anyway. The theater was cool. She sat in an empty row near the rear, while on the screen Anouk Aimée inhaled a cigarette, let out her breath slowly, so that the smoke curled about her face, and leaned back against a pillow. In a tight two shot, a man leaned over and took the cigarette from her hand. They spoke softly to each other in French, but Jessica didn't even go through the process of translation for herself, rather let the musical flow of the French wash over her, less like words than an unknown melody. It was comforting in the dark. Comforting and anonymous. Jessica closed her eyes.

She awoke with a start at the sound of a voice at her side.

"Pardonnez-moi, s'il vous plaît."

The man was trying to step past her into the row. Jessica drew up her feet obligingly. He paused as he stood above her, looking down. In the dark, backlit by the screen, his features were indistinct. He sat in the empty chair next to her.

Jessica bolted toward the exit, not even looking back. She crossed the inner lobby and entered the other side of the theater, stooping low so that she could not be seen from the opposite aisle, took a vacant seat in a row already nearly full. As she slid down, resting her head on the back of the chair, she held her breath, waiting for the door to open behind her. It didn't. Cautiously, she looked around.

Her father had been wrong: fear was not a companion. It crawled inside of you, squeezing your organs and sucking at your breath; it clawed at your thoughts until they were ragged. It wrapped you in a cocoon of altered reality. Jessica sat in the dark, battling the demon possession. Lark's face kept appearing on the screen. She wanted to cry out.

She had no idea what the film was about, couldn't concentrate. If only she could call Peter. But that was fantasy now: somehow, someone had known about her last telephone call to him. How else could the man at Versailles have known about the red handkerchief, about his wife's red coat? She couldn't walk into another trap. She was on her own.

The movie ended and the lights came up. Jessica put her hand to her forehead and stared into her lap as people straggled up the aisle. It seemed to take a long time before the next group of patrons entered and the lights went down again.

This time she sat through the entire movie. Anouk Aimée suffered beautifully at the hands of a chauvinist male. Jessica translated automatically this time, but was distracted by intruding thoughts. Lacking Lucille's last name, or hotel, her only chance of recovering the microfilm was to intercept the tour tomorrow, and it would be easier to find her at the Eiffel Tower or Notre Dame than the crowded length of the Champs Elysées. With luck, Lucille would not have met anyone to take her to lunch or otherwise claim her from the group. What plausible excuse could Jessica give for having dropped the pen into the flower bag?

Once she had the film, she had to find a way to get out of France. But tomorrow was Sunday. The American Embassy would be closed; she couldn't report a lost passport or get another until Monday and the whole bureaucratic process might take days. There was no one to turn to for help. London should have had the foresight to give her two passports for insurance. It was not uncommon to have one's purse snatched, even legitimately. She sighed. Perhaps she could get a message to Peter to send a private plane. But who would meet her on the tarmac? The KGB again?

One solution kept presenting itself to her, but she thrust it aside. By the time the film was over, it had become an obsessive voice. She moved with the audience, larger than for the early show, out into the Champs Elysées. From the booth on the corner, she made the call. It really was her only choice.

"Hello?" The voice was strong and deep.

The sound of that human link made her weak in the knees. Was it feminine instinct to surrender to the male of the species?

"Hi, it's me," she managed.

"Jessica!" The relief in his voice was audible. "My God, where on earth have you been? Do you know what time it is? I was ready to call the gendarmes."

"I'm sorry, Gordon." It was a lifetime ago that she had left him, pretending an interview that was supposed to take only a few hours. She had never even called him. He couldn't know that she had been through hell since this morning. It was an enormous effort of will not to spill out all the details.

"Where are you? What happened?"

"It's a long story. Listen, I have a problem. . . ."

"Are you all right?"

"Yes. Yes, I'm fine. I . . . I was mugged. My purse was stolen."

"What?"

"And my passport."

"Oh, my poor darling. Where are you? I'll be right there."

"No, I'm all right. I can take a cab. I'm on the Champs Elysées."

"Do you have money for a cab?"

"Yes. Gordon, I need another passport."

"Yes, of course, sweetheart. We'll get you another passport."

"I mean right away. Tonight."

"Now don't tell me you have a late date in another country?"

Jessica laughed softly. It felt good. "No. You really are a very sweet man. I'm awfully glad I ran into you on this trip."

"That sounds as if you're saying goodbye. Is that it? You get your purse stolen, and you can't wait to get out of my life?"

"No, silly. But I have to go to London tomorrow."

"London?"

"Yes. So I need that passport!"

"Jessica, my dearest, it's Saturday night. You can't get a passport on Saturday night. Tell me where you are. I'll come get you. . . ."

"You don't have to come get me, I can take a taxi. I thought you might know someone at the American Embassy. . . ."

"Will you stop babbling and get over here!"

"All right. And Gordon . . . thank you for being there."

"It's part of my knight-in-shining-armor routine. I'm always available for damsels in distress. Now please hang up and get in a cab."

Jessica replaced the receiver. Damn Peter Barnsworth and his secrets! If they connected her to Gordon, who knew what they might do to him? She turned toward the glowing Champs Elysées. It had begun to rain, the wetness shimmering the street lamps and automobiles, creating flowing streams of red and white lights on shiny black pavement. It took nearly fifteen minutes to get a taxi.

Gordon answered the bell immediately and swept her into a hug.

"My God, I thought you'd disappeared again. I was imagining you bleeding to death, or with a broken arm." He held her by the shoulders, noticed the black and blue splotch on her neck, the scratches on her face and hands. "You're hurt; I'll get a doctor."

Jessica shook her head. "All parts intact, just slightly damp." She plucked at her hair, feigning a cheerfulness she didn't feel.

"Here, this will take care of you." He crossed to the bar and poured her a glass of sherry. "Now tell me exactly what happened."

Jessica accepted the glass and sank into one of the plush tapestry chairs. She took a hearty sip, leaned back and closed her eyes.

"It wasn't much of anything, really. Someone grabbed my purse. I didn't even get a clear look at him. But I'm fine; he didn't hurt me."

"You've looked better."

"I fell. When he grabbed my bag. I guess he must have hit my neck, I don't remember."

"You were lucky. People kill these days for something as small as a handbag." Gordon poured himself a scotch and sat opposite her. "I was worried when I didn't hear from you."

"I meant to call you earlier. The day got away from me. I . . . I never had a chance to telephone."

Gordon looked at her oddly. "You weren't wearing that outfit when you left this morning, were you?"

"No." She took another sip of sherry. She didn't want to tell him it was her third change of the day. "I spilled wine on my suit at lunch. Between appointments, I ran back to the hotel to change. Please, Gordon, I really need a passport. Can you help me?"

"Yes, my darling. We'll get right to it Monday morning."

"But I can't wait until Monday! I need one tomorrow."

"Tomorrow? But it's Sunday. The American Embassy doesn't operate on your kind of work schedule. I'm afraid we can't start any action until Monday. What's so important about tomorrow?"

Jessica set her sherry glass on the low table between them and crossed to Gordon's chair, sitting on the floor next to him with a hand on his arm.

"This is an emergency," she said, her eyes pouring forth vulnerability. Was she only capable of telling lies? They came so easily it was frightening. "There was a message for me at the hotel. My mother is ill. She and Jim were in London on business and were coming to Paris to surprise me. I don't know exactly what happened, but Jim said I should come as soon as possible."

"Darling, I'm so sorry. You must be terribly concerned. You should have said something right off. Of course, I'll do everything I can." He took her hands in his. "Let me try to work something out; I'll make some calls."

Gordon leaned down, kissed her on the forehead, running his fingers through her damp hair and then along her cheek. She looked up, catching an expression of tenderness she had never seen in his eyes. He averted his gaze and returned to a bantering tone as he stood. "It gives us poor, threatened males a bright spot of hope to think women may need us after all. Wait here." He walked into the bedroom, closing the door behind him.

Jessica went back to her own chair, reached for the glass of sherry, and drained it. She closed her eyes. Lark's face loomed before her. He looked asleep, as he had been in the chair of the acupuncturists's office that morning, except that suddenly his chest opened up and blood poured down the front of him. She opened her eyes with a gasp. The sherry had gone directly to her limbs, making them feel heavy. She wanted to sleep, but she was afraid to close her eyes again. The bedroom door opened; Gordon was wearing a smile.

"Step one completed," he said. "We can get a picture of you taken now. Maybe we can pick up the passport in the morning. My friend, Armand, will meet us at his studio. He owes me a favor."

"And now I owe you one, too." Jessica crossed to put her arms around him, face against the rock of his chest. "And I always pay up."

"I'll hold you to that, lady. But we should go now. I've ordered a cab."

The taxi was at the front of the building as they emerged. Jessica snuggled into the crook of Gordon's arm as the taxi hissed along the wet pavement. They came to a stop in a short, narrow street lit by only one small lamp, which made a pool of light in the center and left the edges deep in shadow. Both sides of the street were lined with seedy-looking buildings. Warehouses of some sort, it looked to Jessica, as she peered skeptically out the window of the cab. Most of the buildings were completely dark.

"Armand has a studio in this building," said Gordon, indicating a four-story brick structure. "Stay here, let me see if he's arrived yet."

The taxi had stopped across the street from the building. Jessica watched him cross the pavement and press a buzzer in the dimly lit foyer. Then he stepped out onto the sidewalk with a motion for her to join him. She ducked her head against the drizzle as she stepped into the street.

She didn't see the car come around the corner, but suddenly she was blinded by the glare of headlights, not more than fifty feet from her. Despite the weather, the driver couldn't help but see her. However, the speed of the car did not diminish. Jessica made a dash for the opposite curb, but her legs, feeling as if they were made of foam rubber, refused to obey. She finally gained the sidewalk. The car was only twenty-five feet from her and still moving.

She screamed. The hard brick of the building wall was in front of her now, the nearest doorway fifteen feet away, impossible to reach in time. She heard Gordon yell, and for a millisecond anger surged through her at the knowledge she was going to die, here in a dark street, crushed against the wall by a crazy driver.

At that second, she looked up. There were iron bars across the window above her. The bottom cross bar protruded about three inches from the brick, the vertical bars rising from in front of the glass. She jumped, grabbed for the bar. It was wet and slippery but held her weight, leaving her body dangling like a puppet. She pulled her knees up as far as she could as she heard the screech of brakes and the hiss of the tires. She could feel the heat of the automobile beneath her.

As her arms rebelled from the strain of her weight, her fingers slowly began to uncurl around the iron bar. She screamed again, but couldn't hear herself. She began to slip. The car had missed the wall by inches, its gray body was beneath her now; the side of the fender hit her dangling foot and slammed it against the brick. She didn't even feel it. Her shaking arms failed, and her body dropped like a stone, but the car had passed the spot. She hit her left hand on the back bumper as she collapsed on the sidewalk.

Beyond the gray mass of the Citroën, centered in the harsh beams of the moving headlights, she saw Gordon. A scream ripped from her throat, this time echoing in her ears. He was thrown backwards into the recessed doorway as the headlights rushed past him. Her vision was blocked by the bulk of the car.

She heard her name, from far off, but her answer seemed to die before it reached her mouth. It was very dark now; she wondered what happened to the street lamp. The quiet was eerie after the roar of the automobile engine. The obstacles to speech and vision became insurmountable and she felt herself sink into the comforting blackness.

CHAPTER EIGHTEEN

Major Nikolayev adjusted the lamp on the table so that it shone directly onto the wooden chair in the middle of the room. He crossed to the light switch and flipped off the ceiling fixture, throwing the rest of the room into shadow. Not bad, he thought. He returned to the table, sat in the chair directly behind the lamp, cracking his knuckles. Yes, it would do.

It was an anonymous room about forty feet square, windowless, stale, with large, unmarked cartons reaching nearly to the ceiling stacked along all four walls, and a pitted floor, worn down to raw wood. When questioned later, those that were brought here found it impossible to give an identifying description; the KGB had made sure of that. Trapped in the circle of stark, glaring white light in the center of the room, the chair was the only place to sit other than Nikolayev's own seat behind the lamp. He approached the chair, faced the burning thousand-watt bulb. He looked away quickly. Yes, it would do very nicely.

Thirty feet down the hall was another anonymous room. He tapped lightly at the door, heard the tread of footsteps, then Kosov stuck his head out. In the sliver of open space, Nikolayev could see a portion of a cot against one wall. The form lying on the cot, facing away from him, was inert. Yuri's knees were all that were visible from his position at the head of the cot.

"Well?" said Nikolayev quietly.

"Yuri gave her the injection just as she was coming to. She never even saw us."

Nikolayev peered past him. After carrying her upstairs, he had thoroughly and completely searched her, checking every item of clothing for the tiny roll of microfilm. At last, he had to admit that she didn't have it. Had she told Yuri the truth at Versailles? Had Alexiekov kept it? The ramifications of that thought were too awful to pursue. Nikolayev refused to accept defeat.

Kosov followed his gaze toward the woman's bandaged ankle.

"Just a surface cut; I stopped the bleeding. Her ankle is strained, but it's not broken. We didn't expect her to jump like that." He was anxious to show his boss that he could succeed. "How did you like Yuri? Pretty fancy driving!"

"I thought he was going to kill her." Nikolayev's voice was a monotone, but Kosov could hear the underlying edge.

"Yuri's the best. Handles a car as if it were part of his body. Never loses control."

"Well, he had me fooled. One more corpse in a report to Barakov and we'll all be shoveling snow."

"There won't be any more accidents," mumbled Kosov. He wondered what Nikolayev had reported. Already he had been demoted, was reporting to Yuri. Losing his seniority boded ill for the future. He longed to be back home with Raya, his fragile wife.

"What about the drug?" asked Nikolayev.

"Yuri says any minute now."

"Good. Bring her in when she's ready." Nikolayev retreated down the hall to the interrogation room, snapped off the glaring lamp, and stood in the shadows behind a column of cartons. Better he should be in charge of the questioning than Kosov, and Yuri had no background in interrogation. He was anxious for this to be over as soon as possible.

The door opened, admitting an anemic, yellowish light from the hall and throwing ominous shadows across the room. Kosov and Yuri entered, supporting the woman between them. As they let go of her, she sank limply into the chair, oblivious as Yuri tied her limbs to the arms and legs with strips of cloth. The bindings actually helped to support her body so that she couldn't fall. Her head lolled forward like a broken doll; her eyes were closed.

While Yuri worked, Kosov walked to the table, turned on the powerful lamp. The shadows sprang up around the room like a silent, ghostly audience of giants. Kosov nodded to Nikolayev, then slipped out of the room, followed by Yuri, who closed the door softly behind him.

Nikolayev sat at the table behind the lamp. He could not

be seen from the chair in the center of the room. He noticed that the woman had reacted when the light came on; now she twisted to avert her face from its glare.

"It won't be on for long," he said. He held a round, metal disc to his mouth as he spoke. It distorted his voice so that the sound was mechanical, almost inhuman, an electronic, disembodied voice floating from behind the sun. The woman peered half-heartedly around her.

"What's your name?" he asked.

Her lips moved, but no sound came.

"Your name!" he barked.

"J . . . Jessica." She blinked several times. Her green eyes were clouded, like wells of stagnant water. She found it easier to bear the light with her eyes focused on the floor.

"Jessica what?" He had to lead her slowly; it was like priming a pump.

"Autland. I went back to Autland after the divorce. I grew up with it; I thought it was my name. But there's Payne in Autland. Now there's too much Payne." She spoke almost dreamily, articulating the thoughts as they came to her.

"Pain in Autland?"

"Yes. Please . . . the light is too bright."

"We'll turn it off if you answer the questions. Why did you come to Paris?"

"To get a film . . . no, to write. To write . . . I must say that. Please, the light. I've been here before. I'm writing."

"Not to write. Tell me about the film."

"It writes even with the film in it."

"What does?"

"The pen. I looked on the ground. I thought it was gone. I almost didn't see it. . . ."

"The film is in the pen?"

"Yes. But it's a secret, mustn't tell."

"Who gave you the pen?"

"Peter. But I call him George now. *George.* That was my husband's name. I don't know why he picked George!"

"Yes. He calls himself George Wheeler."

"Rutford Publishing. Poor switchboard operator, she never gets a day off. Please, the light hurts my eyes."

"You're doing fine. Just a few more questions, then we'll turn it off. Who gave you the film?"

"Lark. But that's a secret, too. Mustn't let them find

him. But he's going to London. Lark was asleep, then . . . then . . . dead. Aahhhhh!" It wasn't a full scream, more of a prolonged high-pitched moan.

"Lark is fine."

"Lark is alive? But I saw blood. . . ."

"Lark is alive. He wants to know where the film is now."

"I should have kept it. I didn't know what to do."

"Where did you put it?"

"I had to put it in the bag. I'm sorry, I shouldn't have done that. I had to run away, that man saw me. . . ."

"What bag did you put it in?"

"The flower bag. I was afraid. It was the only place."

"Which flour bag is that?"

"The one with the orange yarn. It's so cold. There's too much orange!"

"The microfilm is in a flour bag with orange yarn?"

"Yes."

"And where will you find the flour bag?"

"I'm sure it was the Champs Elysées, the Eiffel Tower and Notre Dame. That's the only way to do it, I'll have to try. I shouldn't have put it there, but what could I do?"

"It's all right. You couldn't help it. But where is the flour bag *now?*"

"Now? I don't know. I didn't even get the name of the hotel. I've been stupid. Maybe they've gone to the Folies Bergère!" She made a sound which, under better circumstances, might have been a laugh.

Nikolayev paused. "But you know where to get the bag?"

"I'll try the Eiffel Tower first, that's better than the Champs Elysées. If not there, then Notre Dame."

"How will you find it?"

"She stands out in any group. And she'll wear orange."

"Who?"

"Lucille."

"And who is Lucille?" Nikolayev was making notes as he listened.

"She attached herself to me; just kept talking. De Martino's, she said, but I never heard of it. You see, there are too many women. . . ."

"Does Lucille DeMartinos have the pen?"

"It's in the flower bag, but she doesn't know it. I should never. . . ."

"Does she have the flour bag?"

"Yes. She puts something in it wherever she goes. It's quite full already, but...."

Nikolayev tried to hide his exasperation. For another half hour he continued to hammer at her, but the answers became more elliptical and confusing.

He knew that it was a fallacy that a person tells the truth under drugs. In actuality, the subject merely is freed from a conscious judgment and spills out anything floating around in the subconscious mind, without the normal inhibitions. The trick for Nikolayev was to pull the wheat of desired information from the chaff of the psyche's ramblings. But he had little experience as a thresher. He was accustomed to logical thought, to linear connections that led the mind in a straight line. He had never interrogated a woman before.

"Miss Autland, it's important that we get the microfilm."

"I know. But we mustn't let *them* get it. Have to be careful." Her head was bobbing. Her body slumped forward, straining at the rag bonds that held her. The twilight zone before the drug put her to sleep was almost over.

"What should we do first to get the film?" asked Nikolayev.

"I want to sleep."

"You can sleep after we get the film."

"I can sleep before then."

"No!" His mechanical voice was sharp.

"But it's not until tomorrow," wailed Jessica. "I'm so tired. The light...."

"We can contact Lucille tomorrow?"

"I don't know. I didn't plan, I had to run. We'll have to do our best."

"Where will she be?"

"The Champs Elysées, or the Eiffel Tower, or Notre Dame. The Champs Elysées is too long. We shouldn't try." Her head dropped forward.

"A few more questions, then you can sleep. You're doing fine. When will Lucille be at the Eiffel Tower?"

"After the Champs Elysées, I hope. I think that was the order. Unless she finds a man. Oh, I should never have put it in the bag!"

Jessica's speech was getting thicker. Nikolayev cracked

his knuckles. He couldn't fail! He tried for several more minutes, getting nowhere, until she hung limply in the chair, unable to hear or respond. The sleep phase of the drug had taken over her faculties.

With a grunt, Nikolayev snapped off the light. It would be at least an hour before she was ready to talk again. He walked to the door, flipped on the overhead light and called for Yuri.

"I have most of it," he lied. "We'll resume when she wakes. Let me know." He walked down the hall, rubbing his tired eyes.

Yuri nodded, went to the table, taking out a deck of cards from his pocket. Sometimes his job was routinely dull. Kosov joined him, bringing a chair from the other room. They talked in low voices as Yuri dealt the cards.

A little over an hour later, Jessica once again entered the semi-conscious state in which she could be questioned. Nikolayev resumed his position behind the harsh light.

"Lark gave you the film," he began.

"Yes. Up the dark stairway. He was asleep, but that man came in downstairs. . . ."

"What did you do after you got the microfilm?"

"I put it in the pen. It will be safe there, no one will know."

"And then?"

"Then? I saw the gray car. Have to get away. I went to Printemps. I'm sure someone was following me, but I couldn't see anyone. It was supposed to be simple."

"Did you leave the film at Printemps?"

"No. I still had to get it to London. Stay in crowds, it's safe. The Inter-Continental was crowded, and the tour was safe. But I had to get away from Lucille to get to the Water Mirror Basin. The man stole my purse . . . it was the wrong man, but he knew. . . ."

"But the microfilm wasn't in your purse."

"No. He didn't get it! I fooled him."

"Where was the pen?"

"On the ground and I nearly didn't see it. I thought he had it. . . ."

"So you put it in the flour bag?"

"Yes, in front of the Inter-Continental. It was the only thing I could do. . . ."

"Can we go to the Inter-Continental and get it now?"

"No, she left."

"She? Lucille DeMartinos?"

"Yes. I don't think she was staying at that hotel."

"Where did she go?"

"I don't know."

Nikolayev tried a new tack, affecting a British accent through the distorter. "Jessica, this is Peter Barnsworth. I order you to tell me where the film is now."

"I don't know. I'm an amateur, I'm sorry, I did it wrong."

"Where will you get it?"

"At the Eiffel Tower, I hope. Tomorrow. Or Notre Dame."

Jessica began to hiccup. She rubbed her eyes. The drug would soon wear off. Nikolayev nodded to himself, tapping his pencil against the edge of the table, then walked out of the room, closing the door loudly behind him. Yuri was waiting in the hall.

"Give her the hypodermic."

Yuri picked up the small, black bag at his side and opened the door.

Nikolayev leaned against the wall, eyes closed. He'd handled it badly, he knew. It wasn't his forte. The professionals in interrogation could extract information easily from a free-roaming consciousness, but his own expertise was in another area. He didn't know how to question the subject properly. Perhaps he should have had Kosov do it after all. Under supervision, of course; he couldn't afford another accident. At least he had a rough outline. He didn't know precisely where the film was, but he had a pretty good idea how he was going to get it.

Alexiekov had given him an inspiration and it was the perfect solution to the problem of what to do once the film was neutralized. Nikolayev was going to run his own Department A disinformation operation. A little out of his sphere of authority, perhaps, but it was a brilliant plan to save himself and prevent any more violence.

He had made his report to Barakov over the Embassy scrambler shortly after his meeting with Kosov in the Jardin du Luxembourg. He had begun by hinting at his new plan, but eventually he'd had to report Alexiekov's death. The result was a disaster: Barakov trumpeted like an elephant. Although Kosov was clearly at fault, Barakov was holding Nikolayev responsible—was ready to recall him immediately. Nikolayev had been forced to plead for more time, certain that his plan would salvage the entire mess, even throw Alexiekov's past performance into question by MI6. At last Barakov had agreed to one more day. But Nikolayev had neglected to tell him that he didn't have the microfilm yet. He couldn't afford to fail tomorrow.

Yuri stuck his head out of the doorway.

"She's out cold, Major."

"Good. For how long?"

Yuri shrugged. "Eight to ten hours, I'd say."

"Let's get her downstairs. Then I want you to contact the Embassy. I want a safe house tomorrow afternoon. If this warehouse isn't available, put in a requisition for Beauville."

It was possible he might get his promotion after all.

CHAPTER NINETEEN

Softness was her first perception. Then came pain. Jessica opened her eyes.

The room in her line of vision looked reassuringly familiar; ecru and cream sheets against her face, the buff and black lacquer headboard that wrapped around into a bedside table, the Art Deco lamp. Lying on her side, the position she had been in before the pain jolted her, she blinked twice. The vision remained; she knew she was safe.

She eased over onto her back, testing to see where it hurt the least. Gordon was seated in a chair at the edge of the bed, reading a newspaper, dressed in slacks and a short sleeved shirt, which revealed a gauze bandage on his left forearm and several scratches on both arms. A smaller bandage slanted across his forehead.

"It's about time you opened your eyes." The smile spread across his face like a glorious dawn after a night of rain. He reached over and took her hand.

Jessica managed a wan smile in return. "There's nothing I would rather see at this moment than your smiling face, and no place I would rather be than here in your bed. The last thing I remember was the car heading straight for you. . . ." Her eyes were damp. She turned her head to the window and the sunlight slanting through half-drawn blinds. "What time is it?"

"About 10:30."

"What day is it?"

"Sunday."

"Sunday." She closed her eyes. "Thank God, Sunday. I feel so disoriented!" Bits of memory and dream were still woven together, the handle of reality just beyond her reach.

"What happened?" she asked.

"Your guardian angel has been working overtime. As a

matter of fact, so has mine. We may be the luckiest two people on earth right now."

"I remember the car coming at me, and there was no place to go...." She didn't want to tell him that she recognized the car.

"You rest a minute; I'll bring you some coffee."

He left the room. Jessica moved her body experimentally. Her arms ached hellishly with every motion, as if her muscles had been ripped to shreds, and the top of her left hand, decorated with a gruesome yellow and black bruise, was terribly sore, although the fingers still had mobility. Pushing the sheet aside, she was surprised to find herself nude; Gordon must have undressed her and put her to bed. She pressed her bruised ribs. No broken bones: it was a miracle.

Her right foot ached and, pushing the sheet further aside, she saw that the ankle was neatly bound with an elastic bandage, but the foot below it was the same yellow hue as her hand. It took a great effort to sit up, slowly move stiff legs over the side of the bed. She winced as she put her weight on her foot. Tender, but she would be able to walk.

Leaning back into the softness of the pillow with a sigh, she pulled the sheet under her arms. Tidbits of her dream and the memory of the night before teased her consciousness: blinding headlights, the certainty she was going to die, falling as the car passed and hurtled toward Gordon. It was her fault. If she hadn't gotten him involved.... Thank God he was alive. Did she dream something about Lark and the microfilm? Another headlight ... a voice coming from the sun.... It slipped from her grasp. She put her hands over her eyes in an effort to eradicate the dull ache that was forming behind them. Her arm muscles protested even the simplest order to stretch and contract.

Gordon entered with a tray. "First, some good, hot coffee," he said, putting the tray on the bed beside her and handing her the mug. The hot liquid was a palliative for her abused muscles, seemed to infuse her entire body with warmth and strength.

"Are you hurt badly?" she asked, indicating the bandage on his arm.

"A minor abrasion, as the doctor put it. Someone up there likes me. I fell backward into the doorway as the car sideswiped the wall. Otherwise, I wouldn't be here." He sat in the chair facing the bed. "I hit my head as I fell, and that's all I remember."

"You're right: we must have a guardian angel." She reached out, rested her hand on his knee, and he entwined his fingers around hers.

"I was out for almost three hours," he said. I thought my watch was broken when I woke up. You were still a lump on the sidewalk; the street was deserted. The damn taxi driver was nowhere around."

"He probably didn't want to lose a night's work."

"But he was a witness! He could have gotten a license number, something."

"People are afraid to get involved. It's a miracle you weren't hurt. That car seemed to come from nowhere."

"Probably a drunken driver. We were very lucky, my darling, and for a while I wasn't so sure about you."

Jessica closed her eyes again, a hand to her forehead. Better for him to think it was a drunken driver. "My brain is so muddled! I feel as if I'd fought World War II all by myself."

"You scared the hell out of me. You were breathing, but out cold. Armand was frantic upstairs; he kept calling the apartment and getting no answer. He was about to call the police. He drove us back here once we saw you were alive."

"And you got me undressed and into bed?"

"Nurse Michaels at your service. Although I generally find it easier to undress a woman when she is eager to help."

"And this is your handiwork, too?" asked Jessica, pointing to her bandaged ankle.

Gordon nodded.

"You should become a doctor."

"To tell you the truth, I was coached by Dr. Renaud next door."

"I don't remember him at all."

"I'm not surprised. You weren't at the top of your social form. He came to check you out, said nothing was broken. So he gave you a shot and told me to put an ice pack on your ankle. You strained the muscle, that's all, but it will be sore for a few days. There are advantages to having a doctor next door."

"I had such terrible dreams! The car headlights kept

boring into me, and a voice with no body . . . very weird. It's all hazy."

"You must have been half conscious when Dr. Renaud was here. Wove it into a dream. He was asking where it hurt as he was examining you."

"I still feel funny," Jessica held the coffee mug with both hands, watched the dark liquid swirl around and around.

"Eat your croissant," said Gordon, pointing to the tray beside her. "I'll make you an omelette."

As he reached the doorway, she spoke. "Gordon?"

He turned.

"Thanks," she said.

He stood at the threshold looking at her, a parade of emotions passing across his face, then he winked and was gone. Soon she could smell the tantalizing odor of sizzling ham.

While Gordon cooked, Jessica sat in a hot bath, her foot propped awkwardly on the edge of the tub to keep the bandage dry. As the steam and hot water worked their magic, vague bits of dream evaporated from her consciousness. The car, however, stood out vividly in her memory. Another gray Citroën. The KGB thought she had the microfilm. And they wanted it. At what point had they picked up her trail again? She had thought she lost them after the hotel fire. Did they know she was here, at Gordon's now? She had to get out of his apartment, out of France. But first, she had to get the microfilm.

That brought her to the problem of Lucille. She sighed as she slid further under the soothing water. The Champs Elysées, the Eiffel Tower, or Notre Dame? She would have a better chance at the Eiffel Tower; Notre Dame would be the back-up location.

The hot water had eased her muscles temporarily, but the pain in her foot caused her to limp slightly as she came out of the bathroom. She had washed her hair, and now she combed it out, letting it dry naturally into its own waves over her shoulders. The clock on the dresser said 11:15. If she wanted to take a shot at the Eiffel Tower, she had better start moving.

Gordon had hung her clothes in the closet with his customary neatness. The Japanese wallet with her travelers checks was still tucked into the pocket of her jacket, along with some loose change. She put on the print skirt and blouse, hardly wrinkled from its exposure to the elements last night. Or had Gordon pressed it? The thought made her smile. He was an extraordinary man. As she slid the jacket from its hanger, she noticed the sleeve was torn under the arm. She carried it into the kitchen, where Gordon was putting the finishing touches on the omelette.

"Do you have a needle and thread? My jacket's ripped."

"I'm a man of many talents, but I don't sew. Wait till after breakfast. Maybe Madame Boussard, down the hall, is home."

They sat in the kitchen. Gordon sipped coffee while Jessica ate ravenously. She had to admit he was a good cook.

"Where do we stand with my passport?" she said, between mouthfuls.

"I made some phone calls this morning. I'm afraid my friend at the embassy is away for the weekend. We'll have to wait until tomorrow."

"I can't, Gordon. I must get to London."

"I know you're anxious, darling, but there's nothing I can do. This man is my only contact. Why don't you call your mother? I promise I'll have a passport for you tomorrow. It's only one day."

Jessica banged her fork down in frustration.

"Besides," he said, "you should rest. Your body has been through a trauma."

"I can take care of my body." She grabbed the dishes from the table, deposited them in the sink. She had to get away from Gordon's eternal niceness; it was driving her crazy. Besides, she had to meet Lucille alone. "I'm going for a walk," she said.

"If you stay off your ankle, it would heal faster."

"It doesn't hurt."

"I'll come with you. You can lean on me, if you need to."

"I'd rather go by myself."

"Was it something I said? Or don't you like my cooking?"

Jessica disregarded his attempt to lighten her mood. "I need to be by myself, Gordon. It's nothing personal; I just want to be alone."

"Darling, I know you're upset about the delay. I wish I could help. Why don't. . ."

"Stop giving me advice!" She limped from the kitchen into the bedroom and slammed the door. Her hair had dried and she ran a brush through it. She noticed that Gordon had neatly laid her hairpins in a row on the dresser when he'd put her to bed last night. With a sigh, she picked up the pins, swooped her hair off her shoulders, twisting it into a loose coil, and stabbed the pins in. One missed its mark and painfully scraped her scalp; she gripped the edge of the dresser. This was ridiculous. She had to relax. Frustration and pressure were only going to impair her thinking. Right now she had to get to Lucille, and if Gordon insisted upon coming along, then she would have to work around him. There was no point in alienating her only ally. She finished her hair and opened the bedroom door.

Gordon was in the kitchen, washing the breakfast dishes.

"I'm sorry, that was childish," she said. She picked up the jacket from the chair where she had dropped it. "What did you say about a needle and thread?"

"Ah, Madame Boussard to the rescue."

"Quite a support system you have in this building."

He grinned. "I'll be right back."

Jessica stood in the doorway, watching as he walked down the passage and knocked at an apartment door at the far end. She couldn't see the woman who opened it, but Gordon glanced back with a smile and stepped inside. She hesitated for several seconds, then obeying her impulse, turned and fled down the hall in the opposite direction, ignoring her throbbing foot. She jabbed at the elevator button. Gordon would be furious, but she could placate him later. If only the damn elevator would come!

But it was too late. The door at the far end of the hall opened, and she could hear Gordon thanking Madame Boussard. She was halfway back to his apartment as he came into the hall.

"I was taking a trial walk," she said. "It really doesn't hurt much."

He gave her a peculiar look, then nodded. "Good." He handed her the spool of thread. Jessica followed him into the apartment and went to work on the sleeve.

"I'm through making plans," said Gordon as he watched her needle dart in and out of the fabric. "Where would you like to go?"

"If I tell you, you'll laugh."

"Not me."

She pointed out the kitchen window. "The Eiffel Tower."

Only the corners of Gordon's mouth twitched. "You're a real tourist."

"I haven't been there since you took me, ten years ago. I remember it as a very romantic place; I may be the only woman who's been kissed on every platform."

"Then by all means, let's go and see if it lives up to its reputation."

Mr. Eiffel's tower had borne its share of criticism over the years, reflected Jessica, gazing up at its stupendous latticework of steel, but it was a spectacular monument. No mere photograph could capture its combination of strength and delicacy. She had prevailed upon Gordon to sit on a bench near the ticket booth, pleading a rest for her ankle. The sun fried the plaza before them, sizzling upward into the faces of the crowd, but the bench was in the shade, cooled by the slight breeze. Jessica's eyes slid through the crowd seeking the frowsy, orange-clad figure of Lucille.

Gordon was enjoying watching a group of six children, undeterred by the heat, playing "keep-away" a few yards from their bench. The child nearest them missed the ball and it rolled to a stop at Gordon's feet, several small bodies hot on its trail. With a glance at Jessica, Gordon reached for it, then tossed it to the farthest child, receiving a whoop of victory from the lucky receiver. To the delight of the youngsters, he joined the game.

She laughed as Gordon missed the ball, allowing the smallest child to catch it. He was obviously enjoying himself. He would make a warm, loving father. She experimented with the vision of herself married to him. What exactly did he do for NATO? He had never been explicit. They might live in Paris or Brussels—he had said he divided his time. Would their child have his special vitality?

Looking away from Gordon and the children, Jessica continued her search of the moving crowd. A flash of orange proved to be only the dashiki of an African entrepreneur, peddling his trinkets on a blanket.

Gordon returned to the bench and mopped his brow with his handkerchief. "So much for my father act," he said, puffing.

"Do you ever think about having children?" asked Jessica.

"Once a year, for about five minutes."

They sat in silence, watching the children play, each lost in thought.

"Are you ready to scale this monstrosity?" said Gordon finally.

Jessica peeked at her watch. It was one o'clock.

"Shall we go up? I'll stand in line for tickets. The more you stay off your ankle, the better you'll feel."

"Thanks." She watched him cross to the ticket booth, grateful for the long line which would give her more time to search for Lucille. Surely the entire morning was enough time to do the Champs Elysées. Had she met another married man who wanted to take her to lunch? Had the schedule changed? Gordon worked his way to the front of the line.

The elevator tilted rakishly and shimmied as it ascended the sloping leg of the tower. Holding on to the rail, Jessica stood very still. The ride was better than climbing 1,652 iron steps, but she had felt better on the ground, looking up. Gordon grinned at her discomfort.

"It's perfectly safe, darling. Hundreds of people go up and down all day."

"It's somehow less romantic than I remembered," she said.

They got off at the first platform. Jessica approached the rail with trepidation.

"You see," said Gordon. "There's even a safety net, in case you fall over." Jessica fought the butterflies in her stomach as she peered downward, seeking one flash of orange. It was easier to check the restaurant, but apparently Lucille had not arrived earlier to eat lunch. In despair, Jessica walked around the square of the platform, while Gordon trotted at her side, oblivious, pointing out landmarks below.

"Now, let's see," he said, as they completed the fourth side of the platform, "where exactly was the kissing spot on this level?"

Jessica chuckled, despite her distraction. "Ten years is too long. We'll have to blaze a new trail."

In spite of the number of people surrounding them, Gordon threw his arms around her, making a show of kissing her soundly. Jessica pulled back, laughing, then turned abruptly. A swatch of orange had entered the elevator to the second level.

"Upward," she cried, as she brushed past Gordon and raced to the closing elevator doors, barging through the line. She squeezed herself into the car with the last passenger, amidst the protests of those waiting to board. The elevator operator swung the gates shut without a word. Jessica could see Gordon's astonished face below as the elevator rose. Impatiently she faced forward; the car was too tightly packed to do more than swivel her head, and the tall man standing next to her blocked her view of the rear of the car, making it impossible to confirm the fleeting impression of orange identity. As the doors opened on the second level, Jessica was the first out; she stepped to the side, waiting.

The swatch of orange was topped with a mane of fuzzy brown hair.

"Hello, Lucille," said Jessica.

"Jessica, honey! Well, how are you?" Lucille beamed at her. She was wearing a yellow, sleeveless dress overrun with voluminous, orange poppies. As the occupants of the elevator streamed past them, gravitating to the rail, Jessica dug into her pocket.

"I owe you five francs," she said. "I'm so glad I found you." Her eyes strayed to the bulging straw bag which weighed down Lucille's right arm, the outrageous, flower-shaped loops of orange yarn upstaged by the intemperate print of the owner's dress.

"You tell me this minute what made you run away like that. You scared me. Really, you did."

Jessica's eyes were riveted to the bag. "I'm sorry, I felt ill; I was afraid I was going to be sick."

"I don't wonder, being attacked like that. You were white as a sheet. These things take their toll." She stepped back to give Jessica a thorough look up and down, raising horrified eyebrows when she noticed the bandaged ankle.

"It's only a slight strain," said Jessica. She could hear the whirring machinery of the approaching elevator.

"Lucille, this is silly, but I think I must have dropped my pen in your bag when we were on the bus. Would you mind looking? It's a blue pen. A gift from a friend; I have a sentimental attachment to it."

"Honey, I'd have to empty the whole thing. Let's wait till we get down from here. We'll go have lunch. I can catch up with the tour at Notre Dame."

"I'd like to," said Jessica, glancing over her shoulder at the elevator, "but the truth is, I left this very attractive man down on the first level. Let me put my hand down in and see if I can feel it."

With a roll of her eyes, Lucille reluctantly lifted the bag, holding the handles apart with both hands and resting the bottom on a bent knee to take the strain of the weight off her arms. Jessica reached in, pawing as best she could through papers, postcards, matchbooks, and souvenirs of all shapes, but could feel no pen. Trying not to betray her anxiety, she plunged her hand down on the opposite side. Her fingers closed on a long, narrow object; she pulled it up eagerly. It was a black, plastic cigarette holder with gold letters printed along its length proclaiming *"J'aime la vie Parisienne!"*

The elevator doors clanged open behind her and a familiar deep voice spoke in her ear.

"Desertion is a capital offense."

"Gordon!" Her head turned toward him, but her hand continued to explore the lower reaches of the straw bag. Lucille's eyes were popping.

While Jessica made the introductions, her arm lost in Lucille's bag, she looked at them both, ignoring her busy appendage as if it belonged to someone else. Lucille turned on her megawatt smile and moved toward the man like a magnet, forcing Jessica to withdraw her empty hand or be dragged alongside.

"Hello there," Lucille gushed. She switched the bag to her left hand, out of Jessica's reach, as she leaned sideways. "Some friend," she said, sotto voce. She looked pointedly at the bandages on Gordon's arm and forehead, then at Jessica's wrapped ankle. "You two haven't been beating up on each other, have you?"

"A minor taxi accident," said Jessica quickly. Gordon looked at her oddly. "I didn't mean to desert you, Gordon, but I saw Lucille on the elevator. I wanted to say hello before she got away." The inaccessible orange bag tempted her like forbidden fruit. Gordon followed her gaze.

"Truth is, she was worried about her silly pen," said Lucille with a wink.

"Pen?" asked Gordon.

"I owed Lucille five francs." Jessica's voice overrode his. "And I always pay my debts, remember?"

"Yes, I do," said Gordon. He was wearing a wide grin as he looked at the garish straw bag. "I like your flower," he said to Lucille, who seemed to melt visibly under his gaze. "Do you two know each other from America?"

"We met yesterday," began Lucille breathlessly, like an enraptured schoolgirl, as her eyes roved over his face and curly hair.

"Lucille was there after my purse was stolen. She loaned me Métro fare."

The elevator clattered behind them, pouring out a fresh delivery of tourists, but Lucille was oblivious to everything except the man beside her.

"The poor girl was a wreck," said Lucille, gesturing toward Jessica but not taking her eyes from Gordon's. "All bruised and scraped. You'd think there would be more protection at place like. . . ."

"Gordon isn't interested in the details, Lucille," said Jessica, shooting her a warning look which was totally lost upon its recipient.

"And where did *you* two meet?" asked Lucille, taking Gordon's arm and leading him toward the rail.

"It's a rather long story," said Gordon. Jessica watched the charm fairly oozing from him as he looked at the woman next to him.

"Then I have a wonderful idea," squealed Lucille. "Let's go to some darling sidewalk cafe and you can tell all. Perhaps you have a friend who would like to join us?" She blinked as she looked up at Gordon, her smile as wide as his.

"Actually, Lucille, my ankle is bothering me," said Jessica. "We were leaving when I saw you." She was inexplicably annoyed to see Gordon flirting so obviously. She tried to reach the flower bag. "Let me see if my pen. . . ."

"No, no, I absolutely insist," said Lucille, holding the bag against her bosom, arms wrapped around it protectively. "Your ankle will feel better if you sit down. We're having a reunion, after all! You'll have to give in if you want to find your pen."

Jessica's smile was a tight line, but Gordon laughed with her. "I know just the place," he said.

"Puurrrfect!" mewed Lucille. She linked arms with them and propelled them toward the elevator. Gordon seemed oblivious to Jessica's glare.

The café was within walking distance—although Jessica limped pathetically the entire distance—and they secured an outdoor table with little difficulty. Lucille arranged the seating like a maitre d', then planted herself between the two of them. Jessica sat stiffly in her chair as the flower bag disappeared to the floor by Gordon's side.

"Now, we must have Alsatian beer," said Lucille. She waved a hand in the air for the waiter. "I've heard it's what the natives drink."

"You don't want to miss Notre Dame," said Jessica.

"Oh, pooh. It's only a church. I'm not even Catholic. I'd rather be with friends! Which reminds me. . . ." She fluttered her eyes at Gordon. "Weren't you going to call someone?"

Gordon cleared his throat. "Lucille, I wish I could, but it's the middle of summer. Everyone I know is out of town." He seemed amused and ignored Jessica's toe, tapping his foot under the table. Lucille didn't let disappointment erode her small talk. The Alsatian beers arrived and she launched into tales of Chicago, De Martino's and the single life, sucking up Gordon's rapt attention like a vacuum. Jessica felt excluded and grumpy. She could think only of the pen, but her tentative interruptions were met with an impatient wave of Lucille's hand. At last, she excused herself to find the toilet.

Three people stood in line for the tiny, one-room cubicle at the back of the café. Jessica took her place in line, wondering why Gordon was so taken with Lucille. Men always seemed to respond to that simpering female coyness. She became impatient when the line didn't move and headed back to the table.

Lucille was still talking nonstop, but Gordon no longer sat in silent fascination. Instead, his attention was focused on the straw bag, now in his lap. He pawed through its contents purposefully, dredging paraphernalia from its depths and depositing it on the table. Jessica reached his side in three steps. He looked startled to see her back so quickly.

"Darling, I remembered your pen," He smiled. "Are you certain it fell in here? I can't seem to find it." He held a miniature Eiffel Tower with a thermometer in it in one hand, a sheaf of postcards in the other.

"I hope so." She waited until both his hands were on the table, then reached for the bag, sliding it from under his arms and off his lap. He looked mildly surprised as she crossed to her own chair, where she began spewing Lucille's awesome collection onto the table by the fistful. Postcards and matchbooks abounded; every trinket bore the name of its city of origin: a miniature beer mug from Munich, a windmill salt and pepper shaker from Amsterdam, a double-decker, red bus bank from London. There were several ceramic skunks. "I have a huge collection," said Lucille, not without pride.

Three quarters of the way to the bottom, Jessica pulled out a thickly folded map of Europe. Inside one of the folds, its clip caught by the paper, lay the pen.

"Ah, success," said Jessica lightly, covering her great relief. "It's not worth anything, but it came from a friend." She held it a moment, then slipped it as nonchalantly as possible into her pocket.

"Good," said Gordon. "I'm glad you found it."

"Yes, wonderful, honey, but I'm going to need help here," said Lucille as she began jamming the contents back into the bag. The volume of paraphernalia seemed to have exploded once released from its confines, at least tripling in quantity, and although the bag was filling rapidly, the table remained alarmingly full.

"We'll have to pack it neatly," said Gordon, trying to help. Jessica excused herself again to check if the toilet were free. Gordon stood, but Lucille put a hand on his arm.

"Oh no you don't. You can't *both* go off and leave me in this mess!" Reluctantly, he reached for the bag. By the time Jessica returned, Gordon was leaning over the bag, crushing its contents with the heel of his palm, while Lucille tittered at his side.

"I hate to put an end to the party, but my ankle is throbbing badly," said Jessica.

"And Lucille really shouldn't miss Notre Dame." added Gordon. He had managed to cram everything back into the mouth of the orange yarn flowers and now presented the bag to Lucille with a flourish. "We'll get you a taxi," he said.

"But I don't want. . . ."

He was too smooth to be thwarted by her protest. Suddenly, she was out of her chair, his arm through hers. With the other hand, he gripped Jessica's elbow firmly, then led both women out onto the sidewalk, extemporizing on the history of Notre Dame without a pause long enough for either woman to interrupt. They had to walk up the block to the main avenue to get a taxi, where Lucille was dispatched amid profuse promises to get together before her tour departed for the U.S. The taxi was out of sight before any of them realized no one had asked Lucille where she was staying.

"And now, my girl, we must get you off your ankle."

"It's not too bad, really. I was tired of sitting, I think. Please, Gordon, are you sure there's no one to help me get a passport today?"

"I thought we'd been through all this."

"Yes, but it's so frustrating. I'm wasting time and Mother needs me in London."

"I'm afraid you're stuck here with me. It's a shame Henri is away, he could have helped us. Unless. . . ." He paused, struck by a new thought. Pulling a small address book from his pocket, he thumbed through it quickly. "No, I don't have the number. Perhaps I can get it from the operator." His smile held a promise of hope. "Let me go back to the café and call."

Jessica nodded. Gordon felt his pockets in rapid succession. "May I borrow your pen? I'll have to get the number."

Jessica hesitated for only a fraction of a second, then reached into her pocket, handed him the pen. "I'll come with you."

"No, don't walk any more than you have to. Sit here." He gestured to the flange of a protective wooden box around a young, white poplar planted near the curb. "I'll be right back." She watched him trot back to the café. At the entrance, he turned and gave her a thumbs up sign. She waved in return.

She sat on the edge of the planter and idly watched the traffic, suddenly remembered the gray Citroën and glanced sharply around her. So intent had she been upon finding Lucille that she had forgotten about it. But it didn't seem to be in sight. If only she could call Peter, have him get her out of France. But she was safer waiting to get a passport from Gordon. That way she wasn't signalling her whereabouts to whomever listened to Peter's phone calls.

The window of the shop on the corner near her perch was filled with the souvenir baubles Lucille loved. As Jessica crossed to examine the hundreds of miniature Eiffel Towers that lined the shelves in various guises—as mugs, tee shirts, playing cards, even as a flashlight—she missed the reflection of the gray car gliding to the curb behind her. Kosov leaped out, removed a small vial from his shirt pocket and wrapped it carefully in his large, white handkerchief as he closed the gap between himself and his mark. He squeezed hard. The glass crushed inside the folds of cloth, which quickly absorbed the liquid to give off a faint, sickly odor. He was four paces from his victim. Yuri had leaped from the driver's seat and was coming up behind him.

Impulsively, Jessica decided to go into the souvenir shop and she turned the corner, heading toward the entrance on the main avenue. Around the side of the building she collided with a woman exiting from the shop.

As she moved, Kosov corrected his direction and with two quick sprints, he too was around the corner before his target could move out of range. He grabbed her right elbow and pressed the handkerchief over her mouth and nose. Her body jerked once, then wilted into his arms as Yuri reached her left side.

For a frozen moment, the two men stood with the limp woman between them, staring at the other woman standing barely four feet away. The hunter and the hunted recognized each other and realized the mistake. Jessica was the first to recover.

She turned and bolted down the sidewalk. Kosov cursed in Russian. Yuri shifted the bulk of the woman's weight in his arms over to Kosov and sprang forward.

"The car," he hissed, then he was barreling down the sidewalk. He could hear Kosov telling a passer-by that his wife had fainted.

Jessica hadn't much of a head start. With her bad ankle and high heeled sandals, serious running was impossible. She dodged pedestrians, not daring to take the time to look over her shoulder. The slap of running footfalls was gaining behind her.

As she reached the end of the block, the traffic signal changed to red, freeing a herd of cars in her path; she altered direction, ran into the side street to the right. Yuri caught up with her a few yards from the corner.

He had his own vial, wrapped in a handkerchief, already in his hand; the folds of cloth became damp in his fingers as he squeezed. Jessica managed a muted, guttural cry as she twisted violently to avoid the sickly smelling cloth, but the man held her fast, and at last she was forced to take a breath. Her head pitched forward and she sagged into his arms.

Several curious people had gathered at the corner. As Yuri caught her, his arm around her waist, her head leaning against him, he became aware of the attention he had aroused.

"Irina," he said loudly, "Irina, you know you can't go without your medicine. Nurse will be angry." He turned a baleful glance on the spectators and tapped his head. "She's allowed out with me on Sunday if she takes her medicine." The onlookers backed away uneasily.

Supporting her body, Yuri moved the short distance back to the avenue. The Citroën was cruising down the block. At his signal, Kosov pulled the car to the curb. Deprived of drama, the audience dispersed.

Kosov jumped from the car and opened the back door, revealing the limp body of the other woman sprawled across the back seat. Without a word, and avoiding Yuri's startled glance, he scrambled inside, shifting the body to the far side, then turned to receive Jessica's inert form. He huddled in the center of the back seat, a woman on each side drooping against the doors. As Yuri took his place behind the wheel, he tactfully kept his mouth shut.

CHAPTER TWENTY

Major Nikolayev stood under a tree along an avenue in the Champs de Mars, not far from the Eiffel Tower. The air was still sticky enough to plaster his shirt to his back and he was grateful for the shade. His eyes followed the steady stream of traffic. At last, he spied the gray Citroën making the turn and coming towards them. It cruised to a stop just long enough for him to slide into the front seat, then accelerated into traffic.

"That took a bit longer than necessary. Where did you go?" he asked, addressing Yuri at the wheel, but received only a sidelong glance in reply as the task of driving suddenly claimed Yuri's full attention. Nikolayev looked over his shoulder at Kosov in the back seat. He stared in disbelief.

Kosov sat in the center, staring at his hands in his lap, while on either side of him the two unconscious women were sprawled, eyes closed, jaws slack. In other circumstances, Nikolayev might have found the scene amusing.

"Am I seeing double?" he asked, barely able to control his voice as he looked at the plain, brown-haired woman slumped on Kosov's left. "Would you mind telling me who this woman is and why she is here?"

Kosov swallowed hard. Yuri swerved to avoid hitting an aggressive bus and the woman's body fell sideways, leaning against Kosov's shoulder. He adjusted her, raised miserable eyes to meet the Major's, then haltingly explained what happened.

Nikolayev slammed his fist against the smooth, black leather on the back of the seat.

"Goddam it! Do you know what you are, Kosov? A bungler! You've turned this entire mission into a disaster!"

Kosov listened in silence, eyes lowered.

"You weren't content with killing two people, is that it?

Now we have an innocent bystander unconscious in our car. What's wrong with you? You haven't been able to carry out a single task you've been given. How do you account for it all?"

"I don't know, Comrade-Major," mumbled Kosov as his thumb rubbed his forefinger furiously, working it like an imaginary worry stone. This assignment was driving him crazy. One thing after another kept going wrong and it wasn't his fault; he was having a run of bad luck. Who could have known someone would come out of the shop at the exact moment he came around the corner? He couldn't be blamed for accidents. He shifted uncomfortably as Nikolayev continued.

"I should have replaced you back in Geneva! Thrown you out like garbage! I was trying to protect your miserable hide, to keep your record clean so you could go home to your wife. That was a waste of time, wasn't it! You're through, now. I'll make sure Moscow hears every detail of how you've destroyed this job. I hope you like cold weather because you're not going to be warm for a long time after this kind of performance."

Nikolayev waited until his breathing returned to normal, then spoke to Yuri. "Did we get the warehouse?" he asked.

"No, Comrade-Major. The requisition was approved for Beauville." Yuri's voice was subdued and he didn't take his eyes from the road.

Nikolayev sighed. It would have been easier to effect his plan at the warehouse in the heart of Paris. The Beauville house was a bit remote, but still possible. He had to accept what the Embassy gave him; they controlled all field locations as protection against two operatives arriving at the same place at the same time. He spoke to Yuri again.

"We have to get rid of the other woman first. Go to the Bois de Boulogne."

It took only a few minutes. Skirting the lake, dotted with row boats, Yuri turned into one of the lesser roads that led through an unpopulated, wooded area, devoid of picnickers. He and Kosov unloaded the woman from the back seat. Supporting her body between them, her arms draped over their shoulders and her feet barely touching the ground, they dragged her across a narrow strip of grass to a chestnut tree, laughing and telling jokes for the benefit of a few passing cyclists. No one would remember three people innocently stopping to enjoy the woods. The cyclists safely past, they propped the woman against the base of the tree, then returned to the car.

The atmosphere in the car was thick with tension and deadly quiet. Although the air conditioner spewed forth a stream of coolness, the three men were sweating heavily.

Nikolayev gazed out the window. Even with Yuri in charge, Kosov was still making mistakes. It was unbelievable. From now on, he would keep Kosov out of it completely. He opened the glove compartment, removed a small notebook, and wrote hurried instructions. Then he tore out the page he had written, shoved it into his shirt pocket.

The suburbs gradually surrendered to countryside. Nikolayev turned off the air conditioner and rolled down his window. The air was still warm, but it smelled of grass and recently harvested crops, of cow dung and elder. Yuri turned off the main highway and followed a narrower road for several miles, threading through villages consisting of no more than a cluster of houses. At last, they turned into a rutted road that led to the farmhouse called Beauville, which served as a safe house for the KGB.

It was serene, almost somnolent, as only the country can be in the heat of summer. The dirt road, pitted and overgrown, ambled through a neglected apple orchard where budding fruit was beginning to weigh the branches and which gave cover to the car once it had turned off the village road. The house was completely hidden. A sharp curve brought them to the entrance.

It was an odd, disjointed house. An original nineteenth-century cottage squatted in the center. Looming over it, like the New Age ready to quash the Past, was a charmless stucco box, a two-story addition that grew from the back with complete disregard for its historic predecessor. Its pinched windows were decorated with iron grilles that looked more Spanish than French.

The farm was run by an old man and his wife who lived in the front cottage. The rest of the house was available to those who gave the correct password. The old couple were simple, peasant folks, victims of the spiraling, inflationary economy that plagued the modern world. Small farms were becoming a luxury, no matter that they had been the backbone of the country for generations. The luxury of making ends meet had led the farmer into bankruptcy. The KGB had come to his rescue in the guise of two anonymous, portly, middle-aged men with an extraordinary offer: in return for being cordial to occasional visitors and not asking questions, he and his wife would be allowed to live out their old age on the farm they had called home. It was a mutually beneficial arrangement.

A cloud of dust mushroomed behind the car as it stopped in front of the house. Nikolayev got out and rapped loudly on the thick, wide-planked door. A pleasant-looking woman in her mid-sixties answered, wiping floured hands on a large, embroidered apron, then patting back a stray wisp of gray hair from her face.

"Madame Gilette," said Nikolayev. "I am a friend of Antoine's."

"Antoine Fouchée?"

"Yes."

"Then you must stay for dinner. You may take your car around the back."

"Merci."

The woman closed the door. "Fouchée" meant that no one else was there with her. With a gesture to Yuri to drive behind the house, Nikolayev followed on foot, breathing in the sweet air spiced with the scent of ripening apples. Perpendicular and about a hundred feet to the back of the house was a long, low whitewashed building. It had four sets of wide, double doors. Nikolayev pulled open the first set, and Yuri guided the car inside.

Nikolayev handed the instructions he had written earlier to Yuri, who took the paper to the light by the door, and motioned to Kosov. In strained silence, they eased Jessica from the back seat. Nikolayev spoke over his shoulder to Yuri.

"You have her purse and passport?"

"In the trunk."

"Good. Put it on the table in the foyer."

Yuri opened the trunk, tucked the handbag under his arm, and sprinted toward the house as Nikolayev and Kosov followed, carrying Jessica's body between them. While Yuri worked the key in the lock, Nikolayev looked around. Gentle, sun-washed fields spread behind the garage in green waves, grasses billowing in the breeze. To the left,

197

across a grassy area, the apple orchard gave way to a stand of broadleafed forest. It was an idyllic setting.

They carried Jessica into the dim interior. The curtains at the windows were closed, keeping out the heat of the sun. The air was heavy with the odor of furniture oil, softened by the bouquet of sweet william in a brass vase by the window. Madame Gilette kept a tidy house.

A straight staircase in the foyer led to the bedrooms upstairs. Nikolayev nodded toward it; he and Kosov carried their burden up to the first room. It was identical to the four others; small, two twin beds draped with chintz coverlets, a small chest of drawers, a cane chair and a dry washstand with ewer and bowl. A KGB dormitory in the pastoral French countryside. They deposited Jessica on the far bed.

"Are you certain you didn't overdose her?" Nikolayev asked Kosov, the first words he had spoken to the man since his outburst.

"Yuri administered the drug," said Kosov.

"Wait for me in the garage."

"Yes, Comrade-Major." Kosov shuffled out of the room, feeling like a dead man already.

Nikolayev stood over Jessica's body. Her face was serene, as if in deep sleep. He reached into her pocket, brought out traveler's checks and French money. The other pocket was empty. After placing her belongings on the chest of drawers, he ran his hand over the hem of her skirt, the hem of her jacket and cuffs; then with a sigh, he began to unbutton her blouse. It wasn't easy working with a lifeless form, but at last he had examined every piece of clothing to his satisfaction. He hadn't found the microfilm. He stalked downstairs without so much as a backward glance at the unclothed woman on the bed and went straight to the garage.

Kosov and Yuri were playing cards, sitting in the front seat of the car with the overhead light on. As the garage door opened, they both got out of the car. Nikolayev saw the flask disappear quickly into Kosov's pocket as he stood, but pretended not to notice. It no longer mattered what Kosov did.

"Comrade Yuri, would you mind telling me what you did when she left the toilet in the café?"

"I searched it, Comrade-Major."

"Thoroughly?"

"Yes Comrade-Major. Thoroughly."

"And had she made any contact on the way to the toilet?"

"No, Comrade-Major."

Nikolayev turned to Kosov. "Were you watching her when she came out of the toilet?"

"Yes, Comrade-Major. She returned immediately to the table. No contact with anyone."

Without a word, Nikolayev turned on his heel and walked out of the garage. The two men shrugged, returned to their game in the front seat. Kosov retrieved the flask from his pocket, took a long swallow, then set it back on the dashboard.

Nikolayev returned to the second floor bedroom. He glanced from the clothing on the chair to Jessica's body, then from his pocket he withdrew the blue fountain pen and studied it in his palm. He opened it carefully. The shortened ink refill fell into his palm. The chamber above it was empty.

Impossible, he thought. She still has it and I've missed it. Jamming the pen back into his pocket, he ran his eyes the length of the nude, supine body on the bed. Could she have . . . ? He would have to search the accessible inner cavities of her body. He looked at her unresponsive face.

Suddenly, he leaned closer. A hairpin had slipped out of place and lay on the pillow next to her head. With excitement, he pulled at the remaining pins that held her hair on top of her head. As it tumbled down, he ran his fingers through the tangles, then along her scalp. He felt a lump on the crown of her head. Turning her face gently to the side and parting her hair, he exposed a thick, tight roll of hair held in place with three crossed pins. The microfilm was secure in its own silky, auburn cocoon. No wonder she had given up the pen so easily on the street. She had already removed the film, hidden it in her hair when she went to the toilet in the café.

Working quickly, he unwrapped the roll of hair and extracted the film. As his hand closed on it, he felt a physical sensation of pleasure. He had succeeded! Despite Kosov's ineptitude, despite the death of the Russian traitor, he had succeeded! Let them dare to deny him a promotion now! He wore a huge smile as he pocketed the film.

From his other pocket, he extracted another roll of microfilm. This he wrapped into the cocoon of hair and slid the pins into place. Clumsily, he tried to recreate the loose coil of hair that had camouflaged the hiding place so well. He was awkward at it, but at least he managed to get the coil pinned up. Perhaps she would assume it had become disheveled while lying on the bed.

Next, he crossed to the bedroom door and went to work on the lock with the knife on his keyring. When he was finished, he opened and closed the door several times; it no longer automatically locked when shut. Pleased, he started out of the room, then turned back to the form on the bed, reached for the pile of clothing. Slowly, awkwardly, he began to dress her.

He hadn't heard the sound of a car coming round the house, but he could hear voices in the courtyard and the slam of the garage door. He was at the foot of the stairs when the newcomer entered the house. They faced each other across the foyer.

"Comrade Barakov!" said Nikolayev in surprise. He had been contacting his superior through the embassy scrambler. He didn't know Barakov was in Paris.

"Ah, Major Nikolayev." Barakov pulled his lips back to reveal his teeth in the peculiar manner he had which passed for a smile. He stalked into the parlor, deliberately took off his gray suit jacket and laid it across a chair. In spite of the heat, there was no trace of sweat on his shirt. His inability to perspire added to the myth of his inhumanity. Nikolayev was forced to follow him into the parlor. He stood stiffly as Barakov set his briefcase on the table next to the loveseat.

"I'm surprised to see you, Colonel. I thought you were in Moscow."

"The best way to deal with subordinates, Major, is directly. I placed an important assignment in your hands. I was more than disturbed by your latest report about Alexiekov."

"But how did you know where to find me?"

"Your requisition for Beauville was on file at the Embassy. I am thorough, Comrade, as befits a senior officer of the Committee for State Security—a model I suggest you emulate."

Barakov's reputation was enough to make good men

quake, but in person, his colossal egotism could quash the hardiest. Nikolayev glanced uneasily toward the foyer. He couldn't stay here much longer. Barakov removed his glasses, unhooking one ear at a time, breathed raspingly on each lens, then wiped them with a handkerchief from his pocket. Nikolayev, thus reproached for having created a need for the man's presence, watched the ritual in impatient silence. Comrade Barakov was not a man one hurried.

"Can you give me a reason—one good reason—why a man whom we have a strong desire to interrogate should be killed? Killed before he answers even one question?" His voice was calm, but a holocaust kindled in his eyes. Nikolayev braced himself.

"Colonel. . . ."

"I'm holding you responsible, Major. Leadership means the ability to lead. Rank carries accountability. You let this butcher kill not one, but two men! I wanted those men, do you understand? I wanted them!"

"In spite of Kosov, we. . . ."

"I've already had a little chat with your Kosov. He understands that sloppy work cannot be tolerated. I don't accept excuses, Major. Kosov agreed that his training was haphazard and he has requested that the Party give him further instruction so that he can be useful to the State in the future."

Nikolayev unexpectedly felt sorry for Kosov; he knew that the "training" would be long and cold, that Kosov would probably never see his precious Raya again.

"Kosov will accompany me back to Moscow tomorrow," said Barakov.

Nikolayev glanced uneasily at the foyer again. He had to leave! "Colonel, I . . ."

"And you, Major, are off this assignment. As of now, I am taking over. Your dossier will reflect this little episode. I hold you ultimately responsible. Now I understand the woman is here, and she has the film?"

"No, Comrade, I have it." Nikolayev pulled the film from his pocket. "I have the microfilm right here."

Barakov looked at the outstretched palm before him. He blinked in surprise. "Well, my congratulations, Major. You may have just saved your skin."

"Colonel, I have to. . . ."

"No, Major, you don't have to do anything. You are still off the case. You may have pulled the prize from the fire, but you are still responsible for two dead men. Now I want to interrogate the woman."

"She doesn't know what is on the film, Colonel; she was only a courier."

"I will determine what she does or does not know."

"You needn't concern yourself. I have questioned her. . . ."

"A good officer is never too superior for a lowly task. I wish to hear what she has to say. Thoroughness, Major. You would do well to remember that. You will wait for me here."

"Colonel, please, my plan. . . ."

"I make the plans now!" Barakov stumped up the stairs.

Nikolayev cracked his knuckles. Everything hinged upon his remaining out of sight. Logic told him to go to the garage, but another part of him, a part he didn't want to examine at the moment, told him to stay where he was in case Barakov got rough.

Jessica rose from a deep, black hole, opened her eyes and stared at the unfamiliar room. A hint of a sickly, sweet taste lingered in her mouth and lungs, making her cough; the light and fresh air made her dizzy. She put a hand to her hair in alarm, but the lump of the tight curl was still there and she breathed deeply in relief.

The room gave no clue as to where she was. Behind the chintz curtain, the small window had iron bars, not a promising sign. There was no hotel monogram on the pillowcase. She sat up slowly, fighting the fog of the drug, then lay back as the room undulated. She noticed that the front of her blouse was unbuttoned. The door burst open and a towering, hard-eyed man walked toward her. "I'm Colonel Barakov," he said, with what may have been a smile or a grimace.

Jessica clutched her blouse over her exposed breasts. "I am an American citizen. I have been kidnapped and I demand to see my Ambassador! You cannot. . . ."

Barakov laughed as he watched her fumbling with the buttons. "Let's be realistic. I can do whatever I wish. At the moment, I merely wish to talk to you." He let his eyes slide the length of her body, lewdly. Jessica shifted to sit upright against the headboard of the bed in an effort to counter the psychological effect of lying on her back before this menacing man.

"I have nothing to say." She didn't feel the bravura she pretended.

"What was on the microfilm?"

She finished buttoning her blouse. Her hand involuntarily moved upward toward her hair; she diverted it to her throat, wondering at his use of the word "was." Maybe he didn't know she had it. "I don't know what you're talking about."

Barakov struck her across the face, the blow sending her sideways on the bed.

"What was on the microfilm?"

Jessica sat up, resisting the impulse to touch her flaming cheek. "You're very good at beating women, aren't you?"

Barakov looked at the ceiling, emitted a bored sigh. "There are a great many things I'm good at in order to get information, things you probably never dreamed of. I would be delighted to show them to you, one by one, so it would be in your best interest to answer my question."

"I have no idea what was on it. You could have asked the man who gave it to me, if you hadn't murdered him already."

The next blow caught her ear and sent her sprawling across the bed again. Her eyes were watering and the lump in her throat was so large she could hardly swallow. She lay with her face in the mattress to give herself time to control her trembling. She didn't know how much courage she really had.

"Smart answers are not necessary; it is a simple question. What was on the microfilm?" His voice was flat, unemotional, unconnected to the pain he inflicted.

"I don't know. I was only sent to pick it up."

He hit her again, and this time she cried out before she could stop herself. "If I tell you the truth, and you still hit me, what is the point of my answering at all?" she choked. Her cheek and ear were on fire.

"That's a logical point. But how can I be certain you are telling me the truth?"

The sharp retort of a gunshot cut off her reply. Barakov hurried to the window. The courtyard below lay empty, the countryside peaceful beyond it. He cursed.

"I'll give you time to reflect upon our discussion," he said as he left the room, closing the door loudly behind him. He took the stairs as fast as his bulk would allow. Nikolayev was already outside.

"Was that a shot?" asked Barakov, puffing as he joined him.

"Yes, from the garage."

The two men hurried across the gravel courtyard as Yuri exploded through the garage door, face distorted, arms waving, blood stains dotting his shirt and pants.

"I couldn't stop him, Comrades, I'm sorry. I didn't know he. . . ." He stopped, gesturing helplessly, eyes bulging.

Nikolayev entered first, Barakov behind him. Kosov lay in a widening pool of blood by the front fender of the car, which was spattered with the precious life liquid as if it had erupted with volcanic force, shooting out of the body. Nikolayev turned away, but Barakov leaned over him, close enough to hear the gasping breath and see the rolling eyes.

"Why would he do that?" blubbered Yuri. "We were talking. He was telling me about his wife, Raya. He wanted to give her another baby. Then he started crying that he had ruined her life, that they would send her away because he was disgraced. He said he was finished; it was no use. Then he pulled out his gun. I tried to stop him. . . ." Yuri was stricken by his failure to have prevented bloodshed.

Kosov was moaning now, a low, keening sound, the pool of blood thickening around him. Barakov looked at the wound in his chest.

"The man couldn't even bring off his own suicide," he said with contempt. "We can't take him to a doctor; there'll be too many questions." He put out his hand. "Give me your gun."

Yuri met Barakov's eyes in disbelief, then traveled to the dying Kosov on the ground. He didn't move.

"Our job is to find the expedient solution, Comrade," said Barakov, hand still extended. "Your weapon, please."

Numbly, Yuri withdrew the Graz-Bura from his shoulder holster and handed it to Barakov. Barakov fired quickly, the body at his feet jumping from the impact. More blood spurted into the air. Nikolayev, standing at the rear of the car, turned his back.

"Bury him in the field," said Barakov to Yuri. "And clean up this mess. We don't want our hosts to have any explaining to do." He knew that Monsieur and Madame Gilette would not have heard the gunshot; they neither heard nor saw anything that happened at the back of their cottage. "Major Nikolayev will brief you on the official line," added Barakov as he turned on his heel and walked to the door, the gun apparently forgotten in his right hand. Nikolayev didn't move from the fender of the car.

"Major Nikolayev, you will come with me," said Barakov over his shoulder.

"Colonel, I can't. . . ."

"Now!" bellowed Barakov without looking back as he stalked toward the house.

CHAPTER TWENTY-ONE

Jessica waited until she heard Barakov descend the stairs before she tried the door. To her surprise, it was unlocked; whether Barakov thought she was too afraid to escape or whether he was confident there was no place for her to go, she wasn't sure, but either way there was no point in remaining in the room waiting for his return. How many others might be in the house she didn't know. She turned the knob silently, opened the door a crack. There was no guard outside. At the head of the stairs, she listened, but the house was still; she descended one step at a time, testing for a creaking board, but reached the bottom with only the sound of her heartbeat to break the silence.

She was in a foyer at the bottom of the stairs. The front door was opposite her, a large parlor to her right. She crouched, peered around the corner. The room was empty. As she turned back to the foyer, her eyes stopped at the narrow table opposite the stairs dominated by a large, wood-framed mirror. Unbelievably, on the table, lay her handbag, the one stolen at Versailles. She tiptoed across the foyer, peeked into the sitting room. It was unoccupied, as was the dining room beyond. Sweeping her handbag from the table, she fumbled with its plastic catch, found her passport nestled in the narrow, center section where she kept it. She shoved the bag under her arm.

In the sitting room, the heavy, blue curtains at the window were drawn. Pulling a corner of the fabric away, she could see into the empty, gravel courtyard. There was no sound. The long, low building to the right had no windows facing her, only closed double doors, which meant a reasonable shot at reaching the forest on the right if her luck held.

She opened the front door cautiously. The second gunshot came just as she put her foot across the threshold.

Terrified, she slammed the door. Where were they? She could see no one. If they were guarding her, why were they hiding? She crossed back to the window, parted the curtain a sliver, but nothing moved in the courtyard. Then suddenly the garage door opened. Barakov emerged, striding toward the house. Panicked, Jessica sought a place to hide.

The massive sideboard in the dining room protruded from the wall far enough to conceal her from both the foyer and the sitting room. She hunched into a ball behind its painted panels as the front door opened.

The footsteps stopped just inside the threshold. She waited tensely. Would he go directly upstairs, giving her a chance to get out the door? She heard Barakov's voice.

"Don't concern yourself, Major. I'll report it to the Center as an accident."

Jessica closed her eyes in dismay. There were two men, then. If both didn't go upstairs, she was trapped.

"An accident?" said the other man. Jessica's head jerked up in attention.

"Yes," continued Barakov. "An automobile crash, or better yet, a hit-and-run. You have such good instincts, Major Nikolayev. We wouldn't want a blot on your record.

My record, thought Nikolayev. I just saw *you* shoot the man. But then he saw the trade. "The expedient solution is sometimes difficult to explain, I suppose."

"Exactly."

The two men stepped into the foyer. Nikolayev glanced quickly at the hall table and relaxed visibly, kneading the muscles of his shoulder with a sudden awareness of how tight they had become since Barakov's arrival. He allowed himself a smile. He had won on all counts. Colonel Nikolayev. The sound rolled around his head; he had to restrain himself from saying it aloud. Colonel Nikolayev. His father would be very proud.

Jessica could see nothing and dared not move. She hardly breathed, straining to hear what the men were saying.

"Too many questions." It was Barakov's voice again. "My way is the easiest. I've found headquarters need not be apprised of every little decision made in the field."

Indeed, thought Nikolayev, inclining his head slightly in agreement. Especially when the decision involves murder.

"We both know Kosov was incompetent," said Barakov. "Frankly, I'm surprised you didn't replace him after Payne was killed."

Jessica couldn't hear the reply. Her sensory receivers shut down completely and she began to tremble. This was the man responsible for her father's death. The words repeated in her head like a stuck phonograph needle. This was the man . . . this was the man. . . . She clenched her teeth as her body flashed hot and cold, making her crouched position unbearable, and a sudden cramp gripped her right foot with an iron hold. She could see the muscles standing out in thick cords across the top of her ankle, shifted her position to massage and bend it while fighting to control the rush of tears that threatened to swamp her. This was the man. . . . Then mourning was washed away, replaced by a cold, clear rage more powerful than anything she had ever felt before. It possessed her totally, inhabiting every cell of her body, until she was no longer afraid. The room came into sharp focus around her.

"It was a shame to have lost both Payne and Alexiekov," Barakov was saying. "I'm sure they would have provided us with useful information. We can't be sure others were not involved."

"From the beginning I had expressly requested there be no violence. . . ."

"Requests are perhaps not the best way to exert authority, Comrade." Barakov's tone had changed abruptly, flashed like a knife edge. "Next time I'm sure you will be more in control of your subordinates. But we will keep this little lesson you've learned between the two of us. And you will brief Yuri on the unfortunate hit-and-run accident that killed our friend, Kosov."

"Yes, Comrade-Colonel." The deal was complete: Nikolayev had just traded his conscience for his career, and Barakov's reputation had become even more awesome. Nikolayev wondered if the man would head the KGB one day.

"After all," continued Barakov, "we mustn't lose sight of your accomplishments. We have you to thank for putting us on to Payne in the first place. Spotting the woman as a surrogate courier—splendid! You seem to have established an excellent network in London."

"Thank you, Colonel."

"And, of course, you have delivered the microfilm. I think you have quite a future, Major. I shall put in a recommendation for promotion. Now tell me about this plan you hinted at in your report."

"It's already succeeded, Comrade. I ran a disinformation operation worthy of Comrade Alexiekov." His enthusiasm was somewhat dampened by the incident in the garage. Somehow, he was overcome by a putrid, rotten odor which clung to him despite his attempt to sweeten it with his own success. He licked his lips before continuing. "I replaced the microfilm with one I prepared at the Embassy lab in Paris. I arranged for the woman to escape from here—she's on her way to London now to deliver the bogus film. It contains names it would be advantageous for us to discredit."

"An interesting idea. You're certain she didn't know what was on the film?"

"I'm staking my career on it."

"Noble. For your sake, I hope you're right."

"Her escape will lend authenticity to the film when she gets to London." Nikolayev looked at the empty table in the foyer again. "My network in London is still secure."

Barakov nodded. "Again, congratulations, Major." He looked down, realizing he still held Yuri's gun in his hand. "You may return this." The gun was still warm from his grasp. Nikolayev held it uneasily as Barakov turned and walked into the parlor.

"I have some instructions for you," said Barakov, rummaging in his briefcase without turning around, "now that you will be going back to London."

Jessica couldn't hear as well now that they had moved into the far room. But she had heard enough. She moved to the archway that divided the dining room from the sitting room. Both men were out of her line of vision. Mentally, she measured the distance from her position to the divan in the sitting room. If she could reach it unseen, she could hide there; it would give her a better vantage point from which to see. And she needed to see Nikolayev's face. She crawled on all fours, eyes on the archway to the foyer. The hardwood floor tortured her knees. Barakov's back became visible and she stopped, pulled back quickly out of the line of vision, then crept forward again cautiously. Barakov's back was fully in view now; only a few more feet to the divan and she would be safe. Suddenly the other man leaned

209

forward to take a sheaf of papers from Barakov's outstretched hand. Jessica dived for the back of the sofa. She didn't think he had seen her. His face had been in profile, but she wasn't certain. It no longer mattered.

She huddled behind the divan. As much as she had tried to rationalize the voice, there was no mistaking the face. A jumble of feelings clamored for attention, but she shut them off. He had almost succeeded. She felt the burn of betrayal. She had been duped from the very beginning. She barely heard the front door open and Barakov's voice.

"Goodbye then, Major Nikolayev. I'll see you at the Embassy tonight."

The door closed with a click. Footsteps sounded across the bare floor.

"You can get up now, Jessica."

She didn't move.

"I know you're there."

Slowly, stiffly, she stood. Gordon was facing her on the other side of the divan.

They stood looking at each other, eyes full of pain. Jessica noticed that he no longer wore the bandages on his arm and forehead from this morning. She lowered her gaze to the gun, hanging in his hand at his side like some macabre prosthesis. He didn't take his eyes from her face, but blinked as he saw the broken blood vessels on her cheek where Barakov had hit her. The sound of an engine could be heard outside, a change of gears, then tires squealing slightly as the car rounded the side of the house.

"I thought you were gone." His voice was barely above a whisper. "Why the hell didn't you get out?"

"I didn't have enough time. But it was a good plan. Worthy of the KGB."

"Jessica. . . ." He took a step forward, forgetting the sofa barred his way. He hit his shin on the frame.

She backed away. "How could you do it, Gordon? Or should I call you Major Nikolayev?" She spat the name at him. "How could you sell out your country?"

"My country?" He looked down at the couch, then back at her face. "Sit down, Jessica. We need to talk."

"I have nothing to say."

"Sit down, please." His voice was sharper than he intended. She glanced again at the gun.

"Certainly . . . Major." She walked to the end of the divan, tossed her handbag onto the table, and sat rigidly in the faded armchair. Gordon sat on the couch, put the gun on the cushion next to him, barrel pointing away from them.

"You ask how I could sell out my country," he began. "When I was fifteen, at George Washington High School outside of Chicago, I remember being struck by a quotation I learned in my history class. 'My country . . . may she always be right, but my country, right or wrong.' Stephen Decatur, 1816."

"I don't need a history lesson."

"No, but you see, the point is, patriotism is an accident of birth. I was born in Moscow, Jessica. I'm Russian; my country is Russia. My parents still live in Moscow. My father is a Colonel in the GRU, the military secret police."

There was a pause. Jessica studied him with hostility and pain.

"When I was ten years old," he continued, "I was sent to live with my aunt, who had emigrated to New York and married an American. They had a son the same age as I. When my uncle died, she wanted to return to Moscow. My father was a rising officer and devised the plan of sending me to America as a sleeper agent. I went to the United States on a visit, exchanged papers with my cousin, and he was sent back to Russia in my place when my visit was over. My aunt moved to a suburb of Chicago, where no one knew us, taking me with her as her son, Gordon Michaels, born in America with a genuine American identity. I had been carefully trained; I became as American as I could in speech, in dress, in attitude, in experience. But I was doing it for my country—for Russia."

"What's your real name?"

"Grigori Michailovitch Nikolayev."

Jessica sat like a ramrod in the chair, eyes flatly bright like an animal trapped by the headlights of a car. Nikolayev searched her face, then looked at his hands. He brought his fingertips together and cracked his knuckles. The sound was explosive in the oppressive silence.

"When I met you in Paris, ten years ago," he continued, "I was returning from a secret training trip to Russia. I took a semester at the Sorbonne as a cover. It was easier to slip in and out of Russia from Europe than from the States. After I graduated from college, I began to get assignments from the KGB. An American friend of mine got me involved in a company with offices in London that had important government contacts. The KGB was delighted: I met a lot of people in London and ended up staying there, running a network." He paused, but Jessica still did not meet his eyes. "So no matter how badly you may think of me, Jessica, I'm not a traitor. I am nothing less than what you are: I am doing a job for my country."

"Do you always seduce women for the good of . . . your country?" It always came down to personal betrayal, she reflected. A country couldn't feel hurt.

"What happened between us has nothing to do with jobs, countries, or patriotism."

"You mean you would have made love to me even if I didn't have the microfilm?" She brushed a lock of hair from her forehead.

"You didn't have any microfilm ten years ago."

"No." The room seemed unbearably hot. Jessica stood abruptly and faced the table by the window. She would not lose control. This wasn't personal, it was political. "Tell me, Major Nikolayev, why don't you live in the Worker's Paradise if you think your government is so right?"

"No government is right. They all do terrible things to maintain their power. I don't approve of everything my country does any more than you approve of everything your country does. But I believe the basic principles are right: a classless society can be the only ultimate aim of mankind. And I serve my government as I have been trained."

"But your system doesn't work!" She turned to face him. "Human rights are trampled. It's a vicious, repressive society."

"And you think your system does work? Big business and wealthy corporations running the country on the basis of what is good for them and damn the man in the street? Your precious vote hardly stands up to corporate lobbies for special legislation."

"My country didn't march into Afghanistan and simply take over. . . ."

"It depends upon one's point of view, doesn't it? Your country has supported oppressive dictators in Iran and South America in the name of democracy. Your CIA engineered a coup in Chile. Let's not talk about international meddling!"

She looked straight at him.

"You killed my father."

Nikolayev leaned forward. "I'm sorry, Jessica. Please believe that. It was an accident. Barakov was right, I should have had better control of my subordinates. I didn't know he was your father until after you became involved."

"And Lark?" She saw his face again on the chair in her hotel room. "Are you sorry about him?"

"Yes. I'm not a murderer."

"And what about me, Major? Now that I know who you are, are you going to be sorry that you have to kill me?"

Nikolayev ran his hand across his eyes. "Christ," he said, more to himself than to her. He stood, paced the short distance to the dining room archway and turned back.

"I've done my best to protect you throughout this entire mission, that's why I was running it from the field. I kept track of your every move. When I saw you crawl behind the couch, I could have told Barakov you were there. He would have shot you on the spot. But I protected you. All I wanted was the microfilm." He was standing in front of the chair.

"Well, you have it now."

His free hand went to the side of his hip, unconsciously feeling the lump of film under the fabric of his pants. "Yes, I have it now." He reached into his pocket, tossed the film onto the table, almost with revulsion.

"And I have the other one." She reached into her hair, pulling at the pins, then set the small roll of film beside the first.

"Damn, why couldn't you have escaped, as I planned."

Jessica looked at the man before her, trying to erase the knowledge she had of his body, of his embrace, of the fervor of his lips. She had known nothing about him, nothing at all. She had made love with a Russian KGB Major. What would her father have thought of that? But for an instant, she could see him simply as Gordon. Politics were out of place in the bedroom.

"So what do we do now?" she said. Lover and enemy. Fear had given way to anger, but now all that was left was hopelessness.

Nikolayev paced again, struggling with his thoughts. "I

had hoped that if I could keep my identity from you, there would be no problem. You would go back to America; I would go back to my network in London. We'd lose touch again, and neither of us would be the worse for this experience.

"Not a bad scenario."

"It seems a bit improbable now, doesn't it? Knowledge can't be unlearned. I suppose it would be impossible for you not to report me to your friend Barnsworth."

"What would you do in my position?" she asked.

There was a moment of silence as they probed each other's eyes for answers that were not there. The vanilla scent of her filled his nostrils.

"What would you do in mine?" he said softly.

Jessica stood slowly, running her fingers through her hair. "Perhaps we could make some sort of an arrangement," she said. She walked to the table by the window, touched a crimson petal of the sweet william in the vase. She couldn't smell the fragrance any more; she had been in the room too long.

"What kind of arrangement?" said Nikolayev.

"A compromise," she replied. "Something inflicting minimal damage to both our countries." Her attention was focused on the vase holding the flowers. It was brass, about eight inches high, two and a half inches in diameter, with crudely tooled flowers on the front and sides, the top edge bent down to form a lip. As she studied it, she realized it was a shell casing, probably picked up in a field after World War II, and hammered into a vase. She bit her lip. Killing was all around her. She ran her finger over the raised flower design. Nikolayev came to her side.

"So that we each become only minor traitors, you mean?"

The shell case was firmly in her grip. It was even heavier than she had anticipated. As she turned her head toward him, as if to answer, she swung her arm with as much speed as she could manage, the spin of her body adding force. The flowers arced across the room like a red and green discus, followed by the airborne puddle of the water.

The vase caught him across the cheek and the bridge of the nose, sending him reeling backwards with a cry, blood spurting from his face. Jessica didn't stop to look. She scooped up her handbag and the two rolls of film from the table and ran for the door.

The courtyard was bare. She made her decision in an instant. Although the garage would give her immediate cover, nothing but bare, green fields lay beyond it. At least the woods would give her a chance. But to get to the relative safety of the woods, she first had to cross the gravel courtyard, then the dirt drive, then the small grassy area, all without cover. But there was no choice; she hoped whoever had been shooting at her earlier was looking the other way.

She took off on a dead run. Her high-heeled sandals wobbled and turned once she hit the rutted dirt drive, threatening to throw her to the ground, and her bad ankle forced her into an odd, hopping gait. Impatiently, she kicked off her shoes, but instantly regretted it as the little pebbles from the drive bit into her feet. But she had more speed now, although she still ran lopsidedly.

She didn't see the man with the shovel coming around the corner of the garage behind her. Yuri had finished his task of burying Kosov in the field. He stopped as he saw the woman dash from the house. Then, mindful of his instructions, he turned and hurried to the garage door, closing it behind him. Thank goodness she hadn't seen him! Yuri prided himself on following instructions. If Major Nikolayev said he wanted the woman to escape, Yuri would be the first to let it happen. And his chance appearance at the moment she ran from the house might have ruined everything. After all, poor Kosov had been brought down by just such quirks of fate. Adjusting his glasses, and heaving a sigh, he crossed to the Citroën, climbed into the back seat and turned on the overhead light, closing the door firmly. He would see nothing, hear nothing, do nothing.

Jessica was running as fast as she could, legs pumping, heart pounding, lungs sucking up oxygen like a fire. She had crossed the drive and now plunged into the field. The grass hid the unevenness of the earth beneath. The ground was soft; it seemed to fight her, daring her to make progress, pulling every step downward. Her thighs ached and her ankle throbbed. Her lungs were ready to burst. Please, God, let me make it to the trees; give me the strength to run. She wasn't aware of the tears on her cheeks.

Suddenly she tripped, legs and arms flailing to maintain her balance, body out of control for several paces, but she managed to remain upright. She was only a quarter of the way across the field when she heard the cry, but she didn't turn to look.

"Jessica, stop!"

The woods were invitingly, tantalizingly close now. Over the little ditch there, only a short way to go. Hurry!

"Jessica! Please!" Did the voice sound closer? Was he gaining on her? Don't stop to look, just keep running. Eyes on the ground, don't stumble. God, where are the trees?

At first she didn't hear the sound. Something whizzed past her head. She let out a hoarse cry. Her guttural, inarticulate sob was coming on each panting breath as she ran, an animal fleeing for its life.

The gun cracked again, then there was numbing pain. Jessica dropped to the ground and lay motionless.

"Oh, God, no, no!" Nikolayev was gasping as he reached the spot where she had fallen. Her body was face down in the grass. He stood above her for an instant, not hearing his own incoherent, whimpering sounds. Then he dropped to one knee.

"What could I do, Jessica?" he mumbled. "I had no choice. Oh, God, I had no choice. . . ." Tears streamed down his face. Gently he grasped her shoulder and rolled her over.

The movement took him completely by surprise. Her knee jerked up and caught his jaw, knocking his head back, then her toe crashed into his throat, sending him sprawling onto his back in the grass. The gun flew out of his hand, landing on the ground to his right. Jessica had only a glimpse of his face. The vase must have broken his nose; it was mashed against his split cheek and blood was still running down over his mouth and chin.

She lunged sideways, feeling for the gun in the grass. Her right shoulder had taken the bullet and she could feel the stickiness of blood oozing down her arm. The pain ripped through her with a searing force, but she closed her mind to it, working on pure animal instinct for survival. She shifted her body so that she could use her left arm to reach for the gun. The ground, which had seemed so soft before, now felt like a rock beneath her, unyielding, battering her as she thrashed through the grass. Nikolayev spotted the weapon just as her hand closed over it; he hurled himself at her, but she rolled free, and he ended up with a fistful of grass. As he swung around, she came to a sitting position, her breath harsh, raspy from the pain. They faced each other on their knees in the grass, like puppies stalking one another, each waiting for the other to make the first move.

The gun was now in her right hand, pointed at him. She was motionless, staring at his mangled face.

"Give me the gun," he said.

She didn't move.

Slowly, cautiously, he extended his hand, palm up.

"Give me the gun."

"I can't do that, Major Nikolayev," she whispered, her eyes wide. The pain in her shoulder was excruciating and the gun shook in her hand. She raised her left hand to steady it.

Nikolayev's voice was thick as the blood clogged his throat. "I love you Jessica. I've never loved anyone in my life. When I saw you lying there, I couldn't bear it. Please. . . ." He squeezed his eyes shut as he licked his lips, then looked at her again. "Please. We'll go away, make a new life together. We'll find a country we can call *our* country." He reached out to her.

A tear slid down her cheek. Her entire body was trembling.

"Jessica, please, give me the gun." Almost in slow motion he leaned forward, his eyes locked onto hers. His right hand closed gently over her left wrist.

"Gordon . . ." she whispered.

He brought his left hand up to grasp the gun, still trembling in her two-handed grip. He opened his mouth, but she never heard his reply. The noise reverberated throughout her entire body. In the instant before his hand reached the barrel of the gun, she had pulled the trigger.

CHAPTER TWENTY-TWO

Peter Barnsworth gazed at the Signac painting on the wall, his hands working small circles over the smooth, soft arms of his burgundy leather chair. Suddenly he hated the true, clear colors the artist had chosen to define the landscape. He turned away from the picture. He would sell it. In this business, an early Cubist painting would be more appropriate, a framed cypher of broken planes and fumbled identities within a palette of neutral colors, all intellect without emotion.

He stared morosely at the papers littering his desk. He hated the intelligence profession, wondered if perhaps he weren't past his prime. Human beings were, after all, a sorry lot, he reflected. It occurred to him that the evolution of the ape into Homo sapiens might have been nothing more than a huge, monstrous joke.

He reached for his pipe, but the taste of stale tobacco was strong in his mouth, so he opened his bottom right-hand drawer and took out the bottle of Beefeaters instead. The red uniformed symbol of England mocked him. Pro Patria. . . . His watch read nine o'clock. He could hear the London traffic outside his window gearing up for another day. He had been in his office all night.

The cable had arrived in the early evening: Jessica was coming in to Heathrow on a commercial flight from France and wanted to be met. He had driven to the airport himself, waiting on the tarmac in an official car to whisk her away the instant she set foot on English soil.

The disembarking passengers had edged away from the unsavory woman in their midst, offended by the reminder of the tenuous hold they had on their neat, controlled lives. Peter, too, had been shocked by her appearance. The waif who stepped off the plane bore no resemblance to the composed, attractive woman he had sent to Paris. Her face was ravaged: a network of broken blood vessels spread across her left cheek, a purple bruise puffed her eye and another disfigured her neck. The auburn hair around her face was tangled and matted. She wore a skirt and blouse, wrinkled and torn, spattered with brown stains, and her jacket was rigged into a makeshift sling around her right arm and shoulder. She had wrapped what looked like a white linen table cloth, folded into a triangle, around herself. She was barefoot and limped as she walked to the car. But it was her eyes that disturbed him most. The clear, dazzling green eyes were dead, focused on some inward horror even as they gazed outward.

The story came out in fragmented bits and pieces as they drove. Peter felt a physical pain in his chest as she spoke. In a village not far from the farmhouse, she had found a doctor, whose office was no more than a small room off the kitchen of his home. She was still bleeding; the doctor had attended to the wound before asking any questions. The bullet had passed cleanly through her body, missing the bone in her shoulder by two centimeters; she would regain the use of her arm. But the doctor was adamant: he would have to notify the police, despite her insistence that it was a hunting accident. All gunshot wounds had to be reported.

Jessica had waited until he went to the telephone in the living room to call the police, then she had run through the kitchen and out the back door, grabbing the big white cloth from the table to use as a shawl to cover her bloodsoaked clothes. She had paid an old man in the village an exorbitant sum to drive her to Charles de Gaulle Airport in his beat-up truck. By the time she arrived in London, she was nearly fainting from pain and shock. But she handed Peter two rolls of microfilm.

He had driven her straight to St. George's Hospital at Hyde Park Corner with the command that she spend the night.

Peter had then hurried to the lab to have enlargements made of both rolls of film. The resulting prints, 8 x 10 glossies, were devastating. There were six pay records on each roll of film. Each print had a picture of a Russian agent at the top. He aligned the glossies on his desk in accordance with the roll of film each had come from, then studied the photographs of the Russians. He recognized no one.

The names were another story. Under each Russian's picture were the names of English persons involved in his network, usually ten to fifteen names each, as well as the monies paid or otherwise spent on each. Peter didn't know which set of prints had the correct information, but it hardly mattered; he recognized enough names in both piles, names that made him weep: personal friends, trusted business associates, people in sensitive areas of government, high-ranking officials, journalists. It was horrifying.

Not all would turn out to be spies per se: He knew many would be unaware that they had been used by the KGB, would even think they had been assisting some worthwhile organization that needed information, and in some cases, the information would have seemed harmless. But put together with other bits and pieces collected from a variety of sources, it provided a total picture for the Russian case officer. Peter thought of his unwitting friends with a heavy heart, but wondered how many of the names were actual moles who had purposely deceived him.

He had pored over the material until early morning, reading and rereading the names in a kind of stupor. At last, exhausted, he stacked the photos in two piles in his safe, then tried to sleep on the fold-up cot in his office, but his mind would give him no rest. Now he felt stale and worn.

It was impossible to confront anyone about the lists until he knew which roll of film was authentic. Even then, he was certain that MI6 would want to deal with each penetration individually: a few would be confronted (although the thought of the ensuing scandal made him blanch), some would be eased out of their jobs, never knowing why, others would be fed false information. But it was the people Peter knew personally that hurt the most; he almost dreaded knowing which film was genuine.

He had wanted to bring the prints to the hospital this morning for Jessica to look at, but she insisted upon coming to his office. He arranged the glossies on his desk.

The buzzer on his intercom sounded, then Betty's voice broke into his thoughts.

"Jessica Autland has arrived."

"Send her in. And Betty, bring us some coffee."

Betty held the door as Jessica entered. Peter was glad to see that she looked better than last night: her clothes were fresh and some color had returned to her face. But her eyes were still dull and she didn't smile.

Peter held the chair for her, then sat on the corner of his desk.

"How do you feel?" he asked.

"Better, thank you. The hospital gave me some pills for the pain."

He nodded. His pipe lay empty in the ashtray at his side; he filled it while he spoke, relieved to have someplace to look other than her lifeless eyes. "I didn't have a chance to say it last night, but I want you to know that I'm sorry I put you through this. I had no idea it would turn out the way it did."

"Of course, I know that, Peter. One does one's job."

"If there's anything I can do. . . ."

"I'd really just like to see the photos and get this over as soon as possible. I've booked a flight to the States for this afternoon."

"You should take time to recuperate."

"I want to go home."

"I understand." He wanted to pat her hand, but he sucked on his pipe instead. He indicated the photographs spread across his desk, neatly divided into two rows.

Betty brought a pot of coffee and two cups on a tray. She smiled sympathetically at Jessica as she crossed to the desk to set it down, but stopped abruptly and stared at the pictures arrayed before her. The tray slipped from her grasp, crashing china and hot liquid onto the carpet.

"Betty!" exclaimed Peter, jumping up.

She appeared not to have heard him. Her eyes were fixed on the desk, her mouth open.

Peter felt the thud of knowledge as it kicked him in the gut. "Do you know one of these men?" he asked.

"No . . . no . . . I. . ." She backed away, covering her face with her hands. "No. . . ." Peter was at her elbow. He eased her into the chair next to Jessica.

"I think we'd better talk about it," he said.

Betty looked at him wildly; she was trembling. "No, it's nothing. I . . . I felt faint, that's all."

"Whose picture did you recognize?" Maybe there was some other explanation. He had almost cried last night when he saw her name.

"No one." She looked up at him, her eyes filled with

tears. "Oh God." Suddenly she was sobbing, full wracking sobs that shook her body. "Oh God, oh God, oh God." She pulled a handkerchief from her sleeve and dabbed her eyes.

Jessica had leaned forward to look at the photos. On the left, a familiar, dark-haired face smiled at her. Gordon Michaels, also known as Grigori Michailovitch Nikolayev. Beneath the picture was the list of names. Betty Cowdrick was the second name. The amount listed next to it was £2000.

Jessica picked up the glossy print and stared at it, then nodded and handed the picture to Peter. He looked crushed. Finally he handed it to Betty.

The face in her hand brought a fresh supply of tears. Betty wiped at her face. With a whimper, her hand went to the chain around her neck, and she pulled the diamond ring from her bosom. She gazed at it, then her eyes went back to the photograph. Letting the picture slide from her grasp, she cupped both hands around the ring and held it to her breast, rocking ever so slightly back and forth.

"I didn't know," she whispered. "Honestly, I didn't know." She raised anguished eyes to Peter, the tears still spilling down her cheeks.

"You'd better tell us what happened," he said.

Betty spoke haltingly. She had known Gordon Michaels for a little over a year and a half, had met him at the Embassy party she'd attended with Peter when his wife had appendicitis. They were engaged. She looked away from Peter's expression of surprise. Gordon was president of some kind of trading company, but he really wanted to be a writer. He was working on his first book, one of those thrillers about international intrigue. He was so honest and open with her, it never occurred to her that he was other than what he said. He hadn't even known where she worked when they first met. She had told him she worked for an insurance firm. But as he became more involved in his book, they had begun discussing intelligence services, and she had confessed her real job. Occasionally, after that, he would ask her questions, always stressing that she not tell him anything really secret. Gradually, as she got to know him better, she told him more. Once in a while, she had even brought home documents for him to look at.

"Surely, Betty, you knew that was wrong," interrupted Peter.

"They weren't important state secrets, just little things.

An organizational chart to help him with background, some equipment specs for authenticity. He wasn't writing about British Intelligence, but about the CIA. The information seemed so harmless." She patted her eyes, then blew her nose. "I wasn't telling him where we kept our bombs, or who our agents were. You read about the kind of information I gave him in magazines all the time." She looked at Peter pleadingly.

"What else?" he asked, as kindly as he could.

Then Gordon had asked her to put a transmitter in the mouthpiece of her telephone. At first, she had refused. But he said he was having trouble with dialogue—his characters didn't sound real, and it would help him tremendously. All the really secret information came over the scrambler anyway; he was looking for atmosphere and lingo. He had explained that if he were working late at night, he wouldn't have to disturb her with questions, for the transmitter, drawing power from the telephone, would send to a voice-actuated recorder in an office across the street, and he could call the machine at any time. This one touch of authenticity would probably send his book rocketing to the best seller list. Finally, she had agreed. But she was careful to bring the transmitter with her every morning, and take it home every night, so that it would escape the periodic bug sweeping of the office.

"I don't understand how you could have done it, Betty," said Peter. "You must have known that someone would find out. It's against every rule we have."

Betty twisted her handkerchief. Her voice was barely a whisper. "I didn't want to lose him."

Peter felt as if he were being sucked into a vortex. "So you told him, for instance, that David Payne was on his way to the Italian Alps?"

Betty pinched her lips together and picked at a thread in her skirt.

"And every time Jessica called in to report a contact with Lark, the conversation was recorded."

"I didn't know! I only did it to help him write his book!" She was sobbing again, her head in her hands. "When it was finished, we were getting married. He loved me. We were going to live in New York."

Peter rubbed his hand over his face. "I have to call security, Betty." But he sat for several moments before he picked up the telephone and he had to clear his throat several times as he spoke softly into the instrument.

The room was quiet, except for Betty's sobbing. Jessica had been sitting in her chair, sympathetic eyes on Betty's face, but when she looked away, her eyes had the same, dull, glazed look as when she entered. Peter reluctantly shuffled through the photographs in the now authenticated pile. His breath rasped as he read the names for the umpteenth time. A knock on the door startled them all. As the security guard entered, Betty looked hysterically at Peter and shrank into her chair.

"What's going to happen to me?" she cried.

Peter helped her out of the chair, led her to the man at the door. "I don't know," he said truthfully. "I'm afraid there'll be a lot more questions. Perhaps a trial, in camera."

Betty's red-rimmed eyes pleaded with him as the guard took her arm. "I didn't know. I loved him. I'm not a spy. Oh, please . . . I'm not a *spy!*"

They could hear her anguished voice as the guard led her down the hall. Peter returned to his desk. He looked older, almost fragile, as he sat with his head in his hands.

"I'm sorry," said Jessica.

He looked up. For an instant, he saw her the way she had been when she first arrived in London, so pretty, so full of life. The woman who sat before him bore no resemblance to that other woman: She looked drained, beaten. He wondered if her lovely green eyes would ever recapture that spark that had made them so like David Payne's.

Suddenly, he turned and banged his fist on the computer console at the side of his desk. Controlling himself, he gripped the soft arms of his imposing leather chair.

"We have so much technology! Sophisticated planes, satellites, expensive atmospheric listening devices, photographic equipment that can see, from 40,000 feet, the shoelaces of the Central Committee as they walk into the Kremlin. Why isn't it enough? I wish to bloody hell it could all be done electronically. Leave the human beings out of it altogether!"

"So do I," said Jessica. Her gaze shifted from his face to the broken china on the floor. She walked to the door, then turned back to face him.

"So do I," she said.